Reviews

Creative and delightful… with a wide range of form and tone, fans of speculative fiction everywhere will find something to enjoy, regardless of their political affiliations.

—M.A. Beattie, PhD (Independent Scholar of Media)

Fiction is never more important than when reality "trumps" it in weirdness. The Donald as Wizard of Oz, Ivanka branding the moon, an army of DT clones, and with much more, this anthology of short fiction and poetry will make you think, make you laugh, and hopefully, help you survive the reign of Trump.

—Rick Searle (Affiliate Scholar of the Institute for Ethics and Emerging Technologies and blogger at utopiaordystopia.com)

Essential reading/coping mechanism for The Resistance.

—Tara Dublin (@taradublinrocks, Blocked by Trump since August 2015)

In this world of Alternative Facts, I can honestly say I read every word and loved it more than any book ever. Except the Bible and The Art of the Deal.

—Rocky Mountain Mike (HuffPost featured satirist, broadcaster, and musician)

Trump: Utopia Or Dystopia

A Dark Helix Anthology

TRUMP: UTOPIA OR DYSTOPIA
First published by Dark Helix Press Inc.

Cover design by Dark Helix Press Inc.
Cover element credits:
trump-president-usa-flag-star-2042378 by geralt/Creative Commons CC0
boold by scro2003/Creative Commons CC0
the nut house by cactus cowboy/Creative Commons CC0
American Flag Yin Yang by GDJ/Creative Commons CC0
twitter-tweet-bird-funny-cute by OpenClipart-Vectors /Creative Commons CC0
Bungee Inline font by David Jonathan Ross/Open Font License

Library and Archives Canada Cataloguing in Publication

Trump : utopia or dystopia / ed. JF Garrard & Jen Frankel.

Issued in print and electronic formats.
ISBN 978-1-988416-20-5 (softcover).--ISBN 978-1-988416-19-9 (EPUB)

1. United States--Politics and government--2017- --Fiction.
2. Trump, Donald, 1946- --Fiction. 3. Trump, Donald, 1946- --Influence.
4. Presidents--United States--Fiction. 5. Speculative fiction, American.
6. Short stories, American. 7. American prose literature--21st century.
I. Garrard, J. F., 1978-, editor II. Frankel, Jen, editor

PS648.P6T78 2017   813'.08760835873933   C2017-907196-3
                                                    C2017-907197-1

Trump: Utopia or Dystopia

Edited by JF Garrard & Jen Frankel

a DARK HELIX PRESS anthology

Also By the Editors

by JF Garrard

Fiction
The Undead Sorceress
Designing Fate
Three Microaggressions

Non-Fiction
The Literary Elephant
Feeding The Kraken!
3x Bilingual Series
Baby Shadows

by Jen Frankel

Fiction
Leia of Earth
Undead Redhead
Feral Tales (short fiction collection)

Blood & Magic
The Last Rite
The Red Ring
Living Large in Purgatory (Heaven & Hell Part I)
A Heaven of Fallen Angels (Heaven & Hell Part II)

Poetry
Moving

Anthologies
"CIBling Rivalry," Robotica (Pop Seagull Press)

A Note from the Editors

If you ask anyone anywhere in the world "Why Trump?" you're likely to get as many interpretations of the question as answers. No public figure in modern times has had the power to divide, complicate, and incite like The Donald. From his insistence that Barack Obama wasn't born in the United States to his problematic relationships with underlings and foreign powers alike, Trump has inspired some, infuriated many, and perplexed all. Is he a genius? A moron? Insane? Crazy as a fox? Brilliant businessman, or dangerous bully? Is he self-made, or the entitled scion of wealth? Insider or outsider? Liberal or conservative?

When we set out to create a book in which Trump was a muse to speculative fiction writers, we were met with relentless mocking from everyone from family members to total strangers. They did not understand why we were wasting time on such a project. However, they were also glued to the news about his every move. Trump is the subject you can't believe you're talking about, the way we joke that the only Germans who don't talk about the war are the ones who talk about how everyone else is always talking about the war.

At the same time we began *Trump: Utopia or Dystopia*, we opened up for submissions for a *Canada 150* anthology. Trump stories flooded our inbox at a 10:1 / Trump:Canada ratio. Clearly, Trump was a more powerful muse than our boring, seemingly peaceful country. As Canadians, we read and talk about Trump from an outsider's perspective. His actions will affect us, but it is a trickle-down effect versus direct bombardment. As a character he is larger than life and speaks without a filter with no care about offending anyone. His unscripted moments are genuine and in an odd way, there is a sincere purity to them.

The stories in this book tell of different futures under Trump's rule which are fantastical, bizarre or apocalyptic. Much material sent in told of dire, dark futures. While a some of these were chosen, creating an entire book of doom and gloom was not our intent. In fiction, one can explore and discuss issues without fear while letting the imagination go wild, and our authors certainly did.

We hope that these stories entertain and create debates over what is or is not possible. Perhaps we are naive, but Trump is a human being after all—a husband, father, grandfather—and we hope that he is trying to do some good in this world even if it doesn't appear so. Maybe as writers, we hope that at the end there will be a twist or big reveal, that there is a spark of decency and hope in his leadership tenure.

And if not, at least you can't say we don't live in interesting times.

JF Garrard & Jen Frankel
Toronto, December 2017

Table of Contents

May you live in interesting times.
— Ancient Chinese curse

No authentic Chinese saying to this effect has ever been found.
— The Yale Book of Quotations

On a non-ironic note, we would like to thank a number of individuals who helped make our Kickstarter for this book a success: Kohl Frankel, Bobbi, Matthew, Vivian Mercury, A. Agrawal, Clara, A. Williams & C. Law.

1 Trump Card

by Ramona Thompson

Living under a trump card
It's neither right nor wrong
Just so very surreal
Truth stranger than fiction
A mad or a wise man at the helm?
How are we to know?
I guess we all must
Just wait and see
What the future may bring

Lost in a maze
Does it still not amaze?
This could be
The beginning or the end of
Making America great again
In his eyes
Does there lay a path to salvation?
Or mankind's ruin?
Dare we wait to see?

Where do we all fit in?
In his ultimate plan
Man or cruel beast?
What and who is he?
This creature
We voted in

Will he soon vote us out?
Is he a Jesus who came to save us?
Or a Hitler who will devour the world?
Only time
Cruel or sweet will tell
Lord help us all

Ramona Thompson has been writing over 20 years. Her credits include work with *Calvary Cross, Dead Snakes, Howl, Infernal Ink, Night To Dawn* and many more. She is currently at work on a book and other various music projects. Readers/fans may stalk her on Facebook.

2 A Brief Detour to Oz

by Chris McGrane

Dorothy Gale collected her dog, Toto, from doggy daycare and began to drive home. It had not been a particularly good day. Firstly, Miss Gale had arrived late to work (she had tried to call her supervisor to let him know, but he was apparently participating in "Take Your Hangover to Work Day" and didn't answer). When she finally reached work, Dorothy had been reprimanded for coming in wearing a t-shirt that said "I Voted in the 2016 Election—and All I Got Was This Stupid President."

Then, once Dorothy had changed into her usher's uniform, she made a big mistake while entering the titles of this week's movies onto the electronic display screen. Dorothy rarely looked at the display, so she went about her business blissfully unaware that the cinema in which she worked now claimed to be screening a movie called *Fantastic Breasts and Where to Find Them* instead of *Fantastic Beasts*. While a large number of patrons expressed interest in seeing this movie, the cinema's devoutly Christian owners had not been impressed.

"I'm glad they fired me, Toto," Dorothy said tearfully as she drove back toward the farm. "Now I can follow my dreams." She turned on the car radio.

...Bob, I think our schools would be much safer if the police were allowed to shoot pedagogues on sight...

She changed the channel.

...as a billionaire I am often victimized. Governments ask me to pay higher taxes, and people stereotype me as greedy, just because I'm rich. It is incredibly unjust. That is why I am lobbying Congress to pass a Wealth Discrimination Act to stop people from discriminating against the 1 percent.

Dorothy grumbled before changing the channel.

...Sally, I've always been overweight. But since I joined the US Army, I have lost over 90 pounds... worth of explosives. I think that's why they kicked me out. Suits me, I hated the army, you had to run everywhere...

She changed the channel again.

...you're tuned to AM radio, where great music goes to die...

Dorothy sighed and turned off the radio. She drove along a dirt road until she reached a sign:

The Gale Family's Hardscrabble Farm:
Trespassers will be disappointed.

Toto barked excitedly when he saw the sign. The dog jumped up and down and accidentally tipped open the car's glove box. A number of DVDs that Dorothy's ex-boyfriend had stashed in her car spilled out onto the front seats. The collection included such titles as *Horton Hires a Ho, Harlots of the Caribbean, The Big Wang Theory, How I Humped Your Mother, Pimp My Bride, Miss Grey's Anatomy, The Secret Life of Penthouse Pets* and *The Triple X Men.*

Dorothy was so focused on cleaning up the mess, she didn't notice the tornado until it was upon her. It was strange that the tornado just appeared out of nowhere—almost as if it was merely a convenient plot device. The mighty twister lifted her small car off the road and threw it high into the air.

The car fell back down to Earth with a loud thud and Dorothy temporarily lost consciousness after being smacked in the face by an airbag.

When she awoke, the CD player in her car was playing one of her favorite songs ("F*@k You, Michigan," from *Hillary Clinton the Musical*). The song reached its crescendo, ending with Bill exiting the stage singing his catch phrase "Excuse me while I slip into someone more comfortable."

Looking through her slightly cracked windshield, she saw a sign in front of her that said *Munchkin Country Welcomes Careful Drivers*. After stepping out of the car to check if the vehicle had sustained any other damage, Dorothy gasped when she realized she had run over an old woman who wore a tall black hat and silver shoes. Sweat ran down the side of her face as she pondered about what to do next.

Suddenly, her car was surrounded by a group of little people wearing clothes of many different shades of blue.

"She killed the Wicked Witch!" one of them yelled. The others burst into cheers.

"We're the Munchkins!" they shouted. "Let us be friends!"

This was much nicer than saying, "We are eyewitnesses to your recent act of vehicular homicide."

Dorothy shouted to no one in particular, "It was an accident!"

However, the Munchkins were far too busy singing, dancing and celebrating to pay any attention to Dorothy's protests.

Dorothy was trying to extricate her car from the throng of Munchkins when a tall woman with long red hair and a sparkling white gown walked up to her.

"I am Glinda—the Good Witch of the South."

"I don't believe in witches. You just look mean," Dorothy replied as she hugged Toto tightly.

"A lot of people automatically assume that I'm mean. It's a phenomenon known as 'Resting Witch-Face,'" Glinda said unhappily. "But I can assure you that I am far from mean. In fact, I am positively lovely. I came here to congratulate you on liberating Munchkin Country from the Wicked Witch."

One of the Munchkins intervened at this point and said, "Glinda is a wise woman. She knows how to keep young in spite of the many years she has lived."

"In my world, we call that technique 'Botox'—it isn't really a secret," Dorothy said. "I don't need a cosmetic adjustment, I just need to find a way back to Kansas and my Aunt and Uncle."

"Then you should seek out the Wonderful Wizard of Oz," Glinda suggested. "He can help you."

"How do I find this Wizard?"

"You can take the yellow brick road to the Emerald City. I will arrange a private audience for you with the Wizard. Tell city staff to page me if you have any trouble."

Dorothy decided to follow Glinda's advice, found the stretch of yellow brick road known as the Y-95 and was soon driving through Munchkin Country looking for the exit to the Emerald City.

T

The unfamiliar roads confused Dorothy, and as Oz didn't receive an adequate GPS signal, she eventually decided to stop to ask for directions. As luck would have it, the first building she came across was the *Munchkin Country Fertility Clinic.*

Going in, Dorothy walked through a nondescript waiting room before finding signs of life inside a doctor's office. A young man in a white coat sat behind a desk and spoke to a man who seemed to be wearing a suit and a pig mask. Their conversation was as follows:

"I can't get the woman I love pregnant," Mr. Pig said unhappily.

"Don't worry, our clinic specializes in treating this kind of problem," the doctor said. "What is your wife's name?"

"I'm not married."

"I do apologize. What is the name of your girlfriend?"

"I don't have a girlfriend," the Pig replied

"What is the name of the woman you're trying to get pregnant?" the doctor asked.

"Jennifer Florence."

"The movie star? Why would she find you attractive?"

"She doesn't. She thinks I'm repulsive."

"If she thinks you are repulsive, why does she sleep with you?"

"She doesn't. That's why I can't get her pregnant."

"So you came to the clinic hoping we could persuade this beautiful young movie star to sleep with you?"

"That would be why I took the bus trip, yes."

"Mr Pig, this isn't a dating agency and certainly not a beauty parlor. The fact that you're repulsive to women isn't something we can change. This is a fertility clinic—we deal with problems that prevent men and women from successfully reproducing."

"Being repulsive does prevent men from reproducing. It has been stopping me for years."

Thus began a raucous argument that ended with the Pig threatening to sue the clinic for false advertising and the doctor throwing the Pig out of the building. Abandoning any hope of asking the agitated doctor for directions, Dorothy instead followed the Pig and asked the Pig whether he knew how to get to the Emerald City.

"Yes, I know the way. I could guide you there, but why would anyone want to go to the Emerald City? It is full of beautiful women—all of whom think I'm disgusting."

"You can speak to the Wizard. I think he can make you attractive to women… or at least recommend a stronger mouthwash than the one you are currently using."

The Pig soon agreed to show Dorothy and Toto the way to Emerald City.

They drove for many miles, on a circuitous route that took them past two small porcelain figures, which were standing on the side of the road. The first figure was a little girl in a blue dress, who was waving a sign saying *"Can I hitch a ride?"* The second figure was an old man with a long grey mustache and white hair. He was waving the "hitchhiker's thumb" so vigorously at passing traffic that he lost his balance and stumbled out onto the road.

Dorothy, who was reluctant to run down another resident of Oz, stomped on the brake.

"Please, miss, you need to help us," the little porcelain girl wrote on a notepad.

The grandfather came to stand near to the girl. Grandpa Porcelain had an extremely loud voice.

"Vera. Stop talking to that young woman and come and help me. Grandpa tore his pants when he stumbled. Grandpa needs help to change his incompetence pants before we get into that car!"

Vera shuddered at her grandfather's demand for incontinence pants and then began to scribble on a notepad. *"Three days ago, a twister struck my home in China Country. Our whole town was shattered. My delicate porcelain voice box was broken. I need to find a doctor for me and my Grandpa. Maybe they have some medication that can help me."*

Dorothy looked at the doll with the cracked voice box.

"I don't mean to sound like a certain A-list movie star, but medication won't help you. 'You're not sick, you're cracked.' You need someone to give you a voice."

Vera nodded and then scribbled *"My Grandpa also needs help; he is a little bit… "*

Grandpa spoke up. "I damaged my leg fighting Germans!"

"During the war?" Dorothy asked.

"No, it was during a senior citizens' vacation tour of Berlin in 2013. Those bratwurst-eating bastards kept overcharging me."

Dorothy smiled. "I know someone who can give you a voice and help your Grandpa. The Wizard in Emerald City!"

The porcelain family agreed to travel to Emerald City with Dorothy and the Pig.

"I knew the previous ruler of Emerald City. He was a Scarecrow." Grandpa mused as he settled comfortably into the back seat of the car.

It was a long way to Emerald City so Dorothy gave Vera one of her favorite books to amuse herself—*The Treasury of Classic Fairy Tales*. The book featured classic fairy tales that had been re-written by a very popular American fantasy writer, George R. This writer's later fantasy novels would became famous for their political intrigues, complex characters, amazing dragons and eye-wateringly graphic sex and violence scenes. The novels were later made into a popular TV show in which viewers could often watch their favorite characters die in horrible and unexpected ways.

❧❧❧

Cinderella
(as re-written by a famous fantasy author)

...and so Cinderella and the Handsome Prince were married.

Then they were slaughtered at the wedding feast, along with most of their friends and family.

The End

❧

Sleeping Beauty
(as re-written by a famous fantasy author)

...and so Sleeping Beauty and the Handsome Prince were married. Eventually, Sleeping Beauty had three beautiful children.

With her brother.

The End

❧

The Donkey Prince
(as re-written by a famous fantasy author)

After a great deal of gratuitous nudity, swearing and excessive alcohol consumption, the King and Queen conceived a child ...

The End

❧❧❧

"These stories are full of sex, violence and nudity." Vera wrote on her notepad. *"What kind of fantasy series is this? How can you read this crap?"*

"He writes for a mature audience," Dorothy said defensively.

Meanwhile, in the back seat, the Pig and Grandpa Porcelain exchanged bawdy tales and war stories.

"For my 21st birthday I put a sticker on my underpants that said 'May Contain Nuts!'" the Pig bawled.

Simultaneously Grandpa shouted, "I was watching a fascinating documentary the other day, it said that the Japanese High Command ordered their troops to commit Sudoku if we tried to capture them."

T

After many long hours in the car, the small group eventually reached the Emerald City.

Glinda was true to her word, because as soon as the small group arrived in the shiny lobby of City Hall, they were invited by city staff to a private meeting with the Wizard. They were led into the Wizard's private office, which was a large room filled with golden statues among green sparkling furniture.

The Wizard appeared in a different form for each guest: Dorothy saw a sagacious old man, the Pig met a beautiful (and available) woman and the porcelain people encountered a tall, elegant porcelain woman in a white coat with a stethoscope.

Mid-conversation, Dorothy realized something was wrong with the old man she was speaking with. His image flickered, as if he was a mere projection. Dorothy was no stranger to the cinema business, so she started looking for the projectionist. She followed a trail of light to the far right-hand corner of the room, flung open a curtain behind a potted plant and found a 21st century computer console that controlled the image projector. Seated at the projector was a portly man with blond hair and slightly orange tinted skin in a blue suit and a *Make Oz Great Again* cap. The small man was guarded by a group of Secret Service agents who appeared ready to throw Dorothy out of the building. However, the small man reminded his agents that the media, who lurked outside the building, would probably have a field day if they tossed this nice young woman out into the street.

While the agents prorogued a decision, Dorothy spoke to the small man.

"You're just a humbug," she declared. "What happened to the Scarecrow who used to rule this city?"

"He was a low energy loser. They threw him out."

"Why did they select you replace him?"

"Because I give the people what they want. I promised the people that I would build a wall to keep the Winkies out and that I'm gonna make Winkie Country pay for it."

Behind Dorothy, Grandpa Porcelain cheered in agreement. Meanwhile the Pig and Vera nudged Dorothy nervously.

"Please, Mr. Wizard," Dorothy pleaded. "Can you help my friends? Vera and her Grandpa are from Porcelain Country which is full of little China people who need our help…"

"Don't get me started on China people," the Wizard snorted. "They've been ripping us off for years. Greatest currency manipulators ever. They're spying on us and stealing our intellectual property. We gotta be tougher with them or they'll eat us alive. Fortunately, I know how to beat 'em, I've been doing it throughout my business career… you peace activists have nothing better to do…"

Realizing that the conversation was going badly, Dorothy paged Good Witch Glinda. Several seconds later, Glinda suddenly appeared in a puff of smoke.

"I think you're confused," she said to the Wizard.

"Listen, Hermione, don't interrupt me. You're a very nasty woman. You're ugly, you're old, you have a voice like a chainsaw—I rate you as a three. You're fired."

"Help these people, Wizard," Dorothy said, stomping her feet. "Or I'll tell everyone in the Emerald City that they are being led by a humbug."

The Wizard seemed taken aback and The Pig Who Couldn't Get a Woman took advantage of the momentary lull to step forward.

"Mr. Wizard, I can't find a woman. They don't like me. Can you help me?"

The Wizard frowned for a moment, reached into his bag and pulled out a legal document.

"Here's a contract for your own TV show. Once you're a celebrity, women will put up with you, no matter how big a pig you are."

"Really?"

"You bet. It worked for me."

The Pig beamed and the Porcelain family stepped forward.

Vera wrote a note, in her best handwriting, and handed it to the Wizard. *"Mr. Wizard. I have no voice. Can you help me?"*

The Wizard once again reached into his bag and this time he pulled out a checkbook. He handed a signed check to Vera.

Wizard smiled. "Here is something to ensure your voice will always be heard—lots of money. As long as you have it, everyone will always listen to you."

Vera wrote a follow-up question on her notepad. "Won't the Supreme Court be concerned that I could use my incredible wealth to drown out the legitimate views of other voters?"

"Apparently not," the Wizard said with a shrug.

Vera wrote *"Whooopeee!!!"* on her notepad and danced around the room.

"Mr Wizard. Grandpa Porcelain is sick." Dorothy pointed to the old man. "Do you have something that will help him?"

The Wizard replied, "Yes, here is something every sick person needs." He pulled out a passport. "Canadian citizenship. Now their government will pay all of his medical bills—the treatment won't cost the Porcelain family anything."

"God bless those freedom-hating socialist bastards!" Dorothy and Grandpa shouted with joy.

"But wait… I don't pay taxes in Canada," Grandpa said.

"So what? I don't pay taxes anywhere," the Wizard said proudly. "That's because I'm a very smart businessman. But I still make good use of taxpayer-funded services," he said, pointing to his Secret Service bodyguards. "And you should too."

"OK. So I've helped all your friends. Why? Because I'm a very generous man. I'm very charitable and don't expect anything in return. Remember to tell the media this as you leave. Finally, what can I do for you?"

"Can you help me go home?" Dorothy asked the Wizard.

He grinned. "I love helping people go home, especially if those people happen to be Winkies."

It transpired that the Wizard had been flying to Palm Beach when his jet was struck by the tornado that blew him to Oz. Deciding that he missed his favorite well-done steak with ketchup that was unavailable in Oz, he ordered non-unionized Munchkin technicians to work seven days a week to repair the damaged jet. As soon as the jet was ready, it took Dorothy and Toto back to Kansas before dropping off the Wizard and his entourage in Washington.

Running towards the farmhouse, Dorothy saw her Aunt Em, who was watering cabbages outside. Aunt Em was overjoyed to see Dorothy. She hugged and kissed her beloved niece and asked her where she had been.

Dorothy smiled and said "In the Land of Oz! One of the very few countries in which a complete humbug can rise to a position of great power."

The End

READER COMMENTS

The Wizard
@realWizardofOz

Just read this story, unreadable! Totally biased, not funny, typical hatchet job by the media. Sad!

Chris McGrane loves to write. He has received politely worded rejection letters from a number of prominent literary competitions, publishers and dating agencies. His work has appeared in several anthologies, most recently in the Stitched Smile Publications anthology *Unleashed: Monsters Vs Zombies*. When he isn't dreaming of literary fame, he has a perfectly sensible office job.

3 Love in the Time of Trumpites

by Wondra Vanian

Tristan's first problem was that he had never been able to say no to Callie.

His second was being a vampire. Although… he had never considered that a problem before he met Callie.

Oh, he wasn't one of those sick vampires who became morose when they fell in love with a human. Tristan thought that these vampires, the ones who walked willingly into the sunlight to prove how much they loved some sappy bleeder, deserved whatever angst-ridden end they got. They were an embarrassment to their species.

And it certainly wasn't that Callie was one of the idiot humans who thought any relationship between a human and a vampire was inherently doomed. She loved the could-die-any-moment thrill of being a human as much as Tristan loved the security of being a vampire. Their relationship worked for them.

Or, it *had* worked for them. Until that moment.

Until Callie had come to Tristan, teary-eyed, and begged him to do the one thing they had agreed he would never do.

"Please," Callie said again. She turned her icy blue eyes up to him. They were filled with unshed tears.

"Callie…"

She caught Tristan by the front of his button-down shirt. "Tristan," she said, "please."

Four years, they had been together; a long time for her, none at all to him. In all that time, Callie had never asked him. He had offered once, shortly after their first anniversary, but she had turned him down flat.

"Who wants to live forever?" Callie had joked, quoting a song by one of the classic rock bands she loved.

So that was that. But things change when someone you love is diagnosed with a terminal, swift acting disease.

Tristan could sympathize, he had been a human back in the early fourteenth century, when the Black Death tore through the world. He remembered the fear that had gripped him when the plague claimed its first victim in his village; the mind-numbing terror of watching buboes swell under his brother's skin; the gut-wrenching terror of seeing the flesh rot off his mother's body while she writhed in agony…

Hundreds of years later, Tristan still had no idea how he had managed to escape the plague that had claimed the rest of his family, only that he had. From the moment he watched their bodies tumble into the pit designated for plague victims, Tristan had become obsessed with overcoming death. He went in search of the creatures rumored to exist in the forests outside their village, dark beings that had no fear of the plague because death could not touch them. As it happened, Tristan was lucky enough to cross paths with one that didn't immediately rip him apart.

If the Black Death was still the killer it once was, Tristan was fairly certain there would be a lot more vampires in the world. However, it wasn't and there weren't. Without the constant threat of the plague looming over their heads, modern humans were less likely to seek out Tristan's kind, as he had; less likely to dwell on death when they were busy living the carefree lives the Black Death had stolen from their ancestors.

As for DT2K18, well, a positive test result was rare enough. Rare, but still fatal in 100% of cases.

The mutation, named for the year the first missile flew and the man who launched it, was a remnant of the short but devastating nuclear war between America and North Korea that killed half the world's population and poisoned several generations to come. DT2K18 was the result of that poison—or, more accurately, the radiation that lingered in the atmosphere after the war.

At first, this genetic mutation was easy to identify; many of the early symptoms were external. The infected bore lesions that spread across their flesh at a rate proportional to the internal damage raging through their bodies. By the time a Trumpite's (as the sufferers were colloquially known) internal organs turned themselves inside out, their faces were already crusted over and oozing with stomach-churning green pus.

It had not been a good time to be human. No one knew at that time if DT2K18 was infectious or inherited. They didn't know that radiation could turn a person's already existing cancer cells into something much, much worse. All they *did* know, even then, was that it was incurable. Excruciating, horrific, and incurable.

Being a vampire after the NK-American War wasn't much better. Fresh blood was scarce and, frankly, tasted *awful*. Some idealistic vampires had decided to come out of the proverbial coffin, ending centuries of seclusion, to aid humanity in any way they could. It wreaked nearly as much havoc on the vampire mortality rate as DT2K18 did on the human one. Vampires knew starvation for the first time in their history

Such missiles had flown over two hundred years ago. The fallout eventually dissipated. Vampires and humans ultimately put aside their differences and learned to coexist. Society was rebuilt. Medicines were developed to treat the physical symptoms of DT2K18 so that death, while still a swift agony, was at least easier on the loved ones who were forced to endure it.

Over time, by some miracle of evolution, DT2K18 more or less worked its way out of the human gene pool. Instances of the mutation still popped up in the news every now and then but truth was, you had to lose the genetic lottery in a big way for the mutation to activate, which could happen at any time in a person's life. Callie's sister was terribly unlucky.

Whether Callie was willing to admit it or not, her sister would be dead within two weeks. Tristan felt for Callie—not as much, perhaps, as he would have when he was a human—but there was nothing he could do for the girl, which he had already explained.

"You know there's nothing I can do to help Ingrid," Tristan told Callie again.

A muscle jerked in Callie's jaw as she fought to hold back tears. It was a stab in the heart to Tristan, who had never seen his strong, level-headed girlfriend cry. She lost the battle and a single tear broke free.

"You have to help her," Callie pleaded. "You're the only vampire around for hundreds of miles."

Which might have mattered *if* 'turning' cured the mutation.

It didn't.

Some well-intentioned but ultimately foolhardy vampires had tried, in those post-war years, to save humans infected with DT2K18. The result had been disastrous. Rather than curing the disease, they made what was essentially a horde of vampires doomed to eternal agony. When it became clear that, with constant deterioration and repair, the Turned Trumpites need for blood became unquenchable, they were hunted down and dispatched by the same vampires who had attempted to save them.

Tristan remembered those days all too well. He took his girlfriend gently by the arm and led her to sit on a nearby chair. Desperation made Callie cling to his hand when he would have released her.

"Turning your sister is not going to help. I know how much you care about her," Tristan said in a gentle voice. "Let her suffering be as short as possible. Let her go."

Callie shook her head as she yanked her hand free. For a moment, Tristan thought he'd gotten through to her. Callie dropped her eyes and took a shaky breath. But then rage at the disease destroying her sister burned away any hope of logic or reason. She stood and paced across the room, heels clacking angrily against the hardwood floor.

"Stop lying to me," Callie insisted as she turned back to Tristan. Anger made her voice rise. "I know you can help her. Why won't you help her?"

He sighed heavily. Grief was making his normally down-to-earth girlfriend irrational. If Callie would just stop to *think* about what she was asking of him...

"Don't you love me?"

Well, shit.

The magic words. Tristan had never once had those words used on him and managed to get away unscathed. He doubted any man— vampire or otherwise—had. Callie wanted him to do something stupid and he would do it because *he loved her.*

Love was more dangerous than DT2K18.

"You know I do."

"Then why won't you help Ingrid?" Callie wailed, despair creeping in behind the anger in her voice. "She's a good person, she doesn't deserve to die!"

No one *deserved* to die from DT2K18, but that didn't change a damned thing.

Tristan had been a vampire for over nine hundred years—but he always acted as a noble man. He knew what the outcome would be as he tried, once again, to dissuade Callie.

"Vampirism doesn't cure the mutation," he said reasonably, knowing his words were futile. "All it does—"

"I know what it does!" she snapped. Tristan felt glad that he had kept distance between them; the look Callie gave him stung slightly less than a physical blow would have.

"Ingrid won't thank you for it."

"I. Don't. Care." Callie ground out from between her teeth. "She can hate me all she wants, as long as she's around to do it."

Why couldn't he say no to Callie?

Tristan stared at her for a long moment before he continued. "Are you sure this is what you want?"

She nodded.

Tristan sighed and threw up his hands in defeat. "Alright," he said. "Let's go 'turn' your sister."

T

Nearly a week had passed since Tristan had given in to Callie. Six whole days since he had allowed her to bully him into 'turning' her sister. He hadn't seen either of them in that time. As Ingrid's Maker, Tristan really ought to have been there, helping her adjust, teaching her to hunt, etc. But, honestly, he had been just a little too pissed off.

Anyone who had made it past fifth grade health class knew the effects vampirism had on the human body, that the infection made a person immortal and froze them in time exactly as they were. Forever. Which was why it was highly unadvisable to 'turn' a Trumpite.

The external symptoms of the disease ravaging a Trumpite's body were almost pleasant, compared to the internal damage cause by DT2K18. Outwardly, DT2K18 was disturbing to see. Internally, it was nothing less than catastrophic. Tristan couldn't imagine being trapped, forever, in a body that was destroying itself. He never thought he would be responsible for inflicting that kind of pain on another being, and yet…

Tristan had, in fact, 'turned' Ingrid. Turned a Stage One Trumpite. He still couldn't believe he'd done something so irresponsible—and he blamed Callie for forcing him into it.

Don't you love me?

He'd survived the apocalypse but one vulnerable human had brought Tristan to his knees. He was getting soft in his old age.

After six days of fighting himself, cursing Callie and her entire family, and desperately wondering if they were all okay, Tristan found himself at Callie's door. He raised a hand to knock—and was thrown backward as something flew at him.

Tristan landed on his back on the pavement outside. Ingrid, her chin dripping with red liquid, sat on his chest. He raised an arm to fend off the fledgling as she snapped at his exposed neck.

"You! You did this to me!"

I told Callie it was a bad idea, was Tristan's first thought. He twisted and rolled until Ingrid was beneath him, her arms pinned down by his knees. Her jaws snapped wildly.

"Enough of that," he said in his best 'I'm-your-Maker-you-must-obey-me' voice. Tristan used the telepathy all vampires possessed to send a little mental push with the command. Ingrid immediately stilled.

"I told you both this was a terrible idea. But you insisted. So, here we are."

"It *hurts*," Ingrid wailed.

Tristan rolled his eyes. "Of *course* it does! The mutation is still in there—" he tapped her forehead with rather more force than was necessary "and always will be. Being a vampire only stops it from becoming any worse."

The look he gave her was laced with pity. No patience, but plenty of pity.

"Stage One, forever." A horrendous thought. What on Earth had possessed him to do something so cruel?

Don't you love me?

"I told Callie you wouldn't thank her for—" Tristan paused as a thought struck him. "Where's Callie?"

Ingrid blubbered.

His heart sank. "What have you done?"

"I-I couldn't help myself," Ingrid said through tears. "I was so hungry and the pain—*the pain*. And she wouldn't shut up. She was there, all the—"

Tristan had heard enough. He stood abruptly, grabbed Ingrid by the hair, hauled her to her feet, and dragged her toward the house.

"She kept asking how I felt," Ingrid sobbed. "Over and over. She kept pushing and I-I didn't mean to hurt her. I just—"

The house was in tatters. It looked like a tornado had ripped through the building: tearing, splintering, destroying everything it touched. It was remarkable, really, the amount of damage one pissed off fledgling could do.

Ingrid's family fared even worse. Tristan found pieces of bone and chunks of flesh scattered along the hallway. In the kitchen, he found what remained of Ingrid and Callie's parents. The only things that identified the bodies were the matching wedding rings their severed fingers still wore. He pulled Ingrid through the carnage, and up the stairs toward Callie's room.

"Oh, Callie." A cold hand twisted around Tristan's heart at the sight that greeted him.

If only he had gotten over himself sooner... if he'd just called to make sure everything was alright...

Tristan flicked his wrist and sent Ingrid tumbling into a corner. The wall cracked under the pressure. A shower of plasterboard rained down on her. She stayed where she fell, sobbing loudly.

He turned his back on the lump of mutilated flesh that had once been his girlfriend. His girlfriend, who considered mortality a thrill, who would never accept the offer of immortality herself but had demanded it for her sister.

If he had just had the strength to tell Callie no...

"I just wanted to push her away," Ingrid said miserably. "I didn't know I was so strong. And then, there was all this blood..."

She stared at her blood-stained hands like she didn't recognize them. "It smelled so good. And it tasted even better..."

Ingrid's voice sounded far away. Tristan wondered if she was thinking of her parents. If so, was she thinking of the way she had butchered them—or just the way they tasted? The fact that the thought had even crossed his mind irritated Tristan.

"Shut up," he snapped.

Stupid bleeder, he thought and, for a moment, he wasn't sure which sister he was angrier with. Not that it mattered. He could never be as angry with anyone as he was with himself at that moment. His guilt would follow him through the next several decades as he studiously avoided any entanglements with humans; no good could come from dating humans, he'd decided.

That night, Tristan burned the house to the ground and watched as the smoke carried away all traces of his failure. While the fire still raged, he tore Ingrid's heart from her chest to put an end to her suffering. As he tossed her infected corpse into the fire, he did something that he hadn't done in nearly two centuries.

He cursed Donald Trump for screwing up his life.

Wondra Vanian wrote her first short story at the age of seven and has never looked back. An author first, Wondra Vanian is also an avid gamer, a photographer, a cinephile, and mother to an army of furbabies. She sleeps with the lights on, has music in her blood, and has been known to dance naked in the moonlight. For more information, visit: www.wondravanian.com.

4 Trump Vs the Zombies

by E. Reyes

President Trump had been covertly saving us from a zombie epidemic.

The infamous wall that President Trump wanted to build was not really intended for "bad hombres." No. The wall was not meant for drug dealers, rapists or criminals south of us, it was meant for *zombies*. Upon being elected as the President of the United States, Trump had been granted access to millions of secrets. Of course, there were secrets that not even the President was supposed to lay his eyes on, but Trump being Trump, he found out a lot more than he bargained for.

There was a secret facility in Mexico that tested biological weapons. The most advanced and top secret tests conducted used biological agents to kill people efficiently, which, in turn, lead to an accidental and astonishing discovery—human reanimation. The lab rats were a variety of criminals such as drug cartel members, people already in prison for life and unlucky offenders caught by the Mexican Border Patrol guards. The German thanatologists brought back to life the heads of dogs in their experiments, but the Mexican scientists were able to reanimate the dead heads of drug dealers. It was remarkable work. Late at night, sitting alone in the White House secret room archives, Trump saw video footage of these heads blinking and moving their mouths without a body attached to them. It scared the hell out of him. He couldn't stop the facility from doing these tests, so a wall would have to do. Trump figured that a wall would be able to block a massive hoard of zombies should the day come when the facility lost control of their experiments.

Undisclosed to mainstream media, there were three small outbreaks in Douglas, Arizona, while Trump was in the race for President. He received this information from an unknown source during his campaign. Perhaps it was a Federal Bureau of Investigation (FBI) leaked document. With the Mexico border being so close, three zombies somehow found themselves in the United States. All three of the zombies were brought back to Mexico by soldiers who were hired to protect the facility they were being studied in. Nobody was bitten but it revealed that security was shoddy. Trump felt extremely uneasy about that. He didn't know at the time of his campaign about where these zombies came from, but he knew that they were bad news. Other candidates had no idea about these tests. Trump knew he wouldn't be able to convince the American people that zombies from Mexico might leak into our country, so he told us about the wall, and who it would stop. He was only saving us.

After the Centers For Disease Control (CDC) placed a somewhat comedic image on its website giving step-by-step directions on how to handle zombie wounds and infections, the Federal Emergency Management Agency (FEMA) sent soldiers, policemen, and detectives on a "zombie outbreak simulation" to an undisclosed desert location in Arizona. These events occurred in October of 2016, one month before Trump was elected President.

Many conspiracy theorists and zombie enthusiasts found this to be very peculiar at the time. Out of all possible training, why was there training for a *zombie outbreak?* Hearing said speculations, the FBI released a statement saying that it was in the spirit of Halloween, and it was actually training to handle a terrorist attack in big cities. Years later, the zombie infection would appear in low income areas throughout the country. Soldiers and police fought as hard as they could, but there were too many undead, and bullets run out.

When President Trump discovered that the zombie virus actually originated in the Middle East and not Mexico, he immediately proposed a travel ban. It wasn't to keep out Muslim extremists or ISIS, it was meant to keep possible infections from spreading. There was one zombie incident on an airline from Iraq to the United States in December of 2017 that made Trump push hard for the ban. A man was bitten by an escaped test subject from a secret lab in Iraq. Both were detained and witnesses were paid off. Trump wasn't going to let this happen again.

President Trump and his cabinet tried to pass the Affordable Care Act for only one reason—it covered zombie bites and infections, and paid for a very expensive antivirus in case of a huge zombie epidemic. Obama Care didn't cover it, and wouldn't cover it.

A month later, several vials of the zombie virus were made available on the international black market. It only took two days to cause massive global infection after they were sold to an undisclosed American buyer for $10 million dollars a vial.

There were many different theories on how the virus first spread in the U.S in low income neighborhoods. Many speculated that the Republicans released it to keep poor people from opposing the Affordable Care Act. It was also said that it was actually the Democrats who set the virus loose, since they failed to win the votes and trust of those in poor communities. Nobody took the blame—not even terrorists, but soon there was no time to point fingers or argue which political party caused the infection because everyone was busy protecting themselves from the living dead.

The social justice warriors (SJWs) were the first to die from the virus, become reanimated, then die again. During the early days of the virus, these young SJWs rioted and picketed for zombie rights. They didn't want to see zombies being brutally shot down in the streets. Soon, a lot of them dressed up as zombies and hit the streets to show support, but they were killed after being mistaken for the undead. Sadly, they died because they truly believed that the un-infected could co-exist with the undead. They were terribly wrong. Since Americans were not yet banned from entering most countries, the virus found itself outside of the U.S. and spread like a wildfire around the world.

Trump has since gone underground, after the staff of the White House became infected. He gave the American people one last speech during the first phase of the infection—telling all about the virus—and then simply disappeared. Many speculated that he took refuge in a secret underground bunker. Others believed that he had zombie-proofed his beloved Trump Tower. A YouTuber claimed that Trump was seen walking amongst the undead at a rally for feminist rights. A Reddit blogger claimed that he saw Hillary Clinton shoot the President with a shotgun at this rally. There was a rumor that the video, along with images, had been posted on BestGoreX and 4Chan2. After the videos and images were banned by the FBI, it was also believed that the original video sold for a quarter billion on the black market. Without a leader to look up to, Pence and Ryan drank electric Kool-Aid on the lawn of the White House. The White House had a sturdy cement wall, but soon it was knocked over by a hoard of zombies bigger than the audience at Trump"s inauguration.

I don't know for sure, but it seems as if the world is now ninety percent contaminated with the virus. We—those of us left—are trying our best to survive. I'm leaving this diary for whoever comes along and finds it here in this cabin, so they can get the real story. After all, Trump really hated fake news.

E. Reyes is the author of *7 Deadly Stories*. He lives in Tucson with his wife and three children. Twitter @halloweeneddie, Author page: amazon.com/author/ereyes

5 The President's Man

by Shaun Avery

The President is sitting in his chair as his country burns, watching the parade of never-ending riots on a huge TV, the reflected light from the screen glinting off that fine blonde mane of his.

I keep my eyes on him as I enter the Oval Office.

He keeps his on me, too.

"You here to take me down, Sonny?" he says.

I am.

But even after everything that's happened these last few weeks, after everything I've found out, I still don't have the heart to tell him this.

Instead I say: "He told me, sir. He showed me Dr. Stone's tests."

The President raises an eyebrow, showing his theatrical self, displaying all the star quality that swept him through the polls and into Office.

"*He*, Sonny?"

"Doctor Porter, sir."

"Him?" He waves a hand, dismissing the man in question. "He's in with The Enemies of America, Sonny. On their payroll. You know that."

That's what I want to believe.

What I always did believe, in fact. That anyone who said a negative thing about our beloved President was one of *them*, one of *The Enemies,* a terrorist sympathizer out to bring down this great country of ours.

It was this belief that enabled me to shoot or maim anyone that he had declared one of our many foes; what let me drop bombs on Mexicans when they wouldn't contribute to the building of The Wall; what gave me the strength to adhere to his strong pro-life views by dragging women out of abortion clinics and locking them up until their babies were born and then executing them out on the street.

All of this was filmed, of course, on Trump TV, the world's new favorite channel now that we've taken a couple of the bigger countries over and enforced our religion and our entertainment—often the same thing—on them. All of these were acts that people questioned, elsewhere in the world and online. Still, my resolve never wavered, a firm belief in my master ensuring that I could do whatever was needed to make his word become law.

But all of that changed a few months ago.

When he got a new doctor.

T

Dr. Stone, the man who had been with the President ever since the night that he was sworn in, died suddenly one Thursday night.

The President didn't seem to mind.

"One guy's as good as any other," he declared, a policy he also adhered to when recruiting for his administration. "Find me someone."

He made this request to the office at large, not directing his words to one single person. But I guess someone listened. Soon, we found the President signed up for weekly health visits with a man called Dr. Porter.

Our Leader was always full of jokes whenever we took to him to the surgery, making us all laugh with his gregarious nature. He never told us just why he was keeping up with these doctor's visits, though, as he seemed to be in mostly good health. Well, looking back, I guess he kind of did… though he made a joke out of that, too, telling us that he and the First Lady were trying for another Junior. Saying it in a way that was indeed very funny, but you could never tell if there was a nugget of truth buried in there somewhere.

We were used to that.

We sat outside in the waiting room whenever he went in to see Dr Porter. This made us all a little nervous, as with the number of death threats the President received on a daily basis you can never be too careful about who you left him alone with. The President seemed to trust the guy. And that was good enough for us.

But he was wrong to do this. Because, one day, not so long ago…

T

"Mr. Jenkins? Can I have a word with you?"

"Not now," I said, speaking automatically. "We're very busy today."

"I must insist," the Doctor replied. "It's rather important."

I looked to the President. He was leaning against the limo we had arrived in, regaling the rest of the security people with jokes and tall tales, holding court once more. Technically I outranked all those guys, and should have stayed there watching over them, as ultimate protection of our Leader always fell upon me.

Nodding, the President waved me off with a smile, saying, "I'll be fine with these guys."

I nodded, not quite satisfied but adhering to his words like always.

Briskly, I walked towards the Doctor, standing outside the Clinic, and for some reason that I can't explain even now, I found myself growing nervous. Perhaps it was the look on his face, oddly pensive and worried, or maybe it was a gut feeling, but whatever it was, I felt a sudden urge to reach for the gun in my holster.

"What is it, Doctor?" I said, reaching him.

He motioned me back inside the building, saying, "Come with me."

Frowning, I followed him into his office, where he closed the door behind us.

"Why don't you take a seat?" he said.

"I'll stand," I told him. "Just tell me what's so important. I'm in a hurry. The President has a press engagement."

And weren't *they* always fun. With soldiers and The National Guard off fighting in wars all over the planet—some that we'd started, some that we hadn't—it was all the police could do to keep a lid on the riots that started every time President Trump stepped up to talk somewhere.

Porter's face went a little grey, but he did his best to cover up whatever he was feeling, his voice wavering only slightly when he said, "As you wish."

Swiftly, he went behind his desk but he did not sit down either. Instead, he pulled open one of his drawers and brought out a folder and slapped it down on the table that stood between us.

I saw a familiar name on the folder—*Dr. Stone's Journal.*

"Notes from my predecessor," Porter said. He finally sat down, and looked at me. I met his eyes and saw that the worry he'd displayed outside was still present, but now there was something else as well—he looked exhausted. Weary. Like he had been wrestling with something or someone and it had finally taken its toll on him. Which for some reason made my own nervousness grow, and I tried not to think about the gun at my hip once again.

He glanced away from me. "Care to take a look?"

"I don't think so," I replied. "I doubt it would make much sense to me."

He raised an eyebrow—not quite as theatrically as my Commander-in-Chief but just as dramatically. "You might be surprised. But here, let me do it for you."

He did so, opening up the folder.

I saw a multitude of brain scan images—colorful and dotted here and there with illegible, squiggly handwriting.

"What am I looking at?" I asked, sitting down to get a closer look.

"PET scans," Porter said. "Lots of them. Dr. Stone printed them out, every time he did one."

"Right." I looked up at him. "So?"

"So these images show the mind of a man who has something very wrong with him," Porter replied. "Dementia, and that's just for starters."

I looked up at him.

"And look at the date this was first diagnosed," he went on.

I did so, and my blood chilled inside me, as I realized the date in question was the very first time that Dr. Stone had tended to the President.

The day after he was sworn in.

The day, too, he had called me out of nowhere. I had been out in the field for weeks, hunting an insurgent leader and had just returned to the camp a few hours earlier. While trying to wrap up mission details, I was given a number and told that I needed to call it urgently. When I did so, I couldn't believe who picked it up at the other end.

Our new President.

He told me he had read my file, said he needed a man like me to help him "see that things got done the way that they needed to be done." Went on to explain he wanted to put me in charge of a new group that would handle both military matters and domestic security. A group that he had dubbed The Sacred Services—as in performing our sacred duty to keep this country safe from harm. The job would start immediately.

I jumped at the chance to be a part of this.

I had never cared for any of the former Presidents. I mean, don't get me wrong—I followed orders, performed my duty like any good American should. But they always seemed to be grandstanding types to me, guys who said what they thought people wanted to hear but never really believed their own words.

Not *this* President, though.

I was proud to be his right-hand man.

Sitting under the bright lights in this doctor's office I suddenly remembered all those dead foreigners. The imprisoned, waterboarded rioters. The women who had screamed during childbirth and screamed once more when I pulled out my gun. I felt my blood run ever colder.

"Forgeries," I said, trying my best to dispel my fears. I pointed at the scans. "How much are the Enemies of America paying you to try and discredit our President?"

Porter shook his head.

"Okay," I said. "So it's the Democrats, then."

"Democrats?" He snorted. "*What* Democrats?"

Well, he had a point there. I had been on a couple of the purges myself.

"But," Porter went on, "even if there were some left, they wouldn't have had anything to do with this."

He leant back in his chair.

"Ever visit Dr. Stone's house?" he said. "It was pretty nice. A lot nicer than someone on a doctor's pay should have been able to afford."

I got what he was saying there. Didn't want to, but I did, and I was slightly shaky as I stood and said, "We're finished here."

He seemed surprised. "Aren't you worried about what I'm going to do with these?"

"Not really," I said. "I doubt you're stupid enough to try taking them to the media."

"True," he said. "But what about *you*, Mr. Jenkins? What are you going to do about this?"

A good question. Then he had another, delivered just as I headed out the door.

"Any idea why our President was asking me to recommend a good plastic surgeon earlier?"

T

I tried not to think about it, tried to put the whole conversation behind me. Which, you know, should have been easy since there was always plenty to keep me busy. Not least of all The Wall—people kept trying to get over it, no matter how high we built it or how many of their kids we shot as examples.

All that death should have demoralized me, I suppose.

It did not.

Instead, it further proved that what we were doing was right. Undesirables—The Enemies—still wanted to get into our country. So we must have been truly great. And a country is only ever as great as its Leader.

A Leader I had always believed in.

Still…

What if it was true?

What if all of his decisions had not come from a sane and rational mind but from one riddled with dementia and other things?

I didn't know what to do.

Whatever else might or might not have been wrong with his mind, though, he was still sharp at reading people.

"Something wrong, Sonny?" he asked one morning, while sitting in the makeup chair, getting ready for another TV appearance.

"No, sir," I said sharply.

He glanced over his shoulder at me.

I looked back at him. Trying to work out what he was thinking. But it was impossible.

Still, the doubt was in me. That night, while driving home, I took a little detour.

Went past Dr. Stone's old house.

It was up for sale now. My gut told me it wouldn't be on the market for long. Not with that fantastic ocean view. Not with all of those floors.

And all on a doctor's salary? I thought.

I didn't think so.

I could have gotten past all that, though. I could. I would have told myself he'd inherited it, or he'd won the lottery. Anything. I did not want to believe that Porter's insinuation could be correct, that the President had been paying Dr. Stone off for keeping his mental problems a secret.

Yeah.

I could have lived with that.

Until I saw the President's new scientific experiments.

T

I walked through the gates of the Gold House—once the White House, but redecorated by a bunch of imprisoned Democrat-leaning journalists to suit the new President's favorite color—feeling wary, just like a few weeks ago, after I had spoken to Dr. Porter.

I felt doubt, too. Could not shake that feeling.

The President smiled when he saw me, and it was just like old times.

"Sonny!" he said. "Come with me! I've got something to show you!"

He led me into the elevator, one of the first new functions added to the building. The elevator that only went one way.

Down.

Into the laboratory.

We left the elevator and walked into it. The place where we kept the prisoners that we could not let escape. The people wrongly accused of being terrorists who we had driven mad through water-boarding. Not to mention some of the people who had foolishly tried to sue the President.

As well, of course, the ones we'd messed around with genetically.

The ones we had stuck extra limbs to. The ones whose limbs we had cut off and then tried to grow something back in its place. All the stuff the President liked to sit and watch with popcorn every now and again.

That always creeped me out.

But I'd equally always believed that the voice of the President was the voice of our God.

However, after my conversation with Dr. Porter, I was not so sure.

Still, I followed him. Past the screaming, past all the wailing, on past the captives who slammed their extra body parts against the bars until blood—or something like blood—came gushing out.

We stepped into a huge room at the end of the laboratory.

It had been a while since I was here. It looked, however, like the lab staff had been very busy that entire time.

The area was filled with massive glass tubes that stretched from floor to ceiling, each manned by one of the President's Scientific Staff. Every tube contained murky looking water. And floating within the water of each one...

"The science boys keep telling me it can't be done," the President said, clapping a hand down on my shoulder. "I keep telling them back that 'can't' is not a word I ever want to hear."

I walked over to the nearest tube.

The President frowned as I shrugged his hand off my shoulder to do so.

I didn't care about that.

My focus lay entirely on the thing in the tube.

Half-formed, one eye lumpy and misshapen, the face just a mishmash of random parts in places they should not be. However, there was one thing they did get right.

"You gotta love that hair," the President said. "Right?"

I looked back at him. "You?"

"My DNA," he said, shrugging.

I brought my eyes back to the thing in the tube, bobbing pathetically in the water, looking out at me with its one eye. Not quite alive. Nevertheless alive enough to wish that it could die.

That was when one of the Scientific Staff came over to the President and jabbed a needle into his arm. I took a second to berate myself for neglecting my protection duties, until I saw that the President was smiling, that he actually wanted this.

"Gotta keep trying, Sonny," the President told me. "One day we'll get it right. And then we can have an army full of me!" He looked around the room, raising his arms, performing for an imagined audience. "To help make America great again!"

He didn't say how an army of Trumps would actually be able to do that.

Still, we were all used to this.

I suddenly could not look at him. As I glanced around the monstrosities all around me —knowing that the one just in front was merely the tip of a nightmarish iceberg—I made my decision.

The President must die.

T

I guess he must have known it.

Perhaps he'd had me followed to Dr. Stone's old place.

Maybe Dr. Porter's office was bugged and he had heard the whole exchange.

I don't know.

For whatever reason, I was allowed to drive through the war-torn streets towards the Gold House and then walk inside without anyone asking me why I was interrupting the President's downtime, during which he usually liked to be left alone.

Halfway to the Oval Office, I drew my gun.

Now I stand watching him.

He makes no move to get up from his chair.

Is this because he has something planned?

Or because he doesn't think I will do it?

Will I do it?

I have to.

I think of all the people I've killed, and the poor creatures below us. I'll be heading there next, I know. To put them out of their misery.

And then I'll go to Dr. Porter's.

Yes.

He'll help me break this. People will see that I was a hero! People will...

There are sudden footsteps behind me.

"You idiot," the President says, using the harsh tone he used to employ when he was "firing" people. "You think I didn't have a bug in Porter's office? Why do you think I go back there every week? It's to make sure the secret doesn't come out!"

"But... but why?" I say. "Why go see him at all? Why not just kill him?"

Like you've killed everyone else, I want to add.

But that's not true, is it?

No.

It's me that's been doing all the killing.

Me that now hates him.

I lift the gun.

The door swings open behind me.

I turn around and gasp. It all makes sense to me now, as I remember Dr. Porter's last words:

"Any idea why our President was asking me to recommend a good plastic surgeon earlier?"

"I like to live dangerously." He speaks from behind me. My eyes remain on the vision of hell at the doors. "It's good to keep someone around who could become an enemy. Especially since I've killed all the interesting ones."

"What about Stone?" I still can't turn to look at him, I am frozen by the sight before me. "Why did you keep going back to see him?"

"He liked to listen to me talk," the President replies. "And you know how much I love that."

I hear him get out of his chair, and I know I should look back at him.

But I can't.

The sight in front of me is just too horrible.

A group of twenty people stand there. Staring at me. Hate on their faces. Faces so familiar.

Some stand just within the Office, a few in the doorway, some peer in from the hallway. Men, women and children. All of them armed with pistols. The children and the smaller adults are at the front—so the taller ones behind can shoot over their shoulders.

All of them wear the President's face.

"That's the mark of a good servant," he says to me. "A true servant. Someone who loves me so much they will change their faces to look just like me." He shrugs. "We couldn't get the clones right. But this is even better."

He moves to the side of the room.

Removing himself, I know, from the line of fire. A line that is directed solely at me.

"You... *you* are mad," I say, finally looking at him, accepting this fate I've earned.

He points to his army.

"They look mad to you?" he asks.

I have no words to answer him. No fire to fight him, either, as I let my gun drop to the floor.

"I'll let them deal with you first," the President tells me. "Then we'll pay a little visit to Dr. Porter. It's been fun, keeping him around. But now I think it's time to find a new enemy." He grins. "Think we'll manage it?"

I do.

Thinking of those he has had me kill, all those he has declared foes of America who might have been nothing more than symptoms of the things rotting inside his head—I truly believe him. I know that as long as there are people like those standing at the door of this Oval Office, the President will always be able to find an enemy to attack.

I don't tell him this.

All I do is close my eyes.

The twenty Trump lookalikes all pull the trigger.

Shaun Avery is a crime and horror fiction fan who has been published in many magazines and anthologies, most frequently as a contributing author to the popular *Demonic Visions* series of horror anthologies, now up to its sixth volume. He has co-created a self-published horror comic, more details of which can be found here: http://www.comicsy.co.uk/dbrough ton/store/products/spectre-show/ and recently sold his first comic script, details of which are here: http://shanewsmith.com/allthekingsme n/contributors/shaunavery/

6 Notifications

by Brian J. Smith

My phone is sitting on the coffee table in front of me but it hasn't gone off yet. I'm waiting for my next notification, but instead it just sits there like the space age piece of junk it was before I took it out of the box. I can't wait to get my next notification so I know what to do next.

As the song goes, waiting is the hardest part. I posted an update ten minutes ago, so why haven't I heard from anyone? Maybe they're just too busy to respond to it, running here and there doing this and doing that, living their own lives and—

Bullshit.

If they've got time to post their own shit then they've got time to respond to mine. They're just jealous that my selfies look better than theirs. They can try all they want to, but my selfies will always be better than theirs, always.

Better luck next time, fucktards.

Here's another one of me in the kitchen you can carry around in your pocket. It's a nice kitchen, huh? Oak cupboards, tiled countertop with nice stainless-steel appliances; the place itself is in one of those red-brick buildings that overlooks the city.

My phone beeps.

Oh, goodie!

I got one. I finally got one.

Actually, I got seven but it's not about my kitchen. It's about the tree standing in the back of the building at the edge of the hill; it stands before a pinkish blue sunset, its gnarled shadow stretching across the grass. It would make a good screen saver, that's for sure.

Hold on a minute. I'll be right back.

AHHH!

AHHH!

There I'm back. I had to go out to the back of the building and rip a branch from that tree and whip myself for seven minutes then upload my evidence. Long red scratches crease down my back like a one-night stand; I even got deep enough to draw some blood.

This is how the app works.

You download the app, upload a selfie or a picture and then you base the severity of your self-mutilation on the number of likes, hence the tree branch and the number of whips I'd given myself. When it comes to social media, it's no longer about self-pride and narcissism anymore; they don't care if you smile unless you were going to knock your own teeth out.

It has always been like this since we elected our new President. In order to stay a citizen of the United States, you had to download the app. Some people say he was self-absorbed and wanted to see support through sacrifice from his people. They compared him to the famous cult leader Jim Jones, only instead of "kool-aid," the President preferred a show of pain.

Like me, a lot of people will do anything for him.

If you didn't follow the rules, there was a stiff penalty.

I'm sure it's bad. It gives me the creeps just thinking about it.

Oh well.

Coffee's done.

T

I step out on the front porch to grab the morning paper when I hear a voice. I scan the block of one story stucco houses sitting on neatly clipped lawns when a familiar face steps into my periphery. I pick up the paper, hold up my hand as a greeting and parade across the lawn.

"Hey, Gus."

"How are you doing, Trevor?"

"I'm waiting for my next notification. I got my first one this morning. It was a good one."

"The tree?"

I nod and then slip my left arm out of my sleeve to slide the side of my robe down to show him my back. He whistles and gives me a small round of applause. He is a tall, portly built man with a halo of brown hair around his big dome-like head and has the strict gaze of a grandfather. When I slip the robe back into place, we shake hands like a couple of war buddies.

"President Trump would be proud of you, Trev," he says. "Really proud."

"I hope so. How's Gail doing?"

"She's good." He nodded. "She put up the picture of that new bracelet I bought her last week and her phone has been blowing up all morning."

"Where did you get that?"

"Zeke's Diamonds and More." He gives a proud smile. "She was grinding a paring knife into her right hand when I came out here to find where that little bastard stuck my paper."

"Cool."

"Hello, Trev."

I peer over my shoulder and see Gail Landers crossing the street. She is three inches taller than Gus and has the silkiest mane of blonde hair I've ever seen. She is cradling her right hand inside of her left, her olive tan skin fading to a ghostly pallor. Blood pulsates out from the middle of her hand like a fist pumping the air at a rock concert. Tiny red drops splatter against the front of her cotton-pink nightgown which already has a large stain resembling a poorly-painted strawberry.

"Hello, beautiful."

"I saw your back," she mumbles. "Good job with the branch."

"Thanks." I blush.

"Have you heard back from Mena?"

My throat freezes at the sound of her name. I haven't thought about her in a long time since she chose to go to Mexico with all the others who didn't like the election results.

"Not yet, Gail."

"I miss her. She makes the best tuna noodle casserole."

"She sure did."

Gail teeters toward the ground but Gus cups her in his arm and cradles her tightly against him. Her cracked pale lips tremble as she stares down at the towel wrapped around her still bleeding hand.

"Let's get you inside and get you all bandaged up." Gus nods at me. "I'll see you later, Trevor."

"Take it easy, guys."

I get back inside the house and lean my still-throbbing back to the door. It hurts but the pain has become normal. I wince and accept the pain as much as the rest of the country. I carry the paper to the kitchen table and read the front-page headline between bites of hickory-smoked bacon and scrambled eggs with toast.

MAN BURNS DOWN BUS KILLING SIXTEEN blooms up at me in big black font. According to the headline, the driver was driving a load of people to the border when he uploaded a picture of the bus and received over twenty likes. He then parked the bus along the road, locked the doors on his way out and soaked the bus in gasoline before setting it on fire. He cut his throat before the law arrived to save anyone.

Serves them right.

Patriotism requires sacrifice; if you don't sacrifice anything for your country then you're not a patriot. I finish reading the article when it suddenly hits me from out of nowhere.

Where is my big sacrifice?

Those slashes on my back are just crumbs compared to what I've been seeing these days. Where's my fiery bus full of screaming people? Isn't my right-hand good enough to be cut into?

I'll have to up my game.

After breakfast, of course.

T

There we go.

A selfie of my left hand and another of my right foot. There is a mole on my left hand between my first finger and thumb but I don't know where it came from. I've had it since I was a kid but it isn't like I don't have plans for it; I've got big fucking plans for it.

I've done my work for the day as a stay-at-home accountant for a number of local businesses. I flip on the television to see the news. Glory be praised, our new President is standing tall and proud in front of a podium topped with microphones. Camera flashes throw his shadow against the wall behind him for a split second before disappearing. His thinning white-blonde hair lays over his big head like a failed comb-over but he looks like a glorious dream in a charcoal-colored suit.

"I'm proud of the way things are going right now," he says in a deep monotone voice. "This country elected me to be their Leader and my people will continue to lead America in the right direction for years to come. I love the outpouring of responses to my new app. Keep them coming, America. Good day."

When asked about the bus driver, he shrugs his shoulders and walks away amidst a mix of more camera flashes and questions. I mute the television and let out a girlish shriek. I race into my bedroom to retrieve my cell phone and enter my passcode. My face glows with the glare of the phone.

No way.

No fucking way.

Seven for my left hand and eight for my right foot. A woman I've known since high school compliments me on my pinky toes. I thank her and like two of her recent uploads in return. I set my phone on the table, fix myself a quick lunch and slip off my right sock.

Before I can begin, my high school chum submits a pic of her own. She is standing in front of her bathroom sink with a fist-sized hole in the big mirror. Pieces of jagged glass jut out of her left hand like an extra set of fingers. Rivers of blood pour down her hand and had spread onto the floor.

She titles the pic: *DO YOU LIKE?*

I LOVE IT, I respond.

I wipe my toes with a clean rag and then pinch the pliers onto my pinky toenail.

AHHH! OH MY GOD!

With my grandfather's pliers, the little nail slides away with ease. It always hurts the first time but that is natural, sacrifice requires pain and without one you can't have the other. I stop screaming by the time I get to the biggest nail because I'm already numb from the pain.

I upload the evidence and wipe the blood from my toes. I perch my feet on the edge of the coffee table and lean back against the couch. My foot is still throbbing but otherwise I feel great and—

This is the part I can't—

T

That was a close one.

I don't know how long I was out, but the sun is almost down and all I can think about (thanks to Gail Landers) is Mena. She was walking toward a bus loaded with passengers headed for Mexico when she turned and flashed me a disgusted look. Tears were brimming in her eyes as she stepped aboard. She stepped through the crowded seats, found one and slid up beside a window on the bus facing the driveway and pressed her hand against the glass as if she were visiting me in prison.

Mena and I were your average couple: high school sweethearts who had dreams of grandeur before Life had other plans for us. We loved each other and got married three years after we graduated. She worked as a kindergarten teacher while I worked as an accountant. We had been happily married for seven wonderful years (I had never hit her and she never gave me reason to do so) when the election had gone down. She told me she was voting for the other candidate and I just lost it.

She thought the world would turn into a prison if given enough time. She told me that she would never vote for a man who starved for the admiration of others in a barbaric way. I called her a bitch and threw my dinner plate across the room and sent her running towards the upstairs bedroom. That night, she knew how I felt about all of this and told me that she was leaving the country and even gave me the option to go with her but I refused.

As the bus gave a pneumatic wheeze, she flashed a sad glossy look and pantomimed an "I love you" before the bus rode off into the night.

I woke up before I felt sorry for her. I hadn't thought about Mena like I had done in the past because our love had gone with her to Mexico.

There are times when waking up in a cold, lonely bed isn't the greatest thing in the world but you get used to it after a while. I miss all the flirtatious conversations and the spontaneous late night sex we had, but I love my country and no heavyset blue-eyed brunette was going to tell me who I can or who I can't vote for.

I do miss her and I wish she was here with me. Who knows what kind of damage we could have done together.

I sat up from the couch to reach over for my glass of sweet tea sitting on the coffee table when I hear a car door outside. I push myself up and hobble over to the kitchen sink. I keep my foot bent so I don't put any pressure on it and slide back the curtains.

Three police cars are sitting outside Gus and Gail's place, their red and blue roof lights swirling across the neighborhood. Seven police officers in crisp blue uniforms with shiny black belts and matching holsters stand around talking to the couple. Gus clasps his hands together and his face crumples into a mask half-pleading and half-crying as he kneels to the ground. Gail stretches her hand out toward him when one of the officers snatches it out of the air and holds it down across the hood of a car as two more officers trap her legs in place.

I grab my sweater off the back of the couch and hurry towards the front door as quick as a person can on one bad foot. When I step out, their screams echo across the once quiet suburb. Three of the officers pin Gus to the big oak tree standing at the mouth of the driveway.

"Don't do it please, officer," Gus pleads. "It was my idea, take my—"

"Sir." A tall African-American officer interrupts him. "Don't interfere or we'll have to restrain you."

"She knows the rules," the officer in charge says, while holding down Gail. "She photoshopped the picture and failed to comply with the President's orders. That's considered treason in the United States. She has to face a penalty, Mr. Landers."

"Don't do it please. I'll pay whatever—"

Gail tries to slip free of her captors by kicking her feet at them, but it's too late. The officer slips a stainless-steel meat cleaver from his hip pocket, lifts it up in the air and brings the blade down with such force it sounds like a boot being pulled from the muck. She lets out a loud scream as her left hand slides down the hood on a carpet of slick red blood. The officers toss her severed hand onto the ground, blood spraying through the air, and retreat to their cars as Gus tends to his bleeding wife.

"You fuckin' assholes!" he screeches to their backs.

When the cruisers speed off down the street, Gail lurches over Gus's knee and vomits on the asphalt. I want to join them but I don't know if I'll make a damn difference. I wrap my arms around my chest and shiver from the cold January wind. Gus stares at my house as if he wants to burn it down before helping his wife inside because he knows that I'd hadn't (nor would I) done anything to help him. I hear her scream something at him and then the door slams shut.

I don't feel any compassion for them. They had not only betrayed their country but they betrayed me, too. They got what they deserve. If you don't follow the rules you must pay the price. They should consider themselves lucky that those officers didn't shoot them in the head.

I go back inside and lock the front door behind me. Suddenly, my phone gives off a tiny chime. I race to the living room to grab my phone from off the coffee table as it goes off again and again and again.

It's the picture of my left hand I'd posted before I passed out.

Six notifications.

I stare down at the open tool bag sitting on the floor beside the coffee table and gawk at the tiny claw hammer, which feels good in my hand like it belongs there. I tap the blunt end against the first finger of my left hand, set the hammer down and take another sip of sweet tea before I pick up the hammer again.

AHHH!

AHHH!

God Bless America.

Brian J. Smith has been featured in numerous anthologies, e-zines and magazines in both the mystery and horror genres. His books *Dark*

Avenues, The Tuckers, Uncle Bubby and *Three O'Clock* are still available on Amazon for Kindle. He lives in Chauncey, Ohio with his brother and four dogs. He can be found on Twitter under @BrianJSmith913 and on Facebook under Brian Joseph.

7 Duty

by Maggie DeMay

The pounding on the door intensified after the shot. Hoping she had acted in time she grabbed the open briefcase, slamming it shut before any blood or brains could drip into the electronics inside.

"Stand down!" she shouted as loud as she could. "Stand down! I'm opening the door. Stand the fuck down! It's over!" Or at least I think it is, she thought to herself.

She opened the door to a dozen Secret Service agents all pointing their weapons at her. Carefully, she passed the briefcase to the Marine standing in the middle of the group, and gave her recently fired weapon to the Special Agent in Charge of the detail.

He looked into the room as he took the Sig Sauer P229 from her shaking hand. "Damn, Dupree," he said. "What have you done?"

"My duty," she said as she let them handcuff her and lead her away.

T

Weeks later.

She lay on what passed for a bunk in maximum security, a concrete shelf with a thin foam mattress encased in some horrible waterproof and flame retardant cover. She shifted her head on a pillow that wasn't worthy of the name cased in the same fabric, and burrowed deeper into the two blue wool blankets. The guards had been nice enough to bring her a second blanket when she complained about being cold. She knew they hadn't done it for her health; they just didn't want her to die from pneumonia before she could be tried and executed.

There were no windows in the bare cell decorated with a stainless steel toilet and sink, and a narrow ledge for the few personal items she was allowed. One of the trusties came by every other day, pushing a cart filled with dog-eared paperbacks, most of them former bestsellers geared more to men than women. It didn't matter; she was working her way through them all. It was better than staring at the walls. What she really wanted was the latest newspaper. Or ten minutes worth of internet access. She needed to know if what she had done had been worth it.

How long had she been here? She had lost track of the days. After she had been arrested, as she knew she would, she had been hustled out of the White House and shoved into a waiting helicopter for a short flight to a remote location. From the helipad she had been loaded into a black SUV with blacked out windows. A short drive later she was escorted into a nondescript cinder block building surrounded by an electric chain link fence, the top festooned with razor wire. There were no windows on the ground floor and gun ports were set into the walls of the second. She guessed she was at either Langley or Quantico.

A nondescript employee in a room purposely designed to be boringly plain and forgettable, took her picture and fingerprints. She only spoke when she was asked a question, and only gave 'yes' or 'no' answers. She wasn't saying anything without a lawyer. She was strip-searched, and given a bright orange jumpsuit to wear, her charcoal gray Donna Karen suit and her low heeled Jimmy Choo pumps were bagged and tagged as evidence. Medical testing was next. A male nurse who looked like he ate spike nails for breakfast and washed them down with a cup of steroids, efficiently drew blood and roughly swabbed the inside of her cheek for a DNA sample. When he was done, her hands were cuffed behind her back and she was escorted to her cell by two of the largest men she had ever seen. Trust the government to go in for overkill.

She had as yet to see an attorney. She hadn't been questioned, nor had she been charged with anything. She wasn't too worried about the future. Her fate was now in the hands of others.

One of the guards banged his nightstick on the door to get her attention. She hadn't been expecting visitors. The guards told her to turn around and place her hands through the slot in the door designed for handcuffing prisoners prior to letting them out of the cells. A safety precaution, she had been told, while wondering just whose safety they had in mind. She was a small woman and had to stand on her toes to comply. The guards were both big men. All the guards here were huge. She wondered if they grew them in a vat someplace.

"I take it the world's still out there?" she asked.

The guards ignored her question. She was taken to an interview room furnished with three uncomfortable looking chairs and a wooden table. The guards uncuffed her hands from behind her back and recuffed them in front. To make signing my confession easier, she thought as she looked around the room until she found the CCTV camera. A large mirror set into the concrete wall confirmed that she was being watched. She gave the camera the middle finger salute just to be ornery.

The guards left her sitting at the table. Less than a minute later, two men in black suits entered the room.

The older one gave her a thorough once over. The younger one just gave her a blank stare. She wondered if she was about to get the old good cop/bad cop routine.

The older man sat down and opened his briefcase and took out a sheaf of papers, while the younger elected to stand by the door.

The older agent looked across the table at the small woman and her graying hair and large green eyes with the beginnings of crow's feet at the corners. He gave her a long steady look before he spoke. "I'm Agent Foster with Homeland Security, and this gentleman is Agent Wilkes. You are Ms. Odalis Dupree, Special Agent of the Secret Service and a member of the President's Security Detail. We are here to question you about the circumstances surrounding the death of the President. Young lady, do you know how much trouble you are in?"

Homeland Security my left tit, she thought to herself, more like CIA or NSA. "I'm forty-three so you can just forget the whole 'young lady' nonsense. And for your information, I am aware of exactly how much trouble I'm in. Just one question, before we start. Did I stop him?"

Agent Wilkes raised an eyebrow while Agent Foster nodded his head sadly.

"Yes," he said, "It was a close call, but we manage to stop the process. The Joint Chiefs issued a stand down order and recalled the bombers before any damage was done. At this time, we're still on standby, but it looks like the crisis has been averted."

She dropped her head into her cuffed hands. "Thank the Gods," she sighed.

Do you want to tell us what really happened on the 27th of June?" Agent Foster asked. "You had to have known he had turned off all the recording devices in the office because he thought he was being spied on by the news media. We knew he was not acting in a rational manner."

"Is that how they're describing it? That he wasn't rational?" she said, looking Agent Foster straight in the eye. "He had been ranting and raving all morning, his suit jacket unbuttoned and that horrible red tie flapping in the wind. First about that damned border wall, and then about the press. He threw that scrawny screech owl of a spokesperson out of his office that morning, which, sad to say, was the only sane thing he'd done in months. His toupee had gone crooked and looked like it was about to fall off his head because he kept running his finger through it. He kept going on about people being disloyal. About how everyone was questioning his judgment when they knew that he was in charge. That he was right and everyone else was wrong and how he was the only one who could fix things and make them right again. It was... scary. It was as if he had lost all reason."

"You observed all this?" Agent Wilkes asked. "Were you in the Oval Office from 0800 that morning until approximately 1540 that afternoon?"

"You know damn well I was. I was on his protection detail that day. He was pretending he was all for diversity in the Service. That's why I was on the detail, the token female. He wasn't too pleased by my appearance and said so more than once. Apparently I didn't fit his ideal of what a female should look like. He wanted a younger female agent. That wasn't going to happen."

Agent Foster took out a thick file folder from his briefcase. "I have your 201 file from when you were in the Army. Fairly impressive, I must say, considering that each and every one of your evaluations clearly states that you've had a problem with authority from the time you were a buck private fresh out of basic training until you were medically retired for injuries received in a suicide bomber attack in Afghanistan. It says you did your job, and did it well. You also had very high test scores, which is one of the reasons the Secret Service hired you. That and the fact that you're a damned good shot. Your scores from the pistol range are most impressive."

She shrugged. She had known they'd pull her 201 file. There was nothing in it that she was ashamed of. She would be the first to admit that she had a problem with authority. She had enlisted at twenty and had served sixteen years before an explosion triggered by a suicide bomber left her with two broken legs and a fractured pelvis. It had taken months of physical therapy to get back on her feet.

"Furthermore your record states that you are as stubborn as a mule, and have a very odd definition of duty."

"I thought that duty was doing the job that was in front of you and not dicking around, wasting time." The army was full of tedious little tasks taking up valuable time that could have been better spent on things like target practice, maintaining equipment, and keeping up to date on enemy intelligence and troop movement. Failing to do any of these things meant a lapse in security that allowed the insurgents to achieve their goals using IEDs and suicide bombings.

"You were recruited by the Secret Service two years after you had recovered from your injuries and assigned to the White House eighteen months ago. After the new President was elected, you were included in his security detail."

"Then you should know that I asked for reassignment two weeks later. That so called victory tour was enough to make a happy man cut his own throat on a fine spring morning."

"You didn't like POTUS?"

"That would be a mild word for it. You would have thought his campaign would have ended when he mocked a disabled reporter on national television, or when he was caught on tape bragging about grabbing women by the pussy and getting away with it because he was a star. A star of what? A media circus? I was one of those people walking around in a daze after the election results came in that night. It seemed like the whole damned country went insane at the same time."

"But you stayed on his detail? Why's that?"

"Because no one else wanted the damned job and I needed the money. You've got my record. I put in for a transfer every month, hoping for another assignment. Maybe it's a good thing it didn't go through."

"Let's get back to what happened on the afternoon of June 27th? The only people who know the real story are you and the President, and he's not talking. It's up to you to set the record straight."

She looked up at Agent Foster. "Do I need a lawyer? Not that it matters, I know what I did."

"No, hon," Foster said kindly. "You're not going to need a lawyer. This conversation is off the record, we just need you to verify what happened that afternoon." He nodded briefly towards the mirror, indicating that while the conversation was off the record, it was still being observed.

She raised her cuffed hands behind her head and tried to stretch the kinks out of her spine.

"He had been angry all morning." she started. What the hell, she thought, what's the worse they can do? A bullet in the back of the head and an unmarked grave? She doubted the truth of what happened that day would ever surface.

"Angry as usual?" Wilkes asked, "Or worse than usual?"

She gave Wilkes a quizzical look. "Worse, if that's at all possible. He was livid because a federal judge had filed a cease and desist order over those ICE raids, you know, the ones to round up all the illegals. He was mad because the judge overruled him about using National Guard troops. He couldn't get it through his head that you don't send soldiers out to round up civilians. Then that dimwit advisor got caught lying about some crazy mass murder that never happened. That's when he threw her out of his office and told her not to come back until she had a better story. He wasn't worried about her lying, just getting caught." She stopped to catch her breath.

"Go on, please."

"Then it turned ugly. He said the news media were all against him. He wanted everyone to sign a loyalty oath, not to the Constitution, but to him. He ranted about how he couldn't do what he wanted to do because of the Constitution. He wanted to find a way to get rid of it. He was looking for an excuse to declare martial law. He was pacing around his office and shouting at everyone. No one could reason with him. Not the vice president, not his wife, or his daughter." She looked over at Foster. "You knew, didn't you? You all knew he was losing it."

"That is irrelevant; we just need to know what happened." Foster said.

"Like I said, he was ranting like a lunatic. If he had been on a street corner instead of in the Oval Office he would have found himself on the receiving end of a 51/50 and locked up in a nice quiet room for the next seventy-two hours. But he's the freaking President of the United States, so what the hell can you do?" She paused as if to catch her breath. "Can I have some water please? My throat's dry."

Foster nodded to Wilkes, who left and came back a few minutes later with a plastic bottle of ice-cold water.

She took a long drink and continued. "He had a conference call with the Joint Chiefs and NATO commanders. He wanted NATO disbanded. When he was told it wasn't going to happen, he threatened to fire all of them. Then it got real bad, real fast. You could hear him yelling all over the West Wing. He was livid. He called in staff, yelled at them, called them all a bunch of incompetent idiots, and fired all of them. The Speaker of the House came in and tried to reason with him, but it didn't work. Things really started escalating after that. Then he ordered his security detail to get the fuck out."

"Where were you at this time?" Wilkes asked.

"You ever get one of those feelings that something god-awful is about to happen and you're the only one who can stop it? I had that feeling. I hid in the coatroom that's to the left of the bathroom in the Oval Office. Don't know why, I just did it. I didn't think he should be left alone. Especially after he demanded the Marine carrying the football to hand it over and then used it to knock the kid out. Then he ordered everyone out and told them to take the Jarhead with them. Can you believe it? He spends his youth avoiding the draft with student deferments and a note from his doctor and calls a kid who volunteered a Jarhead, and now he's got the damned football."

"By that you mean the nuclear football?" Foster asked.

"Yes, although calling it a football makes it sound harmless, and you know damn well it isn't. He opened the case and started punching in the codes to launch the missiles."

"Are you sure that's what he was doing?"

"I'm sure. By now you know about Executive Order Archangel. The one he managed to slip past the Joint Chiefs, Congress, and the Senate, or at least I'll bet that's what they're all claiming. Before there was a list of protocol for nuclear launch, one that made it impossible for one person to launch a strike, including the President of the United States. Executive Order Archangel rescinded the protocol, giving him sole authority to launch the missiles."

"And this was what was happening on the morning of June 27th. He was using an Executive Order to launch the missiles?"

"You know he did. He had the codes saved on his damned smartphone! The end of the world codes are all saved on his freaking phone and he's got the football opened and he picks up the doomsday phone and tells whoever is on the other end that this is not a drill, to prepare to launch at designated targets. He's muttering about how when this is all over, the world is going to be a better place because he's going to rebuild it and run it the way it should have been run in the first place. About how this is his destiny and that he knows what's good for the rest of the world, that he's going to be king and no one is going to stop him. And all the while he's punching the codes into the system."

She stopped, looked around wildly, and took a deep breath. Quietly, in a voice so soft the agents had to lean forward to hear, she said, "While he's busy trying to start a nuclear war, the rest of the security detail is trying to break down the door to get back inside. Only this is the Oval Office we're talking about, and the door isn't designed for easy breaching. That's when I came out of hiding. He had no idea I was even in the room, and even if he had, chances are he wouldn't have given me a thought; I am a woman who's over forty and not built like a beauty queen, and therefore a non-person and not a threat. I pulled my weapon, chambered a round. I stuck it his ear and told him to 'cease and desist.' He glanced up at me, and as long as I live I will never forget the look on his face. He smirked at me and kept on punching in the numbers. That's when I fired."

"By that you mean…"

"By that I mean I shot the President in the ear with my SIG P229. It was loaded with steel jacketed hollow points. Exit wound made a big mess. Then I took the football out of his hands and carried it to the door. I think I yelled 'clear' or 'stand down' or something like that and opened the door. I gave the football back to the Marine and gave my weapon to the Special Agent in Charge of the detail. Then I sat down and waited to be arrested."

"You do realize that you have just confessed to killing the President of the United States." Foster said, giving her an intense look.

"No, I did my duty. I did the job that was in front of me. I took an oath to defend this country against all enemies, both foreign and domestic, and from where I was standing, he was the enemy. It was either shoot him or let him start a nuclear war. He was having a temper tantrum because he wasn't getting his way and he was going to start a war simply because he could. Given the circumstances, I would do it again if it became necessary."

"Ms. Dupree, were you aware that we were within two digits of launching those missiles?"

She closed her eyes and leaned back in her chair. She shook her head, slowly, trying to comprehend what Foster had said. "No, I had no idea it was that close. We were two digits from Armageddon."

"That's right, Ms. Dupree. The Joint Chiefs and the State Department have been working tirelessly since to put things back right. Tensions are still running high, but the threat of war has passed. Now all we have to do is decide what to do with you."

"That shouldn't be that difficult. I did it. I suppose it's either going to be the death penalty or life in prison."

"Not necessarily," Agent Foster said, steepling his fingers and giving her a thoughtful look. "The American people don't need to know they elected a madman to the highest office in the land."

"Kinda hard to keep a dead President secret," she scoffed.

"The death of the President cannot be hidden. But with the cause of death, we can, and we have. As far as the public knows, the President died from a stroke caused by a brain tumor, which also explains his sometimes erratic behavior."

She looked at the agents, frowning in confusion. "I don't understand."

"The President died from a stroke. He's already buried in his family plot in upstate New York. The Vice-President has been sworn in as the new President and a new VP has been nominated. All the cabinet members appointed by the former President have been replaced and, for now, America is fine. Although we don't have world peace, at least we still have a world. And as for you, young lady, I want to give you a medal, but since this conversation never happened, I'm going to make you a one-time offer instead." He took a folder from his briefcase and passed it across the table to her.

She sat up straighter, wondering if she heard the agent correctly. She opened the folder and started to read the papers that were inside.

Agent Foster continued to speak. "We can never let the public know that a Secret Service Agent killed the President to prevent a nuclear war. All they need to know is that the government still works the way the Founding Fathers and the Constitution intended for it to work. Here's what we're going to do. You get a new face and a new identity. You get just enough plastic surgery to confuse the latest facial recognition software. We set you up with a new identity, bank accounts, credit cards, the whole nine yards. The only catch is, you can never, ever speak of the events that happened on the 27th of June. You will disappear into the Witness Protection Program with a very nice pension and guaranteed financial stability. You will be taken care of, and it goes without saying that you will be watched, but as long as this stays secret, you will enjoy a long and healthy life. Do you agree with these conditions, Ms. Dupree?"

She thought it over for about thirty seconds. Slowly nodding, she reached for the pen he was offering. "Where do I sign?"

Maggie DeMay is an old cold warrior who never saw combat. Ms. DeMay had always wanted to write, but this thing called life kept getting in the way. This will be her first time being published in a major anthology. Her stories and poems have been published in *0-Dark-Thirty* as part of the Veteran's writing project, proving it's never too late to pursue your dreams. Ms DeMay lives in the middle of the Sonoran Desert with a fat Pomeranian named Loki and a herd of friendly deer.

8 Truth, From the Heart

by Gustavo Bondoni

The room was too bright for Marc's eyes. He squinted as they grew accustomed to the illumination. Two huge windows looked out onto the sunlit lawn under clear blue skies. A girl in a flowered dress who was perhaps seven years old, was playing tag with a toddler under the shade of the single leafy tree.

"Hello, Trent," Marc said as he entered the room.

"Hi, Lieutenant," his platoon sergeant replied hoarsely, his eyes straying slightly from the girl to his visitor, who was dressed in a dark-colored uniform. He shifted uncomfortably on the hospital bed and winced as the tubes running out of his nose shifted.

Marc wanted to tell him not to talk, to save his energy, but there was no point in saving it for anything. "How are you feeling?"

"How do I look?"

"You don't want to know."

"Well, that's about how I feel."

The gas that had ravaged Trent's body hadn't done much to make the man prettier. The hospital had used an experimental new treatment to treat his injuries, but large flakes of skin were peeling away, exposing raw flesh beneath. It must hurt like hell, but Trent ignored the pain and gave his visitor a rictus meant to be a smile.

Marc looked out the window. The girl was chasing a red ball across the grass. He watched her run happily and wondered who she was. The silence stretched out between them.

"Give it to me straight, Lieutenant," Trent rasped. "How long have I got?"

"A few more days. A week at most. There's nothing more the doctors can try. You just got dosed by the gas too hard."

They sank into stillness, neither saying anything. Marc would let the man who had saved his entire platoon at such great cost to himself deal with the news any way he wanted to. He owed him that much and more.

Finally, Trent spoke. "It might actually be better this way. I am so tired of this room and the constant pain."

"Yeah. The doc said that not many survive long after a big dose. She told me that the information they learned about Toxo while they were treating you over the course of these ten months might help save dozens of lives in the future. So you're a hero twice over."

Toxo had come as a complete surprise to everyone. One minute the U.S. had been the world's policeman, keeping rogue regimes from using chemical weapons and the next, anti-secessionist troops had been lobbing Toxo canisters at soldiers who had been their brothers-in-arms until a few weeks before. Trent supposed that it had been stockpiled in secret for emergency use, and evidently, the secession had qualified as an emergency.

Trent turned his head to look out the window. Marc wasn't sure how much he could see, but Trent's eyes seemed to follow the little girl's movements well enough.

"It was worth it, though, wasn't it?" the sergeant said, feebly nodding towards the view outside. "The war's over. And freedom and democracy are standing again, huh?"

Marc was happy to see that the bitterness that Trent had felt at having to fight fellow members of the U.S. army—even before he was gassed—was gone. The man seemed to have made his peace with what he'd had to do. But for the life of him, Marc would never know how his sergeant had summoned the courage to pick up a gassing Toxo canister with his bare hands and throw it far enough away to save the rest of them. Just the sight of a can made Marc's knees go weak.

"Democracy has never been stronger."

Tension seemed to leave Trent's frame as he closed his eyes and laid deeper into his pillows, just a fraction of an inch, but enough for Marc to know that his work there was done. The Lieutenant stood and headed to the door.

"Will you come see me before the end?" Trent asked.

"Of course, Sarge."

"Thank you, Lieutenant."

Marc took one final look at the peaceful grassy scene and closed the door quietly. He took a deep breath of stale air as he stared into the dark corridor. He was twenty stories underground, in the new secure location of the Washington Army's hospital, safe from air raids. They hadn't bothered to move the hospital back above ground because no one knew how long the stalemate would last.

A large woman in a white nurse's uniform with her dark hair tied into a bun rushed over to him and gave him a dour look—the same one she always wore, as far as Marc could tell.

"Listen, Lieutenant, we can't keep those view screens going much longer. We've barely got enough power to run the ventilators in the ER."

He sighed. "It's just for a few more days. He'll be gone soon."

The woman crossed her arms. "It'll cost you double."

Marc glared at her, but said nothing. He had prepared for this eventuality. Pulling out four pink pieces of paper out of his pocket, he handed them over without a word.

She snatched them from his hands greedily. "You've been holding out on me."

"No. The rest of the unit pitched in."

They were going to miss those pieces of paper. Each represented a week's worth of meat rations. The right to eat animal products in the brave, new, utterly civilized vegan world was severely limited by the Washington State government. The new people in charge would have loved to eliminate meat products completely, but that would have been impractical. Too many people, notably within the military, would have revolted at having one of life's pleasures arbitrarily eliminated. As their grip on the populace was already tenuous, the government had had to make concessions. But, under the excuse that meat was a privilege, they'd made life for those who consumed it a living hell.

The nurse wore the green patch that denoted full compliance with a vegan diet. There were advantages to extorting your meat slips from others. Officially, anyone that didn't consume animal products was given preferential treatment when applying for benefits and tax breaks. Unofficially, it was whispered that only fully compliant vegan members of society would ever be considered for promotion under the new regime. Of course, if you could get your meat checks without the government finding out about it, you could have the best of both worlds.

"All right. I'll believe you this time."

"I don't care whether you do or not. Just keep those view screens going."

"Don't you want me to change the weather at least? He can't actually believe it's sunny all the time, can he?"

"Keep it sunny. And make sure that there are plenty of kids playing on that grass," Marc replied in a tone that brooked no argument.

"Whatever. You're the boss." She pocketed the tickets and walked away.

Marc went off in search of the doctor. She was in her office, shuffling some papers around on her desk. There were dark rings under her eyes and her lab coat had a battered-looking Seattle General logo stitched to the front. The Washington Army Military Hospital Seattle had commandeered every doctor they could get a hold of, and hadn't yet gotten around to getting new uniforms.

"How did he take it?" she asked.

"Well enough. Thanks for letting me be the one to tell him."

"I think he expected you to be the one. Bad news, in his world, is delivered by one's superior officer. And I'm sorry. We did try everything, you know. Even some stuff that isn't strictly FDA-approved."

"I know. And I truly appreciate it." He paused, knowing they'd already done more for Marc than anyone had a right to ask. "Can you do me another favor?"

"What is it?"

"Put him to sleep. Don't let him wake up. He's as happy as he's going to be. I don't trust the nurse with the view screens. Just one idiot saying the wrong thing, mentioning how things really are…"

The doctor rubbed the bridge of her nose with two fingers. "You don't know what you're asking."

"I know exactly what I'm asking."

"I guess you do." She paused. "All right. I'll put him under. Just enough to keep him asleep. Not enough to kill him. He'll go when it's his time."

"Thank you."

She nodded. "What's it like up there?"

"Safe, I guess. The People's Committee has finally got control of the countryside. Trump's Reunification Revolutionaries were everywhere. They really want to put us all back under the President."

"I thought we'd get that done much sooner. After all, there hasn't been an anti-secession attack in ages."

"It took them a while to reach a consensus and to send the troops out. Putting every single decision up to popular vote is not particularly efficient."

"But it is very democratic."

Left unsaid was the fact that, if Trump hadn't been busy dealing with the insurgents in his own ranks, the war would have been over long ago.

"Most definitely. Rumor is that that Texas has seceded."

"Texas? It figures. I always wondered why they didn't support Trump in the first place. The rest of the south was quick to reaffirm their allegiance to his policies."

"I think the Hispanics population held them back initially."

"It still sucks. That was the buffer state."

"It had to happen sooner or later. Texans have always liked to follow a maverick. And a lot of them were in favor of the wall in the first place."

"So who's left?"

"I lose count. Washington. Oregon. California. A couple of states back east. D.C. was still under martial law, last I heard. Canada is helping us keep our overland trade lines open."

"Damn," she repeated. Then she looked him in the eye. "Are you staying with him for the final goodbye?"

"I wish I could. But my next unsupervised leave is in three weeks. All former combatants are now required to undergo re-adjustment. Someone went berserk and killed a bunch of people at a mall. Apparently, I can be released from observation once every three weeks without becoming a menace to society. They say I might be re-adjusted enough for society in about six months. If I stop eating meat, it will probably be sooner."

She sighed. "Where'd we go wrong?"

"I think it was when Trump asked Congress to declare his sharing of state secrets with Russia a presidential prerogative and annulled Congress's right to investigate him. Wasn't that when the people of Portland took to the streets?"

Hundreds of thousands of people on both coasts had demonstrated against the changes, but the people of Portland had gone one better. They'd taken town hall and then drove over to Salem and forced the legislature to secede—with the full complicity of the National Guard. They'd been convinced that the new government was on its way to dictatorship. One state after another had followed suit, driven by the purest form of democracy: the enraged, self-righteous mob. The fact that it was probably the most educated mob in world history doing the driving didn't make much difference in the end result.

"Yup. Hell, I was ready to move there if Washington State hadn't followed suit and sided with the Oregonians in open revolt. I mean, where did we go wrong? The secessionists supposedly just wanted to force the central government back to following the constitution. How did we get to the point where we're basically a separate country with the vegans telling us what to do?"

He shrugged. "This is what the people want. Well, it's what the leaders of the mob wanted. A lot of the Portland mob were vegans and it somehow got pushed through the new congress. I hear that this didn't happen back East. Democracy and an extreme definition of what it means to be civilized. Hell, even the animals are safer than ever before. In a way, we got what we were fighting for, I guess. Hopefully the pendulum will swing closer to the middle sooner rather than later."

"And the rest of it? Can we survive as a coalition of states? What if Trump gets serious about destroying us if we don't return to the fold? Will we actually use nuclear weapons we have to fight back?"

"I don't know. That's all above my pay grade. Just put Trent to sleep, will you?"

Marc waited for her to nod before he stood up and left.

Gustavo is an Argentine writer with over a hundred stories published in fourteen countries, in seven languages, and is a winner in the National Space Society's "Return to Luna" Contest and the Marooned Award for Flash Fiction (2008). His fiction has appeared in the *Texas STAAR English Test* cycle, *The Rose & Thorn*, *Albedo One*, *The Best of Every Day Fiction* and many others.

His latest books are two science fiction novels: *Outside* (2017) and *Siege* (2016). He has also recently published an ebook novella entitled *Branch*. His previously published short fiction is collected in *Tenth Orbit and Other Faraway Places* (2010) and Virtuoso and Other Stories (2011, Dark Quest Books). *The Curse of El Bastardo* (2010) is a short fantasy novel. His website is at www.gustavobondoni.com.

9 Tricks Are Not For Kids

by Melissa R. Mendelson

The fires didn't bother me. I thought they were pretty at night. Then, I would remember that a body or bodies were burning, that another family was gone. Bullets sounded like thunder in the distance. They made me think of the one caught in the hailstorm, another life gone. Tires screeched like angry sirens, taking out another poor soul. The housing development across the street had promised a new beginning for families, hopes and dreams. Now, it was nothing more than a mass grave, where bodies were dumped every day, surrounded by the hollow existence of empty homes.

Located on Highway 4, the Go Raspberry rested across the street from the housing development now turned mass grave. Once you could smell nothing in here but sweet baked goods and cooking meat like hot dogs along with pretzels that softly rotated around and around. The cold slushies even filled the air with ice and sugar. You would never think that the smell of burning and rotting flesh would replace these aromas, corrupting them into the gut-wrenching smell that made me grow nauseous and faint. At least, those left stopped crossing the roads, but it didn't matter. I used my bicycle chain to lock the doors of the store. This was my place, a place, where my father had forced me to come and work. "You're going into your senior year of high school," he said, "And you're getting a job, whether you like it or not." I didn't like it, but I lived here now.

Orange balls fell to the floor. I ignored them as I continued to plunge my hand deep into the cereal box, looking for another color. I then kicked the orange balls to the side before popping the red and purple ones into my mouth. People would kill for this. People have killed for this. Prices had gone so high on food, that the only affordable things were cereal and canned goods. All the real good stuff was too expensive except to the rich, who still lived like fat cats, stuffed inside their giant houses with armed guards stationed outside. They probably never left their homes, and they didn't need to. They lived off of the propaganda from the media, telling those still listening to not worry and that better days were coming, and those poor souls bought it, putting their money back into the economy in hopes that things would get better.

But it was a rigged game. The rich held the winning cards, and the deck was stacked against them with the orange Joker on top. And all the little cards fell like the manager of the Go Raspberry. He blew his brains out with his shotgun, but I couldn't bring his body over to that development. I probably wouldn't make it, so I was keeping him in the freezer. We're both better off that way.

More orange balls fell out of the cereal box and onto the floor. I stomped on them, smiling at their hard crunch. Then I kicked the dust aside with my feet. One of these days, I'm going to need a new pair of shoes, but the malls were empty now. If you want to buy, go online, but beware. They will monitor every single move you make, learning what makes you tick, so that they can slowly start to peel you away, draining you into a haunted lost soul like those left in the abandoned mental hospitals. And it's all because you fell for their game, but not me. At least, not yet.

I shook the box, disappointed that lunch was over. I was grateful, though that my boss had been hoarding these. I also found his stash of tuna fish. I used to hate tuna fish. My mother would make it every Sunday night with too much mayo. I wanted something to go with it like tomatoes or onions, but nobody else did. Instead, I would just drop that goop onto white bread and call it dinner. I would love for my mother to come now and make me a tuna fish sandwich. I would love for her to scold me as I made a sour face while eating it. I would love to see her again, but I lost her when the Health Savings Plan was passed. She told me not to worry, so I didn't.

But I should have, especially as time passed and she got weaker. Soon, she couldn't afford the meds or doctor visits, and the hospitals started only accepting the more established while those like us were packed into clinics, coughing and sneezing on top of each other and seeing doctors that called us by a number. She died before I graduated high school, and I'm glad she did. She was a big supporter of education, and all the public schools were shut down right after I graduated. Now those schools like the malls are empty, hollow, distant memories of futures promised, all because we believed in him.

After she died, my father went out onto the road. My brother and I hardly saw him, but he sent money back to us. Then, one day, the money stopped, and he never came home. My brother grew tired of waiting, and he enlisted. The only guarantee for the future was to fight his wars, and some wars were justified. Some were not, but our enemies saw weakness. And maybe, we were, and nobody was protecting us like with the unions in the old days. The police shot first and maybe asked questions later, and the firefighters let fires burn. There were no more heroes, and if there were, they didn't last too long.

I looked outside toward the housing development. So many bodies. So many dead dreams. He made so many promises, so many lies, and we believed him because we needed desperately to believe in something, even him. And all those great leaders of the past were now nothing but skeletal remains. So much for change. So much for making things great again when all that remains is destruction and death. When the day comes for me to leave this place, I know that I won't make it. If anyone out there knew about the food, water, heat and electricity in here, I definitely wouldn't make it. They would plow right through the glass doors, take everything that they could, and kill me in the process. He has turned back time, twisting us into animals like with the old man that tried to break the glass. The old man was bloody and beaten with one eye sealed shut and missing a few fingers, but he hurried across that road and charged the glass. Luckily, he didn't break it. Instead, he fell over with one eye still looking in, and remains looking in. I hope that he will keep others away, but to be safe, I keep the lights off except in the back, where I sleep.

I opened another cereal box, knocking more orange balls to the floor. Crunch. That's how I passed the time, looking out at a broken world, and stomping on cereal. I should have gone to college. Maybe, I should have even enlisted, fighting our enemies, but not all the enemies were out there. I was all for them being found here. I was all for them being shipped out, but then the innocent got caught in the middle like they always do. And families were torn apart. I used to see their faces, their children's faces with tears running down their cheeks on the news as they were dragged away, before he silenced the news. This way, we wouldn't feel bad for them. They were part of the problem as he had said, and the news was forced to speak his words. If the networks didn't, they became a white screen of static like in the movie, *Poltergeist*. No doubt all those children grew up bitter and vengeful.

It was late now. The rabid pack of dogs would be coming through soon to pick at the newly dead. They always seemed to know when to come, and they were never alone. They were once the best friends of man, loyal to the end, but now they viewed us as savage. And they wanted nothing to do with us. They just wanted to survive, and so did I. But how could we survive in a world like this, a world so destroyed, broken by so many lies? Not only were we broken, we were divided. He split us apart, ignoring history once again, and it was history that had said, "United we stand, divided we fall."

It was too late. It was just too damn late, and I'm trapped here. I'm trapped in this store, living off cereal and tuna fish, worrying about how I will die. If only the Joker didn't run wild, but it was all a game, a vicious game that none of us wanted to play. And I would rather the days, where I was just a kid watching Saturday morning cartoons and eating cereal and thinking that everything was going to be okay, but tricks are not for kids.

Melissa R. Mendelson is a published author and poet. Her writing can be found in the archives on *Gadfly Online*, and a variety of her writing is continuously published by *Antarctica Journal News*. One of her short stories has been published by the *Hampton Literary Journal*, and more of her poetry and short stories have been featured in *Names in a Jar: A Collection of Poetry by 100 Contemporary American Poets; Espresso Fiction: A Collection of Flash Fiction for the Average Joe; Voices of the World: A Poetry Anthology; Beast: A New Beginning*. She also recently finished writing her first Horror/Sci-Fi novel, *Lizardian*, and she plans to write her next novel called *Darkness Dreams*.

10 The Great Great Plan

by Mathias Jansson

Behind the great wall
Stands the great tower
Where our leader is sleeping
In his gold tower
In the land of freedom
Where the sun forever shines
Where the wind never blows
And the sky is a crisp California blue
This great land of peace
A utopia frozen in time
Where nothing changes
In short a dead planet
Destroyed and extinct
By corruption and greed
That's the reason my son
We live on the moon now

Mathias Jansson is a Swedish art critic (AICA-member) and poet. As an art critic he is mainly focused on new media art and specially Game Art, i.e contemporary art inspired by video games. He is a writer for Swedish and international magazines and blogs as *DigiMag, Gamescenes, Konsten.net* and *Konstperspektiv.*

11 The Business of Being King

by Bryan Grafton

There was a plague upon the kingdom. The subjects of His Royal Majesty the King were suffering from the lack of affordable health care coverage. They were getting little or no relief under the laws of the prior monarch whom the present King had deposed. So His Majesty the King called together a council of all the vassals of all the dukedoms, fiefdoms, and dumdoms that comprised of his kingdom to remedy and replace the existing health care act with his own health care plan. Thus the vassals now all sat around the round table, for how else would one sit around a round table but to sit around it, with His Royal Majesty at the head of the table. And wherever the King sat, that was the head of the table.

Each one of the vassals had his own plan as to how to save the kingdom and none of them were compatible with the King's. Thus they all collectively defied the King, rejecting his plan in its entirety and consequently nothing was accomplished. All the while the people continued to suffer and die for lack of proper health care.

His Royal Majesty dismissed the lackeys with a flip of his wrist for he was a man of little patience and would not tolerate such foolishness and defiance. He had been a businessman in his former life before he became King. He was a man of action. A man use to getting things done his way. Done now. This health care law was to be his legacy to his loyal subjects so that they could adore and worship him forever. For that is what he truly craved: worship and admiration. So he went to the Royal Magician with this problem and commanded the Magician to cast a spell upon the vassals to ensure that his healthcare plan would became the plan of the land.

The Royal Magician listened to the king, for that was all he was allowed to do: he was never allowed to question or contradict His Royal Majesty. But the King's plan was so complicated, convoluted and incomprehensible that the Royal Magician could not understand it. The Magician asked, for one asks and does not tell a king, the King to write it all down on paper for him. His Royal Majesty did so. It came to only about a hundred pages. Quite a small number of pages compared to the twenty thousand pages plus law now in effect. His Royal Majesty believed in terseness not verboseness, keeping it simple for the simple folk.

The Royal Magician read His Majesty's plan, decided on a course of action, and then told the King how he would work his magic making the King's plan the law of the land.

"This is what I will do," the Magician said. "I will take all the pages of your plan and cut them into little tiny pieces. Then I will have the Royal Baker bake a huge gigantic chocolate pie with all the little tiny pieces of paper in it. I will instruct him to make it extra chocolaty, extra gooey and extra sugary so that no man will know he is eating your words and find them distasteful. I will also have him mix in some special ingredients of sorcery magic, such as toes of toad, silks of spiders, boils of bats, eyes of newts, and other enchanted items. Then I will abracadabra it all with an ancient Druid chant and when the vassals eat the pie they will ingest your words and the magic will make their tiny brains all think alike so that they will all be in agreement. In other words, they will regurgitate your plan and pass it."

"Brilliant!" exclaimed His Royal Majesty. "I hereby by royal proclamation order you to do this."

Soon afterwards, the Royal Magician instructed the Royal Baker about the pie. The Royal Baker began baking, for after all, that's what bakers do: they bake.

Now though the King approved of this magic plan, it did not go far enough as he was concerned. He hated those insolent fool vassals who had dared to oppose him, embarrassing him like that. They must pay for the insubordination. His Royal Majesty must have his revenge, hot or cold, it mattered not. Thus he came up with his own plan to supplement the one of the Magician's.

Before he ascended to the throne, His Royal Majesty had promised to clean out the royal stables. The political horse manure there had been piling up for years and was beginning to stink. True to his word, His Royal Majesty started cleaning out the royal stables with his own hands.

Then when no one was looking, His Royal Majesty bagged up a few bags of horse droppings and hid them in the pockets of his royal robe. He proceeded to visit the royal bakery and told the Royal Baker to take a break, for baking is hard work, to go outside and smoke a cigarette. The Royal Baker didn't smoke but he bummed a cigarette from a homeless person and pretended to smoke it for he dared not defy the King since the King could be a royal pain in the you-know-what sometimes.

Now His Royal Majesty would have his sweet taste of revenge against those who refused to pass his law. He emptied the bags of horse droppings into the royal stirring pot containing the pie filling and stirred and stirred until all the horse droppings disintegrated and were completely mixed into the chocolaty gooey filling.

He then called back the Royal Baker. The Royal Baker returned the cigarette to the homeless person and finished his baking.

The King was in the Counting House counting out his money when it was time to open up the pie and for the birds to begin to sing in celebration. Once again all the vassals gathered round the round table.

"I asked the Royal Baker to bake a pie for you as a gesture of my goodwill and to show no hard feelings over our discrepancies," the King announced. "This is not a cherry pie but an extra rich and gooey chocolate pie.

Oobs and *aabs* came out of the vassals.

"Now this time we are going to accomplish something. But before we do so, everyone is to eat a piece of pie for that will be symbolic of us all coming together, passing a health care bill and giving us closure. Eat!" commanded His Royal Highness.

Everyone took a bite, then more bites, for the pie was quite delicious, extra sugary and extra chocolaty as previously said and the vassals could not resist its sweet taste. But His Royal Majesty did not take a bite for he was suddenly called away by the Queen, he said.

The Queen who was in the Parlor eating bread and honey had not called him at all. It was just a ruse and when the Royal Flunky at Arms informed the King that the pie had all been eaten, His Royal Majesty returned.

Upon returning, His Majesty presented his healthcare bill to the vassals and commanded them to vote on it But before they could do this, they all became sick and had to trot out of the room for that is what they had: the trots. They did not return that day nor the next few days either. And they never did vote on his Royal Majesty's bill.

His Royal Highness was flummoxed. He summoned the Royal Magician and demanded at the pain of death to know why the magic didn't work. The Royal Magician panicked and told him that the Royal Baker must not have followed his instructions and had not mixed up the filling properly. For if his magic formula was altered even in the slightest degree he told the King, then it would not work at all. It was the Royal Baker's fault the Magician said, not his. Subsequently, His Majesty offed the head of the Royal Baker and covered his own tracks at the same time.

Eventually, all the vassals recovered. Before his Majesty took office, they had previously passed special health care bills just for themselves and the treatment they received thereunder lead to a speedy and full recovery, the cost of which was charged to the royal treasury. But when they returned to work they all were just plain sick and tired of all this talk about health care and so they tabled the King's proposed law and put it on indefinite hold. They found all this health care talk distasteful and so they decided to move on to something more palatable like tax cuts for the wealthy. They would deal with health care later, perhaps on the day the whole healthcare system collapsed, went into convulsions and died a painful death. In the meantime, the people would just have to suffer.

His Royal Majesty was disgusted with the whole business of being king because he was not in control. No one would do as he commanded. He might be king but he had less power than a CEO and this bothered him to no end. This king business wasn't a business at all. It was politics, an illogical way of doing things. It wasn't like a simple business deal where he could wheel and deal and manipulate. He realized now that he didn't care for this strange world where nothing ever got accomplished and the more he thought about it, the more he realized that he wasn't cut out for all this horse hockey. Though he had won the election, he was a king without control and it was no longer good to be King for it was certainly not fun anymore. So since there was no point in going on like this being humiliated and frustrated at every turn, he decided to quit. Time for him to go back to what he did best: rule the business world if he couldn't rule the country. Thus His Royal Majesty announced that he was resigning the kingship effectively immediately.

A public cheer went up from the masses and a silent one from the vassals. For after all, it was their secret plan that had come together to oust the King from office. Every politician has a secret plan, just ask former King Nixon or King Wannabe Kerry. And doesn't one just love it, when a plan comes together?

The author's stories have appeared in the books, *The Prison Compendium*, *Tales of Canyon Lake*, and *One Hundred Voices* Volumes Three and Four. His stories have appeared regularly in *Scarlet Leaf Review*, the most recent ones being "Dreaming of Diversity" and "Muslim Time," and every so often in *Frontier Tales* and some other online magazines. He is a retired attorney now living in Texas who took up writing while recovering from a broken foot about two years ago.

12 The Apprentice

by Eli Cranor

Donald Trump is a nice guy. Last year, for his and Melania's twelfth wedding anniversary he started a marriage journal, chronicling each of their years together in tedious detail. Across the front, in crisp black print, he wrote, *"Donald and Melania: A History of Love."*

He sits now, peacefully, in a conservative leather chair toward the back of the Oval Office. He is reading Tom Graves's book, *Crossroads: The Life and Afterlife of Blues Legend Robert Johnson.* Today he plans to work on the healthcare front, a multi-million dollar marketing plan pushing holistic food choices, even going so far as to speak out against red meat.

His phone vibrates in his pocket.

I haven't seen a tweet today, Donald.

He was in a bad place after the last bankruptcy—the towers were falling, so to speak—and Lucifer, Satan, Belial, whatever you want to call him (Donald has him listed as "Butch Taylor" in his contacts, so we'll just refer to him as Butch from this point forward) offered up an apprenticeship of sorts.

Not today. Please, not today, Donald texts back.

You know the deal.

Butch's texts come through in red, always red.

Donald folds the book neatly in his lap. He holds tight to the phone, remembering that fateful night at Mar-a-Lago, the sound of waves slapping against the Atlantic coast like angels' wings. It was years ago, after another bankruptcy, another lawsuit, Melania upset about his latest mistake—the Czech model, and then in walked Butch Taylor to a chorus of third world children singing "Another Brick in the Wall." Red all over, and fat—the Devil is surprisingly fat—Butch took a seat across from Donald and hiked up his pants leg, revealing the red quivering tip of his tail.

Butch got straight to business: "I will call upon you daily, Donald. One stupid tweet a day. I'll even write them for you, and in return, you get the world."

Donald pursed his lips.

"So you agree?" said Butch.

"And you'll give me anything I want?"

"Anything."

"Cool, then why don't you go ahead and make me President."

Thinking back on it now, Donald remembers the last line as joke.

"It is done," hissed the serpent, and didn't so much slither away as waddle, adjusting his pants on account of his tail.

T

In the Oval Office, Donald's orange fingers go white from regret as he taps the screen of his phone. *But yesterday I said the 'fire and fury' bit to Kim. Surely that counts for something.*

Donald pushes Send, proud of his message. Reagan would have never put up with that bullshit. He is tempted to open his book again. But then the typing awareness indicator bubbles up at the bottom of Donald's screen, meaning a response is coming. Anxiety floods the septuagenarian.

TWEETS, Donald. The deal was tweets.

There's a moment, a fully thirty seconds, where Donald seriously considers smashing his phone and calling the whole thing off. Before he does, more bubbles fill his phone.

Don't make the same mistake she did. She's still begging me for a second chance.

Donald closes his eyes. He looks like he is praying, maybe, but Don is not a religious man, despite his recent dealings. After a minute, he picks up his phone again.

Fine. What's the tweet for today?

Donald can almost hear Butch laughing as the bubbles pulse. It is worth it. There are great things to be done in this country—*great* things—and this is the only way.

Donald's phone vibrates. He scans the text, his old heart thudding along with the words. This one is *bad*, as nasty as there has ever been. Take all the misogyny, the racism, even the thrashing of sweet, turtlish Mitch McConnell, and up the evil tenfold. This one will be the worst. There will be hell to pay. But the deal remains. Donald copies the text directly into his Twitter account and sends it out, a small chirp follows, and it is done.

T

Donald and Melania make love that night, a slow, passionate grind. In the morning Donald walks three miles on a treadmill, drinks a protein shake, then settles into the Oval Office for his leisurely morning reading.

Donald concentrates on the book's words, the familiar story, never once turning on the news, a computer, or any other device. He left his phone on the desk yesterday after he tweeted, just left it there, delaying the nightmare that was sure to come.

Shadows creep across the north lawn.

The Tom Graves book closes with a soft thump. It's nearly three in the afternoon. Donald cannot remember ever making it this far into the day without getting word from Butch, or an advisor, a phone call, something, anything.

Donald rises.

The phone sits silent on his desk. Sometimes silence is worse. He stalks the phone, waiting for it to explode, for Butch—or even Hillary— to slither out through the black screen and take him by the throat, but there is nothing.

The phone is cold in Donald's hands.

The screen flashes. His youngest son, Barron, smiles back at him, a reflection of sorts. But there is nothing else. No emails. No texts. Not tweets or retweets, not even direct messages. He turns on the news. George Stephanopoulos is back to reporting rape and murder, and flooding of Biblical proportions in the American South.

A horrible shift has occurred. Donald feels it. The way a cruise ship or a freighter makes for the shore in nearly imperceptible turns.

Donald crumples into the leather chair. Waiting. Waiting for a vibration, waiting for Butch to waddle through the door anytime now and tell him what wicked words he must speak today, but there is nothing left to say. The veil has been lifted. The people have become numb to even the most heinous of tweets, the most vile of men. There is a new level of acceptance in America, a rising or a lowering, a moveable line like the hem of a woman's dress.

Tears well up in Donald's eyes as the sun sets on the two-hundredth day of his presidency. A single wet line streaks down his cheek unearthing sunspots and moles, a trail of pale skin beneath layers of orange.

T

At a resort in hell somewhere along the River Styx, Butch kicks back, Bloody Mary in hand, and smiles amidst the fire and the fury, because, frankly, his work is done.

Eli Cranor writes from Arkansas where he lives with his wife and daughter. His work is forthcoming in the *Greensboro Review,* and has appeared recently in *BULL, Eclectica Magazine,* and the *Arkansas Review.* For more information and a complete list of publications visit elicranor.com.

13 Huge

by Michael Manzer

Klump restlessly shuffled his golf clubs around, picked up several of them one by one and then let each drop back down into his bag. Without taking his gaze off them, he spoke to his android assistant behind him.

"Kush, when the hell is that nacho going to get here? I want to get this over with."

"Sir, I believe the Nichoklu don't appreciate being referred to as 'nachos.' They have not reacted positively to that nomenclature."

Klump pursed his lips. "I don't really care what the nachos like to be called. When they're on our planet, we can call them what we want."

"We're not on our planet, sir."

"Any golf course I build is an honorary part of Earth." Klump paused and looked over the contents of his golf bag. "What do you think is the best club to use to tee off here?"

"A 7-wood is the official recommendation, sir."

Klump grabbed his 7-wood out of his bag and took a practice swing with it. "What are we at here, .6 g? With a 7-wood I think I might hit the ceiling."

"We're at .8 g, sir. The course's Autocaddy program recommends a 7-wood, but of course, an experienced golfer such as yourself knows your swing best."

Klump mulled the options for a moment and then took the 5-wood out of his golf bag.

"An excellent choice, sir. As a reminder, you will also have to aim somewhat to the left to counteract the station's Coriolis Effect on long drives."

"I know that. I built this place, didn't I?" Klump teed up a ball and hit a long, curling drive that landed within fifty meters of the green.

"Excellent swing, sir!"

Klump smiled. "This is a first-rate course. It's going to be huge. No doubt it'll be another of my really great investments once it opens to the public. And I haven't even been to my gold suite in the hotel section yet. None of the other clones owns a course like this. Not even the members of the Council." A wistful grimace flitted across Klump's face. "It reminds me a bit of the Old Course at the Winter Residence."

"The fact that the Council banned you from entering North America is a travesty, sir."

Klump turned to face Kush for the first time since hitting his shot. "I was born to rule and, mark my words, I will rule more territory than the whole Council of Drumpfs put together when I'm done. I'm out of the planetary rulership polity now, Kush, but politics is a game and there's always a way to get back to the table if you know how to play. And I know how to play to win."

"Yes, sir, Mr. Klump. You certainly do."

Klump fiddled with a knob on his 5-wood to adjust the density. "And this little errand"—Klump spat out the word like a grapefruit seed —"will get my comeback started. When I get these idiot nachos to hand me a few quadrillion dollars, it'll be a huge win. And then we're going to keep winning. I'm going to show those double-crossing, lazy stiffs on the Council what a real clone can do. I'll have them calling me, begging me to do a deal. It's going to be a big win, Kush. We're going to win and then win some more, just like I always do at golf. We're going to win so much, we'll get sick of winning, Kush."

"I'm sure we will, Mr. Klump. I would love to be privy to your master plan, sir. It is undoubtedly ingenious."

"It's on a need-to-know basis, Kush. Need-to-know. Besides, I couldn't tell you half of it before the nachos show up." Klump teed up another ball and hit it. It landed closer to the green than the last, but took an awkward bounce and ended up buried in the rust-red Mars-dust trap.

"Rest assured that it's a tremendous plan, though. Worthy of the Original."

"I have no doubt it is, sir. I would expect nothing less from you."

"Have I ever told you, Kush, that the DNA I was cloned from was ninety-nine percent pure, right from the Original?"

"You have told me that on multiple occasions, sir."

"Well, none of those little losers on the Council are over ninety-five percent. How they managed to get on the Council of Drumpfs, I'll never know. Sad."

"It is certainly unfortunate and puzzling, sir."

Klump took another ball out of his golf bag and set it on his tee. "You never answered my question, Kush. When the hell are they going to be here, anyway? They had better not keep me waiting."

"Well, sir, the agreed meeting time was twelve noon. It is currently 11:59 GMT according to the station's central clock. The station has not reported visual contact with an approaching craft, but past encounters have shown that the Nichoklu's ships can be difficult to detect and may..."

The perfect blue sky overhead—really a collection of video tiles programmed to display artfully designed Terran skyscapes—flickered once and then showed an enormous, jet black object that looked like it was composed of a jumble of platonic solids fused together at odd angles.

Klump planted his club in the turf and leaned on it as he looked at the overhead display. "I guess their negotiator heard I was going to be here, so he brought a whole law firm."

"That may be the case, sir. However, we do not understand their technology well. Perhaps such a sizable ship is necessary to house their propulsion systems. A vessel of that size likely requires a significant crew."

Klump shook his head dismissively. "That sleazy nacho is trying to intimidate me. But it's going to find out I don't get intimidated by funny-looking spaceships." He punctuated his point by jabbing his fingers into the air. "At least it didn't keep me waiting."

Once it began docking procedures, the image of the alien ship faded from the overhead tiles, leaving blue skies and puffy white clouds. Subsequently, a door opened in the course's wall to admit a trio of aliens.

Klump had seen plenty of videos of the Nichoklu, but he'd never seen any of them in person. The lower part of their bodies sprouted a multitude of arthropod-like armored legs, which rippled as the aliens propelled themselves over the terrain with a flowing gait similar to a millipede's. The main part of their bodies was made up of a fleshy trunk mottled in dark grays and greens. They had no obvious human facial features that worked like eyes or ears, though they did have an ellipsoid opening in their trunks that served as a mouth. Long tentacles—which they reportedly used to sense their surroundings—snaked out from various points on their bodies, moving about in a wavelike manner.

The Nichoklu moved a short distance onto the grass and the lead Nichoklu stretched out two of its sensory appendages in front of it like arms and fanned the others out to the sides and rear. Its two companions mimicked it. Klump ran his hands through his hair to fix his comb-over for the thousandth time. Keeping his eye on the Nichoklu, he messaged Kush via neural implant. *They come in that huge ship and now only three of them bother to disembark? Probably for the best—God those things are ugly. Are we sure this is Convex?*

Kush responded the same way. *I believe the negotiator's chosen name is Caurvex, sir. Our ability to identify individual Nichoklu is not yet perfect without a full physical examination, but I can say with approximately 84% certainty that the largest Nichoklu is in fact Caurvex.*

Who the hell are the other two, his wife and his caddy?

Unknown, sir. We can only speculate about Nichoklu familial and social structure at this juncture. If it is his wife, however, let me just say she is nowhere near as beautiful as your Melawnia.

The three Nichoklu quickly crossed the distance to where Klump and Kush were standing. As they got nearer, Klump noticed they were quite tall—at least six or eight inches taller than he was—and larger in width, giving them significant mass. He was surprised by their size—in the video footage he'd seen of the Nichoklu, they hadn't looked particularly big.

No matter how large or how alien they were, though, this was still a negotiation. Klump smiled the smile that every member of his genetic line had perfected in countless offices and diplomatic events, a sharp curvature of the mouth that never touched his eyes. "Caurvex! Welcome to Klump International LaGrange Links at L2."

The lead Nichoklu, presumably Caurvex, quickly manifested a fleshy lump that approximated a nose and two eyes from the mass of its body. The eyes were whitish gray, with a greenish circle that might have been a pupil. Both the eyes and nose were too close to the mouth. The whole effect was like looking at a badly designed Halloween mask.

"We thank you for the invitation to meet." Caurvex's voice took Klump off guard for a moment—it didn't come from the creature's mouth, which didn't move at all. The voice seemed to originate from somewhere outside the alien's body.

Kush, what the hell is going on with its voice?

Unknown, sir. Nichoklu have not been observed using verbal communication among themselves. It is likely that they do not have vocal chords. Our scientists have speculated that all instances of recorded verbal communication are through some sort of technological implant.

Caurvex extended one of its tentacles, which then sprouted five small appendages in the rough imitation of a hand. "We offer you a handshake."

Still smiling, Klump forced himself to shake the alien's tentacle. It was stiffer than he would have thought and the "fingers" encircled his wrist in a vaguely unsettling way. He tried his usual arm-tugging handshake, but he couldn't move the alien's appendage more than a centimeter or two. "It's a pleasure to meet you, Caurvex."

The Nichoklu's mouth turned upwards in an attempt to mimic a smile. "It is also pleasant to meet you." It disengaged its hand from Klump's. "It can be difficult for us to make the ritual of 'hand-shake' with humans, but your hand is pleasingly small."

What a jackass. I can't believe I'm going to play golf with this thing.

Yes, sir. You are willing to do whatever it takes, sir. That is just one of your many admirable traits.

Klump used his club to indicate the surroundings. "My company, Klump Exploration and Investments, has just finished building this tremendous hotel and golf course. You wouldn't believe how many celebrities I've had call me wanting to play golf here. People call me about it all the time. I'm not sure if you're familiar with our Earth game of golf, but this is the best course in the solar system. A great place to try out the game. I'd be happy to gift you with a really great set of Klump-brand clubs from our pro shop so we can play a few rounds together while we discuss matters."

"We are not interested in playing this game."

Klump's smile got more strained. "Oh, well, it's traditional on Earth for leaders to play golf together while..."

Caurvex cut Klump off mid-sentence. "You bear striking resemblance to all other leaders on your world. Are you a member of the leadership clade on your planet?"

They didn't even bother to find out anything about Earth customs. I'm going to enjoy screwing these lazy nachos over.

Yes, sir. I'm sure you will find it diverting, sir.

"I'm mostly a businessman at present, but I have, let's say, friends in planetary government and they asked me to help them out. I have full authority to negotiate on behalf of the Council of Drumpfs and Planet Earth, if that's what you're wondering."

"Good. Then we wish to ask why you have summoned us."

These things get right to it.

An excellent observation, sir.

Klump tossed his 5-wood toward the bag and Kush dutifully retrieved it from the ground and put it away. "I'm sure someone in your outpost on Titan has noticed the fact that Earth now has a planetary defense shield."

"Yes. We were perplexed. We were not aware your world was in an interplanetary conflict. If there is any danger to our colony in your system, we greatly appreciate any notice you can give us."

Klump smiled briefly. "That's not it at all. There is no interplanetary war going on. Yet. That shield was built to keep your kind off of our planet." He jabbed a finger at Caurvex. "And Earth expects you to pay for it. The total cost of building the shield adds up to around a hundred quadrillion dollars."

Caurvex's facial features didn't move a millimeter, but several sensory appendages extended further out behind it, and the other two Nichoklu grasped them with their own tentacles. The silence stretched on for a few seconds before the contact was broken and Caurvex spoke. "We are perplexed by your claim. Our dominion on Titan has never made aggressive action toward your planet, nor do we intend to. Why is it that you deem a planetary shield a necessity?"

These things are going to be pushovers, Kush. We're going to fleece these meat-tubes for so much money we could make a road out of the cash and walk back home from here.

I believe that idea to be problematic at best, sir.

I didn't mean that literally, you stupid circuit-brain.

Of course, Mr. Klump. Should I arrange for the hotel restaurant to start cooking us a victory dinner, sir?

Yeah, tell them to make me a steak—well-done with a side of ketchup, like usual—and add the Grande Fiesta Taco Bowl.

"Don't give me that crap. A number of you nachos have visited Earth. You've met with humans, talked with humans. You've tried to spread your ideology. You've already colonized a major planetary body in our system. We can't be sure you're not gathering information about humanity or using some kind of technologically advanced info-weapon. My friends in world leadership think that what you're doing is a tremendous threat to the Earth. We've taken steps to prevent that threat. You owe us for that. We expect to recover our investment."

Caurvex again entangled its sensory appendages with those of its companions before replying. "Our species is composed of clusters of modular communalist hive-minds. The concept of individuality is fascinating to us. We simply wished to interact with members of your species and pass on knowledge that may be beneficial to your civilization. It is not clear to us what harm there may be in these actions. We have never intended harm."

Klump made a chopping motion, as if to cut off the Nichoklu's point. "I don't care what you intended. The reality is that you owe Earth a hundred quadrillion dollars."

Caurvex's eyes withdrew into its trunk and then re-emerged onto its face in something that resembled a blink. "Our society does not use money as you understand it. We are incapable of what you request."

Klump shrugged. "We've already thought of that. I've had some friends in Manhattan who work in commodities price out some other options. In lieu of dollars, we would accept a delivery of ten million tons of stabilized astatine or francium."

Caurvex paused again for silent communication before speaking. "Your species is subject to a phenomenon called humor. This is surely an example of that, although we cannot understand why you have used it in the middle of our discussion."

Klump shook his head and grimaced. "I'm not joking. This is a serious demand. We expect to be paid."

"We will not pay you. We cannot pay you."

I've got them right where I want them, Kush.

Yes you do, Mr. Klump. Your negotiation skills are spectacular, as usual.

Klump smiled. The smile didn't reach his eyes. "I know what kinds of toys the Council has at their disposal and you don't want to mess with that stuff, believe me. That would be a huge mistake."

"You are threatening aggressive action against us. Do you intend to attack our settlement in the system?"

"No, I would never threaten you. But, you know, a lot of our advanced weapons testing has taken place in the asteroid belt. Now that I think about it, though, some weapons need an atmosphere to really see what they can do. Titan does have a pretty good atmosphere. If we started testing some of our stuff there... well, let me just say I wouldn't want to be living on Titan at that point."

"We are a peaceful civilization. We do not wish conflict, but we cannot create a ship capable of returning to our system of origin for many more cycles. Our voyage to your solar system was intended to be one-way."

How did these idiots make an interstellar craft in the first place? My golf clubs are smarter than these things. Maybe that's why they didn't want to play.

I'm sure it is, sir. You're right, as usual.

Klump shrugged. "Not my problem. That's your problem. And it's a huge problem, unless you pay me the money you owe."

Caurvex again communicated via its appendages with the other two Nichoklu. "If you pursue this possibility, then we will have no choice but to respond. We will use short-range craft to travel to Earth."

"A minute ago you were saying you were 'a peaceful race'—now you're going to invade us?"

"We are peaceful. We will not invade your planet, only travel there. You will be hesitant to use destructive weapons on your own planet."

"There is no way you would even get to Earth. You wouldn't get through the planetary shield we just built. That's why we built it."

"Not true. You have ships constantly coming and going from your moon and major colonies. You need to open passages through the shield to let these ships in and out constantly. With our superior stealth technology, you will not be able to keep us out."

These things just don't understand that they've lost.

Clearly not, sir. They have no hope of matching wits with you.

"But once you get to the surface, we'll have police or military units there to arrest you. You can't hide forever. You'll be deported back to Titan. Or maybe we'll throw you in prison on Mars. I don't think you aliens would like Martian jails."

"You would imprison us because we took an action you forced us into?"

Klump was disappointed he couldn't hear fear in the alien's voice, but it was difficult to hear any emotion in it at all. "I didn't force you into anything. You're the ones who are talking about invading Earth. But, look, all this can go away if you just pay me a hundred quadrillion dollars. Then you don't have to worry about anything."

The Nichoklu didn't have expressions in the human sense, but Klump was sure something changed in the alien's features before it spoke. Something about it put him on guard. "It will not be possible for you to imprison us. When we come to your planet, we will have a safe haven. We will be welcomed."

"What, do you have some sleeper agents ready to hide you? Believe me, we know how to deal with that kind of thing. You aliens talk like you're all one big happy family. You don't spy on each other, do you? You don't have experience with conflict the way we do on Earth. You might think you're being sneaky, but you're not. You'll get caught. And if you've done some kind of slimy alien mind-control on any Earth citizens, there will be a response. A huge response." Klump jabbed a finger at Caurvex to make his point.

Kush, query some law enforcement databases and see if there's anything to what this thing is saying.

"We do not yet have any agents on your planet. But we will when we arrive."

"And you're telling me now? We can increase surveillance of your colony and block any kind of electromagnetic signal you produce. You won't be able to control anybody."

"You will be our agent, Mr. Klump. That is why we arranged for you, and none of the others of your clade, to meet us today."

"You jokers had nothing to do with me being here today. I just came to get the money you owe the Earth." Klump paused and looked at the Nichoklu behind Caurvex for any sign that they were doing anything. Trying to look calm, he ran a hand through his hair.

Kush, is there any evidence of some kind of mind-control device on the station? Do we know if they have this kind of technology or are they just bluffing?

"Are you planning on kidnapping me? I won't bow to threats."

Caurvex attempted to twist its mouth into a smile, but only succeeded in showing off the three rows of sharp, bony plates it used as teeth. "No, Mr. Klump. Threats will not be necessary. You are going to help us of your own will, without any kind of coercion."

Kush, contact station security. "Why the hell would I do that?"

"As we understand your system of rulership, every political entity on your planet is governed by a clone of the same long-deceased individual, who you call The Original. When you are birthed, each of you is assigned and educated to rule a specific area."

"What does this have to do with anything? If you're planning on attacking Earth, I'm not going to confirm anything."

"You were originally birthed to be the leader of a group of islands, but before you assumed leadership, those islands were subsumed into a larger country that already had a ruling line. Because of these events, you are not currently part of your world's ruling class. Is that correct?"

Klump tried to look Caurvex in the eyes, to stare it down, but he found it difficult to look at the flat gray-green pupils and broke eye contact after only a few moments. "Are you... have you been spying on me? I take that very seriously. Very seriously. I'm going to notify my security team."

Kush, have you gotten in touch with station security?

There was no response.

Kush? Klump glanced back at his android. Kush was standing at attention, but his gaze was focused straight ahead and his facial features were frozen.

Kush?

Klump turned back to the Nichoklu and pointed at the android. "What have you done to my assistant?"

"He was attempting to contact the authorities. We do not believe that is productive. Please hear us out."

Klump took a step back. His brain sped through escape plans. He had foolishly not even considered the fact that the diplomatic envoy could be a hit squad. Killing a member of Earth's ruling class could be their declaration of war. He had little idea what these creatures were capable of physically, but their sheer size was suddenly unnerving.

"...nothing less than complete power over your entire planet."

The phrase penetrated through Klump's building panic enough to get his attention. "What did you say?"

"We arranged for you to meet us today for a reason. We wish to offer you nothing less than complete power over your entire planet."

Klump took a breath and tried to pull himself together. This sounded like an offer—the beginning of a negotiation. That was something Klump understood. "Why would you want to do that?"

"We find it difficult and tiring to have a multitude of unpredictable political entities so close to our colony. It causes undesirable uncertainty in our predictive models of the future and makes communication with your world unnecessarily complex. The fact that every polity is governed by a clone of what your species terms a narcissistic megalomaniac also increases your race's aggression to unfortunate levels. It would be preferable if your planet was controlled by a single entity. Who that entity is does not matter to us."

"I'm not going to betray the human race so we can be controlled by some slimy aliens. No matter what the stakes. No way." There was just a moment of hesitation in Klump's response.

"As we said, we have no desire to control your planet or dominate your species. It would be much too tiring for us. We simply wish to be left alone and have a neighbor whose actions we can predict. In return for these considerations, we will use all necessary and appropriate resources to place you in total control of your planet. What do you say to our offer?"

Klump thought for a long moment. *Could he really trust the nachos? Could they really do what they said?* There was no way to know, but sometimes in life you had to roll the dice. The Original had understood that well. Klump thought about the Game—all the tit-for-tat, the sting of losing, the rush of victory. An hour ago, he had been out of it, looking in from the outside, trying to formulate a plan to get back in. Now, though... this was a game-changer, if it was genuine. Not since the Original had anyone been able to dominate the entire world.

"The Council of Drumpfs won't take this kind of thing lying down. Believe me. If I start taking other clones' territories, there will be open war. You're talking about killing millions of people, wrecking hundreds of investments, damaging the portfolios of dozens of major banks. I'd need tens of millions of troops on my side and at least half that many drones."

Caurvex's tentacles swirled. Klump wished Kush was functioning so he could explain what the gesture meant. "We believe you are capable of raising such a force, with appropriate assistance. We can provide undetectable, intelligent, self-replicating persuasion algorithms that will infiltrate your terran social media networks and influence the neural states of large masses of humans. Additionally, we have studied your system of commerce and we anticipate that we should be able to create significant sums of your currency as needed. Our predictive models indicate that, with this help, you will eventually triumph in any prolonged conflict. How you assert your dominance concerns us not."

Klump mulled over the possibilities. "But people are stupid. They're short-sighted. They wouldn't see what a tremendous opportunity this could be. If they knew I was being backed by aliens, my own forces might rebel against me. I wouldn't have any troops left after a while. I can't fight the Council of Drumpfs and the people I'm supposed to be ruling."

"That will not be a problem. We will completely disguise the origin of our aid."

Klump pursed his lips. "If any of those sleazy media bots ever caught even a hint of this, they would never shut up about it. It would be a fake press field day. My real estate investments might be damaged. The Lunar Putinocracy could even take sides eventually."

"We trust you are capable of avoiding unwanted attention. On our end, this will not be a problem."

Klump paused, out of questions. It was a risk, but he knew what his answer would be. It was time for him to make Earth great again. It was time for him to win and win and keep winning. He stuck out his hand to shake.

"We have a deal. This is going to be huge."

Michael Manzer is a writer and ELL teacher who lives with his family in the Seattle area, where he reads lots of books, writes fiction, and thinks a lot about languages, aliens, space, magic and the future world he is imparting to his son. You can follow him on Twitter @nevtelenuriembr (a handle which makes total sense if you happen to speak Hungarian).

14 The Trump Brand

by Marleen S. Barr

Professor Stella Diamond, feminist science fiction scholar par excellence, was strolling with her metrosexual French Canadian art historian husband Pepe Le Pew. Stella shook her head when she looked at the moon and saw a logo emblazoned on it. Stella had heard that astronauts were mounting a billboard on the moon. After Trump built the wall, he signed an executive order which restructured NASA funding. Decreeing that science had no connection to space exploration, he reconfigured NASA to comply with his self-interest. The Trump-era moon landing, no small step for mankind, was a great economic leap forward for the Trump family. Astronauts mounted a neon sign on the moon which could be easily read from Earth. No one could miss the nightly lunar message:

BUY IVANKA'S CLOTHING LINE

Stella was outraged. "This is the limit," she said to Pepe. I thought that Trump turning the White House into a hotel was the last straw. I was incredulous when he placed huge golden letters over the White House main entrance which read 'TRUMP HOUSE.' The nerve of him, renting out the Lincoln Bedroom for ten thousand dollars a night. Who could have imagined that the stately White House Red, Blue, and Gold Rooms would be transformed into convention venues?"

"My breaking point came when Trump changed the White House lawn into a golf course," interjected Pepe.

"No! The worst was when he had 'TRUMP' painted on the side of the Mother of All Bombs he dropped on North Korea."

"I beg to differ. The biggest outrage was his law mandating that Trump Steaks were the only food that could be sold in American grocery stores. I'm a vegan. Now I'm being forced to eat dead cows with Trump's name stamped on them."

"I was most surprised when CUNY and SUNY, and then Harvard and Yale, merged with Trump University. Trump University has taken over every university in the country."

"Ditto for the airlines. Trump resurrected the Trump Shuttle and merged it with the entire American aviation industry. Remember the outrage after United Airlines overbooked a flight and dragged a sixty-nine year old doctor off the plane? Those were the good old days. United, of course, no longer exists. The Trump Shuttle routinely treats passengers in the manner of Mitt Romney transporting his dog on a car top."

Taking a last look at the besmirched moon, Stella and Pepe walked back to their Park Avenue apartment. Pepe almost keeled over after picking up the paper and seeing the *New York Times* headline: "PRESIDENT RENAMES USA DRUMPFHEIM."

The entire American economy had become tied to the Trump family business. "Trump impersonator" was the most lucrative occupation available to men now. Alec Baldwin's wealth recently surpassed that of Bill Gates. With the exception of "super models" and "beauty pageant contestants," Drumpfheim women could no longer hold jobs. Trump decreed that all women look like ladies at all times. No more jeans, sneakers, and scrunchies. Women were mandated to resemble Ivanka and Melania clones.

Stella hung her head when she told Pepe the latest news. "My name isn't Stella anymore. I have a new name."

"Which is?"

"Ofdonald. All female Drumpfheimians have been renamed Ofdonald. Melania and Ivanka are the only exceptions. The exemption applies to two women. Who ever heard of anyone else being named Melania and Ivanka?"

"If all but two females in the country are now named Ofdonald, how will we differentiate between individuals?"

"Trump, although he didn't use these exact words, ostensibly said that female subjectivity is a lie. He claims the right to grope any pussy at will."

Drumpfheim men became bored of seeing all the Ofdonalds wearing Ivanka brand clothes. Attired in their Trump impersonator guises festooned with blue pussy hats, they gathered to protest by participating in the Men's March on Washington. The concentration of men worked to Trump's advantage.

"The Trump brand has become the most important thing in Drumpfheim," bellowed Trump through a microphone on a stage set up in the gated White House lawn. "In the wake of the Ofdonald plethora, I will also apply Fordism to men. I put my brand on the moon, the food, the universities, the airlines, and the entire Drumpfheim economy. I will now brand all Drumpfheim men. I mean this literally," screamed Trump as he brandished a branding iron at the blue hatted marchers.

The branding iron contained five letters: "T" "R" "U" "M" "P." All men were required to roll up the right sleeve of their oversize Trump impersonator suits as they were herded and concentrated within corrals. They were branded on their inner arms just above their wrists with the five ubiquitous letters.

Former feminist science fiction professor par excellence Ofdonald, dressed in Ivanka brand clothing, cried as she took Pepe's hand and saw his "T" "R" "U" "M" "P" brand. During her entire career publishing articles on feminist dystopias, she never imagined that real women would carry placards which read "Make Atwood Fiction Again." She never imagined that, like her German immigrant parents and men residing in Drumpheim, her French Canadian immigrant husband would be branded for life.

Marleen S. Barr is known for her pioneering work in feminist science fiction and teaches English at the City University of New York. She has won the Science Fiction Research Association Pilgrim Award for lifetime achievement in science fiction criticism. Barr is the author of *Alien to Femininity: Speculative Fiction and Feminist Theory*, *Lost in Space: Probing Feminist Science Fiction and Beyond*, *Feminist Fabulation: Space/Postmodern Fiction*, and *Genre Fission: A New Discourse Practice for Cultural Studies*. Barr has edited many anthologies and co-edited the science fiction issue of *PMLA*. She is the author of the novels *Oy Pioneer!* and *Oy Feminist Planets: A Fake Memoir*.

15 Twice Upon A Trump

by Timothy Carter

On August 26, 2017, three very interesting things happened in the city of Houston, Texas.

One, an energy discharge ripped the air inside the Lakewood Megachurch Stadium.

Two, a figure emerged from the energy discharge in the middle of that stadium.

Three, part of that discharge hit Air Force One, which happened to be flying by overhead at that exact moment. The plane broke apart and rained destruction down on the already hurricane-battered city, but the emergency escape pod landed gently on the stadium floor.

T

President Trump waited in the pod for someone to open the door and help him out. He could have emerged on his own, but he had people he paid for that kind of thing. *Whoever's job it was is getting a pay cut,* Trump thought. He'd been waiting nearly five minutes!

The pod door opened, revealing only darkness beyond. Trump waited for the door opener staff person to reach a hand in and help him out.

Instead, a gruff and pushy voice said:

"Get out here, you lazy self-absorbed shit-fucker!"

At first, President Trump was astounded. Then he was hurt. Then he was covering that hurt with bluster.

"You can't talk to me like that!" he said, climbing out of the pod in spite of himself. "Don't you know who I am?" He had to admit he was intrigued; who would dare speak to him in that tone of voice?

A somewhat familiar voice…

"I know exactly who you are," said the disrespectful cretin, who stood just outside the pod. "You're a narcissist and an idiot who's destroying this country." He was broad-shouldered, elderly and fat—and stark naked. He had tiny little hands and a very distinctive mane on his head.

My God, Trump's eyes squinted and his mouth engulfed flies. *That disrespectful cretin is me!*

T

President Trump stared back at his older, nakeder self as he explained how he'd come to be here. They were alone in the stadium; Pastor Joel Osteen's heroic efforts had kept the place refugee-free. There were also no Secret Service agents rushing to the younger Donald's rescue; his older self informed him that the time travel effect had produced an EMP that had blacked out the entire state.

The President was of two minds as well as two incarnations. *Time-travel from 20 years in the future? Puh-leez!* It was ridiculous, and stupid. Like Hillary Clinton's hair.

But at the same time, the man was clearly, undoubtedly him. The tiny hands were unmistakable, as was the… not so tiny other part. And even though the man before him was older and fatter, he was still seriously gorgeous. The clincher was the hair, of course. No way anybody could fake that.

Yeah, it was him, all right.

"Why the nudity?" President Trump asked.

"The time travel," his elder self replied. "Terminator rules. James Cameron was right. Who knew?"

"Huh," said President Trump. "Well, we gotta put some pants on ya. Can't have the president swingin' his... Chief of Staff."

"Heh, staff! Good one," said the naked Trump. "There's a track suit in one of the cabinets in that pod. Get it for me."

"Whoa!" said the younger Donald. "The president doesn't play fetch for anybody. Even himself."

"I'm Emperor of the United Continents of America," the elder said. "I outrank you."

"Emperor?" said the younger Donald. "Continents?"

"Yeah. Kind of what I need to talk to you about. But first, pants. Go fetch. And grab the emergency stash while you're at it."

T

They sat in the stands, popped some booze from the pod's 'emergency stash,' and got down to the business of things to come.

"After everything went to shit," Emperor Trump began, "there was another civil war. Not about blacks this time, although there were a lot on the other side... mostly it was about Mexicans. Anyway, after I won that war I declared myself emperor, and it just made sense to keep going. Mexico and Canada first, then Alaska. They tried to tell us they were already Americans, if you can believe that!"

"Let me guess," said junior, "then we went after South America, right?"

"Yeah, that's right!" elder replied. "Every place that called itself America became the United Continents of America."

"Heh," younger replied. "I thought continents were what you put on hot dogs."

"I used to think so, too."

"Doesn't sound so bad," President Trump said. "The world, I mean."

"I guess that part's kinda okay," the Emperor conceded. "But the civil war sucked. We had to nuke New York."

"Oh man," said younger Don. "I love that place. What about San Francisco?"

"That city we nuked just on principal," Old Don replied.

Emperor Trump went on to detail the next twenty years, and how things had gone from their present conditions to their shitty war-starting ones. President Trump tried to listen—he did love to hear himself talk—but his desire to dominate the conversation was overpowering. Especially when the Emperor started talking smack about him.

"Nope. That is not true," the President said.

"I'm telling you it is!" said the Emperor. "I was there, I cut the funding for climate change research…"

"Which is a liberal hoax."

"No it isn't!" the elder Don cried. "Look where we are, in the middle of a city getting its ass kicked by a hurricane, with four more on the way, all because…"

"There are only two hurricanes, this one and Edna. And that one that's gonna hit the Caribbean, which is not America's concern."

"Will you shut up?" Emperor Trump shook his fists at his counterpart. "I'm trying to protect my legacy, here. And save America, too."

"Well, the hurricanes are not my fault," the President replied. "I haven't even been in office a full year yet. And I didn't get the anti-funding bill passed yet, either. This," he gestured at the inclement weather around them, "is on Obama."

Emperor Trump opened his mouth to retort, then paused. His younger self had made an excellent point.

"Okay, I'll give you that," elder Donald said. "But your response to the hurricanes—all 5 of them…"

"Three."

"…make the situation worse."

"Nope."

"It did! You… I made George W. Bush's fumbling of New Orleans look like a smart game plan."

"Nope. Didn't happen."

"Well, not yet!" the Emperor roared in exasperation. He'd known this was going to be hard, but… "I'm talking about things you're gonna do. In the FUTURE!"

"No I won't."

"Yes you will!" the Emperor lunged forward and grabbed his younger self by the tie. "Now shut your stupid mouth before I do something to your face that I'll regret."

"Okay, okay!" younger Trump threw up his hands in surrender. "I'll be good."

The Emperor released himself, then sat and put his face in his tiny hands. *God, had he always been such a pussy when confronted directly?*

"Did we get the wall built?"

"Huh?" the elder raised his head.

"The wall across the border," younger Trump elaborated. "To keep the illegals out. Did you build it?"

Elder Trump sighed.

"Yeah, you did," he said. "And it pretty much bankrupted the country."

"No, not true," the younger said. "We've always been great with money."

"Well, yeah, but it led right to the civil war…"

"It created new jobs, didn't it?"

"It did, sure, but it cost a lot more than we figured."

"So? Didn't you get Mexico to pay for it?"

The Emperor stood up, walked away a few steps.

"You didn't, did you?" the President rose to his feet and approached himself. "Well, there's your problem right there. Why didn't ya make 'em pay? I thought you said we conquered them."

"That was after." The Emperor looked back at his younger self, but would not meet his eyes. "They said no."

"Huh?" younger Trump said. "They said no? And you took that from them? I woulda…"

"Well, we didn't, okay?" elder said.

"So we become a complete wimp?"

"We become Emperor!"

"Yeah, *Emperor Wimp!*"

"You take that back!" Emperor Wimp said.

"Why don't you make me?" President Pussy replied.

The Emperor lunged. The President freaked. And kicked his older self in the balls.

"Ow!" younger Trump cried, clutching his foot.

"Ball shield!" elder Trump tapped his nutsack proudly. "You think you're the first one to try that?

"Besides," he went on, "if you really think I'm a wimp, just ask North Korea."

"North Korea?" President Trump said. "We go to war with those chumps?"

"Yep! And we kicked ass."

"No kidding?" younger raised his hand, and elder slapped it. "Doesn't sound to me like you're doing all that bad."

"Well... I mean, it depends on your perspective..."

"Perspective?!? We became fucking Emperor!"

"But... say, that's right!" the Emperor said. "And... all the bad things that I did..."

"Nope. Wasn't you."

"Right. All that stuff led to me becoming emperor!"

"Oh. Then I guess it was you. Because that was the plan all along, right?"

"Yeah! And you know what? The United Continents of America is pretty darned great."

"Of course it is."

"Okay. You just stay the course, my friend."

"You know I will."

"Okay." Emperor Trump turned his head to the sky. "Covfefe!"

President Trump frowned.

"What did you say that for?"

"Sending me back in time," the Emperor said, "is Operation Covfefe. The science nerds told me when my mission was over, I just say the word and they'll bring me back."

"What word?"

"Covfefe, you moron!"

"Oh, right. Well, see ya."

"You will," Elder Trump assured him. "Hey, Covfefe, already!"

The Trumps waited. Absolutely nothing happened. And continued not happening.

"Maybe you have to say it louder," the President said.

"I'm sayin' it plenty loud," the Emperor replied. "Covfefe!!!"

An hour later, it still hadn't worked.

"How was it supposed to work?" President Trump asked.

"Just like this—I say *Covfefe* and they pull me back."

"That's what the science nerds told you."

"Yeah."

"Hmm…" they both said.

"You know, it's possible they were working with my enemies," the Emperor mused.

"How do you figure?"

"Well, they were science nerds."

"Hmm, good point."

A helicopter appeared over the side of the stadium walls, bearing the presidential seal.

"Well, my ride's here," President Trump said. "Good luck with the whole getting back to whenever thing."

"It'll work," Emperor Trump said. "Covfefe! Covfefe!"

President Trump left his future self and walked over to the landing helicopter. Several Secret Service agents jumped out to assess the situation and verify that their charge was all right.

"Who's that, sir?" asked one agent, pointing his gun at the Emperor.

"He looks like you, but older!" said another, also pointing his gun.

President Trump turned to look back at his future self. The man was emperor of half the world where he came from, and the man he himself was destined to become. But here, in this time, he was basically an illegal alien looking for a handout.

"He's an ISIS impostor, responsible for this blackout," the President replied. "Arrest him."

The agents ran over to the elder Trump, beat him more than was necessary, beat him again, then dragged him back to the helicopter in handcuffs.

"W...why?" the Emperor asked his younger self as he was manhandled aboard the helicopter.

"What can I say?" the President replied. "This country's not big enough for two of me."

T

Timothy Carter is a writer of far-fetched fiction for young adults and the young at heart (and mind). Born in England during the week of the final lunar mission, he has a great love of outer space and tea. Timothy is the author of *The Five Demons You Meet in Hell, Epoch, Evil?, Apoca-Lynn* and *Section K.* He lives and writes in Toronto with his cat.

16 The Trivia Room

By Jared Bennett

What is Perdition. I'm not asking—I'm telling.

Question number 5 on season 33 episode 81 of Jeopardy.

"I'll take 'Invisible Places' for $200, Alex!"

Alex reads, *"Tom Hanks took the road to this place in his 2002 release."*

Becky, "Big Tits" as I know her, buzzes first. Carl on the left is getting agitated. Doris, in the middle, seems confused. Her expression makes her look like an elephant seal.

"What is Perdition!" Big Tits says in her ridiculous southern accent. When the crowd begins to applaud, she giggles as if she is embarrassed by giving the right answer. Carl remains the champion in the end.

"But how will he fare against our contestants tomorrow? Tune in to find out. So long."

Fade to black.

Blip.

Jeopardy 33:81 appears in white letters on a black screen. Sporadic lines of static glitch up and down.

Pause.

1 Mississippi. 2 Mississippi. 3 Mississippi.

"This is Jeopardy!"

The music plays and the episode starts over again. I've never watched episode 82. I have a panic attack anytime I hear the jingle.

Before my room, I didn't mind Jeopardy. I wasn't very good at it, but my ex-wife enjoyed the show. After dinner, when there was nothing more entertaining on, we would watch it and she would try to impress me with her knowledge of useless trivia. Of course, I really had no reason to watch the show after the divorce. To be honest with you, I don't think I watched an episode of Jeopardy after our divorce until they took me.

I thought about my ex-wife a lot when I was in my room. I blamed her mostly. I wouldn't have been out walking that night if we had still been together. I would have remained home with her, eating dinner and sharing a bottle of wine. But she just had to say it, she had to tell me before she walked out our door for the last time. "You've let yourself go! You're not the man I fell in love with! Look at yourself!"

"What is the Atkins diet, Alex."

"I'm sorry that is incorrect."

I started walking in the evenings a few months after our divorce was finalized. I guess I thought if I lost some weight and started looking better I could at least hold on to some of my dignity.

On that night, which now seems like endless ages ago, everything seemed normal. It was my usual route through the usual neighborhood— everything the same, except for the van.

I thought they needed directions and I wanted to help.

I never saw their faces.

It's all a blur now. The sound of the van's door sliding open. There was a sharp twinge in my neck and my body went numb. Then I was gliding backward—pulled along by some unseen force. My heels bumped along the pavement. Black closed in around my vision and my head swam. There were muffled voices and a vehicle's gears shifting. Then there was nothing.

I woke up during Final Jeopardy between four walls of grey concrete. Encased within one wall and behind a shield of Plexiglas, *Jeopardy* blared. Its catchy jingle bounced around the room reverberating in my pounding head. I was naked and lying on my back. The cold of the concrete floor seeped into my bones. Whoever had brought me here didn't even have the decency to lay me on the pathetic piece of yellow foam that would serve as my bed. I felt exposed and vulnerable. I tried to hide my nude frailty, but the ceaseless fluorescent glow from the out-of-reach ceiling gave me nowhere to hide.

It wouldn't serve me to tell you about those first endless hours in the room. I spent my energy on pointless activities. I screamed until my vocal chords tore. I pounded my body on the expressionless walls of grey concrete. I wrenched at the door handle until my hands bled.

I hoped.

I hoped against all hope that someone would find me. I thought of my dad. We were supposed to meet tomorrow. Was it tomorrow already? Had tomorrow already passed? He was coming into town on business and he wanted to get lunch. I couldn't tell how much time had passed but surely he would realize something was wrong. Surely he would be out there looking for me—mustering cops, search and rescue volunteers, the fucking National Guard! Surely someone would find me. All the while, as my brain scrambled itself in desperation to escape the same episode of Jeopardy, played over, and over, and over, and over again.

I can't remember when I stopped all that nonsense. I can't remember when the empty void of my room gradually became a dimension of its own and my hope was drowned in the endless blaring loop of *Jeopardy 33:81.*

Gradually my body adjusted to the chill and my nostrils accepted the stinging smell of bleach that filled the room. I started keeping time by how often I was fed. There was a plastic tube in my room that ran straight from the ceiling to the corner where I kept my bed. It worked like the tubes at the bank. Every 75th episode, right when Double Jeopardy was about to end and Doris would fail to answer:

"Birth of Borders for $1600."

"This 1964 birth occurred with the merger of Zanzibar and Tanganyika"

"What is the United Republic of Tanzania."

A cylinder-like capsule holding a shrink-wrapped meal would shoot down the tube and another day in the room would pass. The meal was more liquid than solid. It looked like someone put a 3 course dinner in a blender set it to liquefy. But my hunger had little pride. I scooped the meal out with delight each time it arrived, gagging past the putrid smell that exploded from the plastic when I tore it open and sucking at the remaining paste that clung to my fingers after I had licked the wrapper clean. I kept the wrappers piled in the corner furthest from my bed. I recounted them after every meal to remind myself how long I had been in the room.

Five meals had been delivered before Alex and the others started talking to me.

Alex was reading the Final Jeopardy question, *"This 19th Century inventor revolutionized communion by creating a non-alcoholic grape beverage,"* when I saw Doris smiling at me.

"Hey Becky, look at his tiny dick." Doris said.

Becky covered a giggle and pointed at my naked form.

Carl and Alex soon joined in. The crowd began to applaud as they hooted and cawed with laughter. I sobbed and they mocked my tears. I hated them. I begged them to stop, but they continued.

My despair turned to anger. I wanted to kill them. To punish them. To shut them up. But how could I—they were safe behind their window of Plexiglas. The hum of television laughter twisted my insides and tore at my mind.

I was a joke to them.

This was a joke to them.

Everything was a joke.

Then it hit me.

This was a joke. This was a joke to them—the people who put me here. No one could seriously do this to a person. No one would seriously do this to me. I was good. I was nice. I never hurt anyone. I paid my taxes. I donated to the Salvation Army. I used my turn signals. I voted. I was vanilla. Not even my ex-wife would be this cruel to me. This was a joke. And if this was a joke, then someone had to be watching.

I dragged my body across the room and pressed my head on the window into the world of Alex, Doris, Becky, and Carl. I could feel the hum of the television vibrations working through my skull. I closed my eyes and clenched my teeth. A cold sweat began to drip down my neck and my body trembled. I steadied myself. I took a deep breath. I pulled my head away as far as my neck would allow and I began to pound.

The first smash of my head into the Plexiglas made my eyes water, but I returned with a second blow of renewed vigor. My brain exploded. My body screamed please stop, but I knew. I knew that anytime now they would come in—the ones who brought me here. The door would open and they would grab me and say: *"Please, stop! It was just a joke. We are sorry. We never wanted to see you get hurt. We will let you go."*

I felt warm liquid pour down my face as I continued to pound. My blows began to glance off the window as it became slick with crimson. My sight grew dim and my neck muscles ached. I screamed and pounded over and over, until I could only muster one last mighty blow. I strained and screamed and launched myself forward with every last piece of hope I held on to.

When I came to, the blinding fluorescent lights that hid in the ceiling welcomed me back. The audience applauded with admiration. My eyes struggled to focus. I moaned in pain, grabbing at an enormous open gash on my forehead. I had only succeeded in knocking myself out. The door remained locked. The episode continued to blare.

That was the first time I tried killing myself.

Gradually, I became grateful for the television. I came to an agreement with Doris and Becky and Carl and even Uncle Alex, an agreement that gave us all some semblance of purpose. They needed me to laugh at their jokes and cheer when they answered correctly, and I needed them for playmates.

"Alliteration Groups for $200."

"English band of Sherwood."

"Who are the Merry Men."

I invented new endings for the episode. I built new conflicts for Alex and his contestants and pitted them against each other. I paired them with the forgotten faces of my memories. I made them marry and fall in love. I made them divorce. I locked them in the studio. I fucked every one of them. I made them fuck each other. I beat them to death. I loved them. I hated them. Every possible dimension that my degrading and decomposing brain could create was their destination.

Sometimes my ex-wife was there too. She said she didn't recognize me anymore. She said I had let myself go. She said I needed to clean my room. I argued with her. I told her I wanted to grow this beard and she always said that I needed to lose some weight. I ran my fingers up and down my exposed ribs proving that I had, in fact, finally lost the weight she railed on so much about. I was just what she wanted now. I apologized to her for the smell, but at least I had the decency to shit in the corner furthest from my bed and out of the view of my friends in the television.

When I wasn't watching my friends play, I wondered who was at the other end of my feeding tube. I reasoned that it must be Uncle Alex or maybe Doris. It wasn't in Big Tits or Carl's nature to feed the tortured.

With my 258th meal, I received a special delivery in the tube.

It was a photo of a tombstone. The tombstone read:

Loving Father and Husband
Steven Greene Sr.
Born: February 4th, 1941

The date of death was cropped out of the photo.

"Who is Steven Greene Sr?"

"I'm sorry that is incorrect." answered Uncle Alex.

I asked Becky and Carl and Doris, but even with all their combined knowledge they couldn't tell me. My mind turned for the next four episodes as I played with Doris and Carl. She was fucking him while smashing his head in with a hammer. That's when I remembered my name. It sounded like a curse when it fell off my lips.

"Steven Greene Jr."

I hid my face in my mattress because I didn't want them to see me cry.

After my dad's tombstone picture was delivered, I stopped eating. Doris told me not to and that she still wanted to play, but I was tired. My meals stopped arriving when I stopped sending back the capsule that held my meals. It was the only thing that connected me to the people on the other side of the tube. Somewhere someone opened that cylinder and put my shrink wrapped meal inside. Somewhere, another set of human hands touched the item that I touched. But I was done with them now, and since they never sent another cylinder I supposed they were done with me.

Eventually, I lost track of the days. My characters were left to play on default.

Eventually I couldn't lift myself off my bed. Every time I shifted, the smell of shit and piss that saturated the foam mattress wafted around me. I thought of death and peace and escape. I thought of endless darkness far away from blinding fluorescent lights. I thought of warmth. I allowed myself to remember things best forgotten. This was going to be it. I had found freedom. I closed myself up. As the world around me began to dim, I saw the door open and they stepped in.

The next time I opened my eyes I was sitting against the wall next to the television. Alex was asking about Thomas Bramwell Welch again and a new foam mattress was in my room. I scratched at a small puncture wound just above the bend of my arm. They had been here. They had revived me.

It seems strange now that I didn't cry or wail or scream or break down when I truly realized that even death did not exist in my room. I suppose a part of me was glad to see my friends on the television, and another part of me felt strangely comforted that somehow and somewhere someone was watching to make sure I didn't die.

Uncle Alex and the others threw a big party for me.

I received two more surprises from the tube during my stay in the room. Around 177 days after I returned, a picture of my mother's tombstone was delivered. I tried suffocating myself in my mattress.

The third surprise came with meal 764 It was a yellow post-it note stuck to the packaged food. In delicate handwriting it read:

"good-bye."

I carefully counted 176 episodes go by before I decided that something had happened to the ones on the other side of the tube. When no more food came, my stomach twisted into knots; not so much from hunger but from the haunting notion that there was no one watching me now and I was truly alone.

I asked my friends on TV if they knew what was going on, but they couldn't answer. Becky offered to show me her tits but I knew it wouldn't help.

My mind raced. I wondered if I had done something wrong. *Were those who put me here mad at me? Did they leave me? Was I dead?* A thousand questions flashed in my mind, until I began to stare at the door.

I hadn't thought about it in so long. The world on the other side of the door seemed unreal. It seemed fake. All that existed on the other side of that door now was only a projection of my dreams.

Right?

"It won't work. Why would you try?" asked Uncle Alex

"But how long has it been since we tried?"

"Don't fucking try it, dumbass. It won't work."

"You're only going to be let down in the end." piped Doris

"I'm going to try."

I attempted to push myself off the foam mattress, but I had grown too weak. My arms trembled and I collapsed back to the floor. My only option was to crawl. My hands and feet smacked against the concrete as I dragged myself across what seemed like an endless expanse from my bed to the door. My joints ached and popped. What remained of my muscles burned as they tore from my exertion. I panted for breath. My lungs felt like they would explode. Hand over hand I pulled myself along while my feet frantically kicked and slipped behind. Slowly, I reached the door. It had been a while since I had been near the door. Bloody fist marks still adorned the entranceway. The scars on my fists told me they were mine, but the details seemed lost to me.

I reached high and clutched for the handle. The muscles in my back strained and I felt the blood pounding in my veins. My hands swayed and trembled with the effort as they closed around the handle. With my last ounce of strength, I was able to pull myself to a standing position teetering on feet that were now only skin and bones. I paused to catch my breath. My throat burned as I sucked in gallons of air. It had been so long since I stood here. It had been so long since my hands knew the cold metal of the door. It had been so long since I hoped. I centered myself and took one last breath. Then everything stopped. I pulled at the handle. Electricity ran through my fingers and up my arm at the sensation. The door gave. I pulled again, frantic now. My body groaned and strained liked the hinges of the door that screamed with a metallic howl. Darkness from beyond the door began to pour in and I began to weep.

My knees buckled and my body trembled. I vomited bile. In an instant my reality had been shattered. All that I had created to survive—all that I had come to rely upon was suddenly gone. I was terrified. *How could I leave?*

This was my room. This was my world.

Beyond my room, I heard voices and footsteps. I moaned and bawled. Voices called out from beyond. Beams of light sliced through the darkness. The steps grew closer. I heard voices cry out and hands grab hold of me. There were men in black helmets clutching guns that only shot beams of light. Some of their voices assured me I was safe. Others cursed or called to God at the sight of me. They hoisted me to my feet. Pulling me away from my room. My head grew light and began to swim. I couldn't understand. I couldn't process what was happening around me. I collapsed—spinning into oblivion. Then the room was gone.

There are people around me constantly now. They help me walk. The help me piss and shit. They feed me and wash me. Doris, and Carl, and Becky, and Uncle Alex still visit sometimes when I sleep, even when I ask them not to.

My new friends tell me that I had been in my room for over two years. They told me people looked for me after I disappeared. They told me my mom and dad never gave up hope. They told me that I wouldn't have to worry about the people on the other side of the tube anymore. They let me watch TV sometimes, but never *Jeopardy*.

Yesterday, I got to watch the news. Two men were side-by-side looking at me. They wore stiffly-pressed suits. The man on the right seemed very upset by something. His face was flushed and a vein pulsed in his forehead. He was talking very loud.

"Did President Trump decide, at the beginning of his term, that our methods to extract information from foreign militants was exceptionally ineffective and weak-handed? Yes, he did! Did President Trump actively work to improve those methods? Yes, he did! But to suggest that that leader of the free world was..."

The man on the left interrupted.

"Please, Mr. Grimes! Then how do you defend this memo? It comes directly from the desk of the President and describes the ideal candidate for these sites. The memo reads, and I quote."

The man on the left looked down at this desk and read from an unseen document. *"The preferred candidate should be: single or widowed; few family/social connections; Democrat, i.e. someone who will not be missed...'"*

It was now Mr. Grimes's turn to interrupt.

"I'll tell you what I think of that memo, Chuck. I think that that memo is a fabrication. It is a fabrication created by those who would see our great country in ruin. I think that whoever created that document should be hung for treason! I think this is just another lame attempt to disgrace our great President, and you, CHUCK, and your

network seem interested in only giving more volume to these treasonous terrorists who create such nonsense!"

The man on the left seemed unimpressed. *"Well, Mr. Grimes you are entitled to your opinion, but unfortunately that is all the time we have. Thank you for being with us today."*

"Thank you, Chuck," said the man on the right as he faded from view and the man on the left filled the screen and continued talking to me.

"If you are just tuning in, we are awaiting a statement from CIA director George Humboldt regarding reports of possible black sites in several major cities across the nation. Early this morning, The Charleston Tribune reported that the CIA has been practicing torture and interrogation techniques on possibly hundreds of American citizens. This report comes on the heels of a massive cyber-attack on the Pentagon last week in which thousands of classified and top-secret documents were released to the public, including a memo that ties these allegations directly to President Trump."

A nurse turned the TV off.

"Alright, Mr. Greene, time for your bath."

"What is Perdition," I said as she rolled my chair down the hall.

Jared Bennett is a writer from West Virginia who was inspired to create "creepy" stories after years listening to the tales of ghosts and demons that thrive in the Appalachian countryside. He can be reached at bennettjs29@gmail.com or followed on Twitter @jaredbennett3.

17 Trio Interstellar

By DJ Tyrer

Norville had no love for the eggheads. Damn scientists, messing about with things they didn't understand. Fooling with alien technology like kids playing with matches in a basement filled with fuel oil and sawdust. Opening a wormhole in Earth's orbit to who-knew-where-or-what…

It was Norville's job to monitor what came through. The people of Earth weren't supposed to know about it, but if an alien invasion force popped through and began their conquest in Times Square, the cover-up would be over. So, he watched for what came through and prayed the agencies, the Army, the Air Force, that one of them knew what to do and still had the budget to do it.

The office he worked in was pokey and mostly filled with a bank of CRT monitors installed years before, which showed the vicinity of the wormhole, and all kinds of readouts, a few of which hadn't been covered at his induction, and that was long ago enough that there was nobody left to ask.

A campaign poster for Donald Trump was tacked up on the wall in defiance of workplace protocols. Norville had voted for The Donald, once in each state, thanks to the multiple IDs his post provided, on the principle that someone who stood firmly against Mexicans was bound to take a stand against aliens arriving from other worlds. His department could sure use a funding boost.

He gave the screens a quick glance—one of the images of the wormhole was rolling as it had been for weeks, but this wasn't covered in his manual or training, so it didn't matter. He stood and stretched, thinking about how he needed a coffee.

Norville's office was in a tiny underground bunker beneath a shack somewhere in western Nevada. Steve, night shift, was asleep on a camp bed in the shack. The only other room down here contained a coffee machine and a microwave they weren't supposed to use, since it interfered with their equipment. He shoved a burrito into it and poured himself the dregs from the pot while the burrito turned about. He paused to consider his bladder, but it wasn't full enough to wander out through the half-finished hallway to the porta potty for relief.

Done, he carried the scalding-hot burrito and barely-lukewarm mug of coffee back to his office.

He swore. One of the screens was flashing.

Cursing the microwave, he gave the screen a bang. Then, he spotted activity on another screen, the one that tracked objects in the vicinity of the wormhole. This wasn't a glitch: something had come through and was headed straight for Earth!

He grabbed the telephone off the wall and yelled into it, before realizing it was still ringing. Typical—probably on their lunch break.

"Yes?" Someone finally answered.

"We've got a bogey."

"Sorry?"

"Something has come through the wormhole. It's headed for Earth. Are you tracking it?"

"We'll take a look, keep monitoring it."

He slammed his phone back into its cradle, wondering what the point of an early-warning system was if nobody was much interested in heeding the warning.

Next time—if they survived and there was a next time—he just hoped The Donald would have things working properly.

Norville slumped back into his chair and watched the screens as the alien craft sped towards Earth. With a lurch of his stomach, he realized it was heading for Nevada—*western* Nevada—their corner of western Nevada. Here.

He really wished he'd relieved himself.

If the Air Force had chosen to intercept the craft, they had left it too late; no jets appeared as blips in its path as it sped at an unearthly speed towards the bunker. Norville really hoped they were friendly.

"Why me...?" he moaned. He was supposed to be an observer, not an active participant. If humanity were wiped out, he was meant to be one of the last to go, having watched it happen, not one of the first.

He supposed he ought to go wake Steve.

Norville gulped down his coffee, wishing it were something stronger, and abandoned his burrito beside the flashing screen to head upstairs.

"Wassit?" burbled Steve as he shook him awake.

"Aliens!"

A moment later, the shack began to shake and Steve finally woke up, wide-eyed and confused.

"'Sit, an earthquake?"

"No—aliens! Something came through the wormhole and it's headed straight for us." The shaking stopped. "And, I think it's arrived."

They looked at each other. Steve yawned.

"Guess we'd better go take a look," he said, stumbling from his bed.

He picked up the old Second World War-vintage rifle that was issued for their defense, then tossed it back down: it seemed doubtful any beings capable of interstellar travel would be deterred by a simple popgun. They probably had force-fields and deathrays and all manner of hi-tech nastiness.

"Okay," said Norville and they stepped outside.

Normally, midday out here would be extremely bright and extremely hot in the desert, but right now it was pleasantly cool and overcast.

They looked up. A sleek silver vessel a full mile long was hovering overhead.

"Well, there's a sight we don't get to see most days," said Norville, jaw slackening in surprise.

They stood for a moment in silence, staring up; the vessel made no sound as it just hung in midair. Nothing happened.

A few minutes later, a dark circle opened in the underside of the craft, although it contrived to appear without them quite seeing it do so. Something similar to a long silver tongue unravelled from within it and extended in front of their feet, all in total silence.

The two men looked at each other, shrugged, then walked up the ramp a little way before stopping, uncertain if they were being invited to ascend into the vessel. Their training manuals never outlined the contact scenario, which would involve employees above their pay grade.

The decision to continue up the ramp was taken away from them as a trio of figures appeared at the top of the ramp and began to descend towards them. Assuming the biological conventions were the same on their homeworld as on Earth then, despite the green skin, they appeared to be two women and a man. Each carried a long-barreled weapon of some sort slung across their backs, which looked suspiciously like rifles. Steve and Norville stepped off the ramp nervously at this sight.

"Greetings," the male-looking alien called out as they neared the bottom of the ramp. Norville was a little surprised that the alien spoke English, but NASA had been sending all manner of probes with information about Earth through the wormhole, along with explorers, , so it wasn't impossible for them to learn the lingo. Plus, for all he knew, radio and television signals might be making it through, as well.

"Uh, hi," said Steve.

The alien nodded. "We would like to request sanctuary."

"Sanctuary?" Norville wasn't even entirely certain he knew what the word meant. Something to do with hunchbacks and chiming bells... but, beyond that?

"We are refugees seeking asylum in your United States."

"Well, it's not mine, personally," murmured Norville as he considered the claim. Asylum seekers he understood. He didn't approve of them, but they had to be better than alien invaders. Given the choice, he would have told them to go back through the wormhole, or at least to France, but decisions about granting asylum to green-skinned folk was *well* past his pay grade.

"Uh, you'll have to talk to my superiors about that. I'll put in a call."

"And," Steve gave a nod to the object on the alien's back, "you'll have to disarm."

"Disarm?"

"Those rifles you've got slung on your backs. Can't have aliens walking around with rifles."

"Rifles? These aren't rifles. They're guitars."

The male alien unslung his guitar and they winced as he pointed it towards them, until they saw it was, as claimed, an instrument akin to a guitar.

"Well, I'll be..." Norville rubbed his chin.

"We're a band."

"Oh?"

"We're called Trio Interstellar."

"I guess it does what it says on the tin," said Steve. The aliens looked at him quizzically, but he left the statement hanging.

"I guess you're on the run from an alien North Korea, eh?"

The alien looked at Norville and nodded. "Something like that."

"Well, I guess I'll put in that call."

T

Norville tugged uncomfortably at the collar of his suit. Having acted as the aliens' welcoming committee, he and Steve had been roped into attending the ceremony conferring asylum on Trio Interstellar.

The intelligence agencies had wanted to keep the landing secret, 'to prevent panic,' while the White House had wanted to publicize it, in the hopes of deflecting the ill-feeling towards the President over the latest iteration of his travel ban. In the end, Trump had tweeted all about it, making it impossible to keep the aliens under wraps without making him appear loony. The CIA tried to argue that a cover-up was the way to go, but the gala was announced by Trump, and then Norville and Steve had been ordered to appear.

It was a celebrity-studded event. Norville spotted Meryl Streep who kept a wary distance from the President. Apparently, the presence of alien superstars, as Trio Interstellar was being touted, was enough to bury loathing for an evening in the hopes of a photo op. Not that there was an overabundance of press at the event.

"Hey, everybody, if I could have your attention." The President was onstage with the aliens. Meryl tried to push past his aides to join them, but the Secret Service intercepted her and bundled her off into the wings.

The crowd in the ballroom looked towards the stage and Trump preened a little in their gaze.

"It is my delight to grant asylum to these three victims of otherworldly oppression and persecution. But, do not think I've gone soft. No, these three have unique talents. But, should more of their kind, feckless green-skinned folk who have nothing to offer our great nation, come to Earth seeking to settle here, I shall say 'no.'

"Be reassured that I have approved funding for a new generation of space-based defenses, an 'orbital wall' if you like, to deter unwanted off-world immigrants."

Norville nodded vigorously and clapped with the half of the attendees who didn't hail from Hollywood.

"But, now, let us enjoy the amazing music of our new guests: Trio Interstellar."

The President clapped and everyone in the room, regardless of their view of him, joined in. The aliens began to play.

Norville's first thought upon hearing the music was that it was, in fact, alien. There was something vaguely similar to it amongst the many musical styles on Earth, but none he had ever heard. The second thought he had was to wonder if anyone had bothered to check they could actually play; the sound was pretty awful. His third was that everyone around him seemed to have gone oddly silent.

Surely, he thought, *they aren't enjoying it?*

Norville turned to Steve, who had the same blank, drooling look he'd had on his face when he was shaken awake to greet the aliens.

Norville gave him a shake now, but it made no difference.

Looking around, Norville saw that everyone had the same blank look as Steve. The music seemed to have put them all in a trance.

Norville had no idea why he was immune, there were too many possibilities, ranging from the damage his brother did to his hearing by shooting him in the ear with a BB gun, to his exposure to radiation at Area 51. It could even be the fact that he'd drunk about two-dozen Redbulls before rolling up to the White House and was completely jazzed. What he did know was that the alien musicians had entranced the President, his staff and his most vocal critics. America was defenseless before whatever evil scheme the aliens had planned. He had to do something.

He looked around for the nearest Secret Service agent, thinking to get a gun to defend his country in the time-honored American fashion. Then, he spotted Meryl. The actress was struggling in the frozen grip of several entranced agents. Except, it wasn't the actress because she was as green as the trio playing onstage.

Norville ran to her.

"Who are you?"

"Get me free—I have to stop them!"

Norville began the difficult job of prying the agents' fingers free from her. "This will take a while, you might as well tell me. Don't tell me that Meryl Streep's been an alien all this time. Although, I guess, it might explain a few things."

"Of course not. The actress is at a spa retreat without any contact with the outside world. Arranged by me, of course."

"So, you're an imposter. You came for these three?"

"Actually, no. I was here observing your President, this Donald."

"Don't tell me he's an alien!"

The alien woman shook her head. "No. Well, we thought he was, at first, but all my observations indicate he's all yours. However, when he tweeted about Trio Interstellar's arrival I knew I had to act."

She was almost free now.

"But, who are they?" Norville asked as he pried the last few fingers off her.

"A lousy band," she said, reaching into her handbag for a ray gun, "who invented instruments capable of mesmerizing anyone who heard them play. At first, they just used them to get to the number one slot on the music charts. But, soon, they began to build an interstellar empire of mindless slaves. A terrible war followed and they were imprisoned."

"But, I guess they got out?"

"Uh-huh."

The band ceased playing and the green man spoke to the hypnotized audience, announcing himself as the new ruler of the United States.

"And soon," he concluded, "the world."

The alien who wasn't Meryl Streep stepped forward at that moment and raised her ray gun.

"Stop her!" The male alien yelled out.

The command came too late and the trio were struck by the ray and began to shrink in size. Guests and agents, under the command of the green man, advanced upon Meryl, but the three aliens had shrunk down to a tiny, inaudible size before anyone reached her and, without further commands, the crowd halted, bemused.

"Grab them and put them in a container," fake Meryl Streep ordered Norville.

Norville did as she said, dropping the three miniature musicians into a champagne flute he found on the floor. He covered the top of the flute with his hand before jamming a square of toast with caviar smeared on it to act as a temporary seal.

People began to shake their heads as if to clear their minds and there was a tentative buzz of confusion.

Norville handed the glass to the alien.

"I'd best be going," she said, turning and slipping off through the crowd.

He wondered if people would see the actress leaving the building or if the alien had multiple guises. Indeed, *how many more aliens might there be, lurking amongst humanity?* As grateful as he was to her for helping save the day, he felt rather shaken by her revelation. After all, given the chance to grab a gun, it was entirely possible he could have saved the day alone.

People were looking around, now, asking where the aliens had gone.

Steve stumbled over to him. "What the heck happened?"

"I haven't got a clue," said Norville. He didn't know if the CCTV had caught his involvement, but there was no need to draw attention to himself in case not. All he wanted to do was get back to his bunker and return to watching his screens.

The President stamped his foot in annoyance at the disappearance of his guests and yelled something incomprehensible. The Secret Service smoothly shuffled him off the stage, not knowing what else to do with him.

The crowd continued to discuss the event, despite an almost total absence of any facts.

"Hey," Steve said, while looking around.

"Yeah?"

"Did you see where Meryl Streep went? I wanted to ask her for her autograph. Not for me, of course. For my niece. She's a big fan."

Norville suppressed a smirk. He knew his co-worker didn't have a niece.

"No, sorry." Which was true to a certain degree. "I didn't see where she went."

"Oh."

T

DJ Tyrer is the person behind Atlantean Publishing, was short-listed for the 2015 Carillon 'Let's Be Absurd' Fiction Competition, and has been widely published in anthologies and magazines around the world, such as *Warlords of the Asteroid Belt* (Rogue Planet Press), *Strangely Funny II* and *III* (both Mystery & Horror LLC), *Destroy All Robots* (Dynatox Ministries), *Steam Chronicles* (Zimbell House) and *Irrational Fears* (FTB Press), as well as issues of *Tigershark* ezine, and also has a novella available in paperback and o n   t h e   K i n d l e , *T h e   Y e l l o w   H o u s e* (Dunhams Manor).http://djtyrer.blogspot.co.uk/ & http://atlanteanpublishing.blogs pot.co.uk/

18 The Cymbals of Progress

by Emad El-Din Aysha

You carry
All the ingredients
To turn your life into a nightmare—
Don't mix them!

You have all the genius
To build a swing in your backyard
For God.
That sounds
Like a hell of a lot more fun.

Let's start laughing, drawing blueprints,
Gathering our talented friends.
I will help you.
With my divine lyre and drum.

— Hafez

"Are you sure this is going to work?" she asked.

"It's got to work," he replied too confidently. He was holding the lapels of his ominous lab coat as he answered. While of medium build, he looked taller than he should in the outfit he wore like a uniform. He didn't wear a tie—he had as much trouble with them as he had with shoelaces—and his hair was short, closely cropped like he was heading off on pilgrimage.

"But how can you be *sure*, Dr. Al-Tharthar?" She was almost pleading now. The white blandness of her own compulsory lab outfit contrasted to the multi-colored, flowery mosaic of her headdress. It left her looking like a nurse assigned to the fashion police.

"He's volunteered. We're not doing anything wrong," he justified, avoiding the eyes of his subject, a man who didn't so much as stir despite his hefty, well-fed bulk. The experimental chair the subject was strapped into resembled an interrogation chair. The long, braided wires attached to his scalp made him appear to have silver and red dreadlocks emerging from a shock of blond hair sitting on top of the pink smudge that was his face. "And think of how many lives we can save if we can 'reform' the leaders of the world with this technique. No grunt will ever have to die again doing the dirty work of an elected official."

"That's not what I asked," she reminded him.

"It's worth the risk, Concepción." He had as much difficulty in pronouncing her Iberian forename as she had in saying his Arabic surname.

"And call me Hassan," he added for measure. She pronounced the word *sure* as 'shu-wur'. She also pronounced sugar without the 'sh', with just a flat s instead.

He fell silent as his assistant finished attaching the last of the electrodes to the subject's cranium. The shadow cast around her eyes in the hazy lighting of the laboratory made her the spitting image of the bride of Osiris.

Dr. Al-Tharthar had only eyes for her. In addition to her wonderful name, she had a delightful accent, emerging from behind a gorgeous toothy grin. And dimples, but only when she was happy.

How had they first met?

T

"Cortical stimulation," Dr. Al-Tharthar said in front of the gathered audience in the packed lecture hall, a hastily converted music hall with ill-fitting seats. In the distance, on the wall, were two giant portraits of his intellectual heroes while growing up. The first was of the pianist and literary critic and defender of Islam, Edward Said. The black and white photo of Said portrayed a man deep in thought who did not stare into the camera.

The second was of that epidemiologist of the global village, Marshall McLuhan. His picture was in color, with a vainglorious smile on his face. Dr. Al-Tharthar *should* have been more like the first photo, as an Arab and Muslim, but he tilted more towards the second. "That's the key," he went on. "The problem is isolation. Hemispheric isolation. The analytic, linguistic, erstwhile 'rational' side of the brain, in men especially, is cut off from the emotional side, the synthetic, the creati..."

"I thought your thesis centered round music. 'The Sound of Morality' you called it," someone in the crowd scoffed.

"Yes, that's right. I'm just giving you the technical details here, the neurophysiology of it," Dr. Al-Tharthar explained nonchalantly, his voice booming. The hall was designed for that kind of thing, an echo chamber of certitude.

"How did you get such an... outlandish idea?" the man persisted.

He had expected such a response, and from someone dressed in grey. From the podium, his opponent looked like a blur. "From the Great War," Dr. Al-Tharthar finally replied. The First World War was no longer the 'great' war. Even World War Two didn't qualify anymore.

"How so?" someone else in the audience asked, with the same obstinate tone of voice.

"Some person, some 'intellectual.'" Dr. Al-Tharthar said the word with distaste. "Someone who uses his brain too much, or some *portion* of his brain, had the nerve to describe the bombs hitting the capital of his native country, the explosions and destruction, as sounding like music to his ears. Like an orchestra. That got me thinking."

It got him angry at first, but that never lasted long with him. Thought always replaced anger. But there's nothing like a little emotion to *nudge* you in the right direction. "Culture shock, gentlemen. Culture shock! It often manifests itself as hypochondria, the fear of contagion. Fear of touching and smelling and drinking things, fear of infection. It's an extreme form of isolation, of *alienating* yourself from your surroundings, people and places and things. The same can happen to a person in his own homeland, with what was once familiar becoming foreign and hostile."

He stopped for dramatic effect, holding onto the lapels of his tuxedo for added show. It was all just for show. If it was up to him he'd go to work in his jimjams. On one occasion, he did, ever the absent-minded professor. "We've focused too much on physical and visual stimuli in neurology and cognitive studies. We've forgotten the auditory. Sounds can be just as alien and threatening, haunting, scary." He almost wanted to say 'boo' to startle the audience.

You didn't need a PhD to figure this out. *Just watch any half-decent horror flick*, he added to himself, before plodding on. "We need to *re*-integrate the mental functions and faculties of the brain, bring back the sensory balance so people can *hear* the consequences of their actions and future plans." He gestured as he spoke with his hands, about McLuhan, the great media theorist of television, but also of radio. Sound wasn't nearly as easy to pin down as sight. Sound was too subjective, indefinite, too 'stimulating.' To paraphrase McLuhan, image was all about perspective, taking you out of the picture. Sound pulled you right back in again; an emotional must, if you called yourself a human being, but *so* hard to quantify.

Dr. Al-Tharthar paused, revving up for the climax to his presentation. "Do you think it's a coincidence that the superpower that launched the Great War insisted on filming its soldiers raiding people's homes, searching for terrorist hideouts and 'terrifying' families?" The pun was intended. "Do you really think it was a coincidence that they broadcast those horrendous images to the world, images I tell you, with the sound turned *off*?"

Then something unpredictable happened.

"You're trying to recreate the Garden of Eden in the laboratory. It won't work," a woman spoke up against him, oh so melodiously.

"We do the same thing every day when we go to the opera or listen to legendary Egyptian singer Om Kulthoum on the radio or put on a Sinatra album." They were in Canada but the place was teeming with Muslims and Arabs, the detritus of the Great War. "I'm just doing the same thing in a more targeted fashion, with pinpoint precision," Dr. Al-Tharthar added in a voice as flat as a concrete slab, as if he was programming an intercontinental nuclear missile at a firing range.

"There's a reason why the Garden of Eden doesn't exist anymore. There's a reason why you have to *wait* for Paradise in the afterlife," the speaker continued. As intense as her words were, he thought he was listening to a bird chirping.

Dr. Al-Tharthar had to squint to see the speaker. Although she spoke like a Muslim, she just didn't *sound* like one. He could not quite identify the accent, having become accustomed to thinking of his people as only ever hailing from the Third World. "Are you saying my thesis is wrong?" Now *he* was on the defensive.

"No. I think you are right." The woman he would come to know as Concepción stood up to face him. "I just don't think it can be applied practically, in real life, under laboratory conditions. This world is imperfect and is meant to be. And God is my witness," she said

There was some hubbub from the crowd, with sneering remarks. Dr. Al-Tharthar didn't like theological restrictions any more than the next guy, but he couldn't stand seeing a woman being shushed into silence. He could see her clearly now. Concepción. She was of small stature—slender, with maternal hips—but someone who clearly made up for it with that delicious mouth of hers. And she was religiously dressed, to boot.

"Please let the wom… let her speak," he said a little bit more loudly than he intended, into the two microphones strapped to his suit. His thumbs tickled them while he was showing off, creating a deafening screeching sound. Regardless of all the fancy communication technology they had in the 21st century, some things just never got fixed.

"There is no Laghw in Paradise," she said triumphantly, using a phrase from the Quran. She gave a prompt explanation for the benefit of the audience. "No idle talk, no sneers and rebukes. No 'noise pollution,' only the sound of peace."

He knew the verse all too well: "They shall not hear therein (in Paradise) any Laghw (dirty, false, evil vain talk), but only Salam (salutations of peace). And they will have therein their sustenance, morning and afternoon [19:62]."[1]

"Be that… as it may," Dr. Al-Tharthar said slowly, trying to unscramble his brains. He had trained himself for criticisms from Westerners, not people from his own 'camp,' so to speak. And it rang true too. Milton's *Paradise Lost*. "We should at least test my thesis. See if it is in fact practicable. You can… set 'moral' limits to experiments, but *theory* has to roam free."

"But wouldn't it just be easier to give soldiers compulsory music lessons?" Concepción replied. "To use the Quran, not as a restriction, but as a guide?"

"Ah, music soothes the savage beast." Dr. Al-Tharthar said, after regaining his bearings. "Soldiers, yes. But *politicians*…" he trailed off, not entirely prepared to question himself.

T

Concepción was a European convert to Islam, from the Mediterranean. She had a better ear for music than him, and no doubt a deeper heart. So he simply had to hire her as his lab assistant since he only

---

[1] Muhsin Khan translation, https://quran.com/search?q=vain%20talk.

had an eye for equations. He could see them floating through the air, or—better still—splayed over a woman's body.

She was at it again. "Wouldn't it just be easier to, how do you say it, pump Arab music and song into his nervous system?"

"That's cruel and inhumane. That's just like using heavy metal to interrogate people in Gitmo. The Arabic sound-spectrum is as offensive to them as their music is to us. That's the whole point of my thesis." *Well, not to all of us,* Dr Al-Tharthar muttered to himself. He was a metal head, the one branch of pop music that girls hadn't turned into mush, he was glad to say. Not that he would admit to any of it in public.

"But you can't force people to be kind, or good or generous," she retorted.

"We're not. He wants to do these things, we're just helping him along the way." Or at least, that's what the financiers had told them. "Clearing out the mental clutter, so to speak, so he can strike a path through the wilderness."

"Yes, I know. The straight and narrow path, of good intentions." Concepción looked away for a moment. In the short time—very short time—they'd known each other, she had become his better half. "You always tell me that Englishy saying, how does it go about the horse?"

"You can lead a horse to water, but you can't make it drink." *This was a saying we men always use with women, when it comes to marriage and other unpleasantries.* Dr. Al-Tharthar made sure he kept *that* comment to himself.

"Sounds like the concept of *irshad*[2] in Islam, 'showing' the way instead of *telling* people what to do," she replied intelligently.

---

[2] In Arabic, a *murshid* was a guide, whether a tourist guide or an usher in a cinema. *Irshad* means guidance. Paradoxically, the ministries of information in many Arab countries were also called ministries of *irshad*.

Were her eyelashes teasing him? He'd never known Concepción to behave that way before. They were still only colleagues. Dr. Al-Tharthar shook the notions out of his head and resumed the conversation.

"Right you are. So, in that case, we're just… 'showing' him there's more than one way to go in life, but he has to make the final choice about which path to take." *Hearing the sounds of destruction and hostility the subject had inflicted on others is what's going to do the trick and take people like him down the pre-conceived path I chose,* he said to himself. The mind was like a maze, with multiple options leading you to your desired goal. The catch was some of these paths were not so desirable as the outcome might result in others getting hurt by your decisions. But imagine that the cries of their pain could be heard in your head; this would force you to take a different, more universally benign course. *Once I'm through with this guy, his brain will be a minefield of noisy stop-signs!*

"So, here goes nothing." He was about to depress the button to start the procedure, but hesitated for an instant.

"The readings are a bit off," Dr. Al-Tharthar finally said. "Could you check the electrodes again? He's sweating, for some reason."

Was that a look of worry on the subject's face?

T

"You were right, you know." Dr. Al-Tharthar felt that he had to say it. They were now sitting at an adjoining table in the experimental theatre which was covered in probes and semiconductors along with other odds and ends that made it look like the room Galileo had been tried in. Dr. Al-Tharthar should have been in the hot seat. Playing God with another man's nervous system.

Concepción was right. Tried and tested techniques existed to tame the beast within man. You can't force someone to be kindly any more than you could force an occupied country to be free. *Maybe it was my quest for revenge, hidden from my supposedly too-objective mind,* Dr Al-Tharthar said to himself.

"About what?" Concepción asked with a non-too-humble smile on her face. Her dimples were showing. All four of them.

"It would have been easier, and more effective, to just teach grunts to play the bagpipes or the guitar or how to compose a tune." He was looking over the test results. The charts weren't promising. Staring back at Concepción, he noticed the pattern on the *hijab*[3] she was wearing round her head. Flower patterns and other abstract plant forms. *It was as colorful and detailed as...* "I'd read somewhere, that many years ago in Iran, they dealt with drug addicts by teaching them how to hand-weave Persian carpets. It got them off their drug habits and made them think and see things in a completely different way."

It was the same hijab she had had on when they first met. Iberians were such colorful people. *Could you turn pictures into sounds and measure the wave formations in the brain?* he wondered.

He decided to prattle on instead. "A nice humdrum, inexpensive and thoroughly homegrown, solution. I just forgot, for some reason. I guess I talk to myself too much."

Concepción giggled. He had explained his name to her before. Al-Tharthar in Arabic meant someone who spoke too much. It is the curse of being a genius. For some reason, he had never bothered to ask her the meaning of her name. He just loved how it trickled off the tip of his tongue, tickling his taste buds all along the way.

She continued, "It was worth a try, as you said. At least we tested your thesis. What one application can't do, another can do, with time."

"Right you are. And we did, at least, make a 'pacifist' out of him. He won't be invading anyone else's country any time soon," Dr. Al-Thathar said in a further effort to console himself. "He won't have the inclination to push the button either. He won't be *able* to 'push' anything, even a piano key." They had turned the man into a pacifist, *inadvertently.*

---

[3] Loosely translated, a headscarf.

Too much electrical clutter, with sporadic spasms. It was interfering with the subject's motor functions, and specifically those related to musical composition. "If the price of total world peace is to banish music and song, it's *not* a price worth paying," he added in a footnote to his conscience, the lovely lady sitting right next to him.

Concepción was right to quote that verse from the Quran, Dr. Al-Tharthar thought to himself. On the Hajj, the pilgrimage to Mecca, people weren't supposed to argue and bicker and disagree. It was a world of passionate near-silence, with nothing but religious chants to be heard. Hajj was to give believers a *taste* of the afterlife. But nothing more than that. He should have seen it coming.

Dr. Al-Tharthar shot Concepción a look from the corner of his eye. She looked like she wanted to hold his hand, to comfort him, but she shied away from her own impulses by moving away from him abruptly. It appeared that she was only outspoken in the middle of a crowd. In one-on-one confrontations, she clammed up. You could see it in her shoulders. That delicious restraint.

"So, do you think the Pentagon will approve the backup plan?" she asked instead.

"Your backup plan? The compulsory music lessons? Yes, I think they will. It was *their* idea to hire a couple of Muslim academic hacks to pacify their elected fanatics, as a symbolic gesture for the new, post-war era of reconciliation." *Was the word they used pacify, or neutralize?* "And we've finally got the measurement equipment sorted out, thanks to this," said Dr. Al-Tharthar, as he jabbed towards the guinea pig with his thumb, like he was hailing a taxi.

"We can measure the success or failure of *any* policy they enact with mathematical precision now. And they were the ones who got us our subject." They'd decoded the wave patterns of the acoustic centers of the brain and put Dr. Al-Tharthat's computer model to the test.

The doctor stole a glance or two back at said guinea pig. The same silly, drugged smirk remained on the man's features from before the experiment, when the grunts carted him in.

Dr. Al-Tharthar paused for a tentative moment of all too deep introspection, then said, "You don't think they forged the signature on the consent form, do you?!"

T

NOTES

[1] Muhsin Khan translation, https://quran.com/search?q=vain%20talk.

[2] In Arabic, a *murshid* was a guide, whether a tourist guide or an usher in a cinema. *Irshad* means guidance. Paradoxically, the ministries of information in many Arab countries were also called ministries of *irshad*.

[3] Loosely translated, a headscarf.

Emad is an English-language academic, freelance journalist (political columnist and movie reviewer) and translator currently residing in Cairo, Egypt. While a British citizen, by birth, his parents are Arabs , Muslim by faith and English by natural predisposition. He completed his undergraduate and post-graduate education in England (BA, MA, PhD). His field of study covers international politics and Arab society. The two great loves of his life are history and science fiction. After years of procrastinating he thought he'd finally try his hand at SF, Arab-themed, and is already an active member of the Egyptian Society for Science Fiction.

19 Ma Gohardy's Shop

by Paul Williams

Ma and Pa Gohardy had a shop.

A grocery store built before the great depression and not renovated since. Once it was in the center of town but gradually fell into the outskirts. People wanted to turn it into a cafe but never offered enough money. One rainy day, just after my fourteenth birthday, a kid walked in with a gun and shot Pa Gohardy between the eyes. Right in front of the President Trump poster. The kid ran off with five dollars from the till and a packet of butterscotch mints. Ma Gohardy saw it happen but didn't have the energy to scream. Old Man Lloyd, thirty minutes later, found her cradling Pa Gohardy's body and trying to force a biscuit into his lips. She told the inquest that he liked biscuits.

The cops did their best to catch the killer. They rounded up every black man with a criminal record and some without. Ma Gohardy's description didn't specify color or anything apart from gender and height. Eventually they persuaded someone to confess and stuck him on death row, where he died during the appeal process. Ma Gohardy died first but I'm jumping ahead of myself.

We all tried to help her. Everyone shopped there for the next few weeks and took turns to cook meals. My mother made breakfast on the Tuesdays. Others bought juice, at her prices, and served it to her. Some, with retail experience, kept the shop open when she went to the funeral and afterwards to the grave. Then she started shutting an hour early every day, giving her time to catch the last bus to the cemetery and the last one back. Except on Sundays when it didn't run at all. Nobody offered her a lift; they were all too busy going to church. With a shooting in town at least once a week, Pa Gohardy was soon forgotten by everyone except Ma Gohardy.

The regulars kept shopping at the store, although they couldn't buy biscuits anymore. It was the one stock change that Ma Gohardy made. She kept the butterscotch mints, displaying them proudly below the Trump poster. Ma Gohardy kept them with the symbol of hope that Pa believed in. My father remembered Ma and Pa Gohardy arguing about Trump before he was elected. It was a rare public disagreement. She refused to consider voting Republican. Pa Gohardy picked a candidate, not a party. I never understood the divisions. Never realized that one man could offer so much hope and bring so much despair. Gradually people realized that she was going senile. She forgot prices, a fact some exploited, and sometimes their names. Then she stopped going to the grave and the shop opened as normal before the death.

One afternoon, it closed at lunchtime. Ma Gohardy was seen visiting the optician and then, two hours later, my father, her doctor. She opened the shop next morning, wearing a pair of giant glasses that hung down on a string like a cobweb. Her appointment with my father resulted in rumors of a heart condition. Pa Gohardy had died at the age of 82 and she was a year older. In some places, the poor can retire but not in our town. Not with all the welfare cuts that Trump introduced to offset tax reductions. My father refused to discuss her condition with me. He was more concerned about my relationship with Delmore. Ma Gohardy told him. She saw us together in the shop and, despite her illness, must have guessed.

I didn't mind. It's never easy to keep a secret in a town and, knowing that Delmore was my boyfriend kept some of the other boys away. Father insisted that we keep going to Ma Gohardy's shop to support local businesses, even after they opened a supermarket near the center of town. Delmore got a job at the supermarket, stacking shelves to help pay for his education. In his spare time he helped Ma Gohardy even though she couldn't afford to pay him.

Ma Gohardy carried on living in the flat above the shop. Every time we went there, the shelves looked more and more empty. Delmore guessed that she had been cancelling deliveries. He challenged her; nobody else would. She said it was temporary then asked Delmore to do her a favor. He agreed, he was good like that. She pulled out a large suitcase stuffed with banknotes from under the floorboards and asked him to carry it. They went to the gun shop. The owner, one of the few white shopkeepers in town, greeted her with the sympathetic look that successful people always give to failures. Someone had to make a legal profit from increased crime. President Trump gave this guy an award once, for business innovation. In return, Trump's poster was on the wall in a special golden frame, with smaller copies in the windows. This was a business surrounded by boarded up drug dens that benefited from Trump's tax cuts. The owner spent the revenue on security cameras, which protected shoppers, and his stock.

Ma Gohardy got Delmore to open the suitcase and told the owner that she wanted to buy a gun. There were no rules on eyesight or an upper limit on age. The only stumbling block was Ma Gohardy's failure to show a driving license. She had never learned to drive. Eventually she proved her identity and the owner sold her an automatic with a free loyalty card. The gun rested on the counter of her shop, pointing over the newspapers at every nervous customer. Some said it was a greater deterrent than any camera. Six months earlier, President Trump had pardoned a shopkeeper convicted of shooting a shoplifter. He called him a hero. The media, most of which had been bought by Trump's companies, compared the shopkeeper to the police who routinely shot dangerous criminals. One was a boy at my school, crossing the road with headphones on. The police said he failed to stop when shouted at. In the days before Trump, officers were prosecuted for manslaughter. Now they carried on as normal with the President urging everyone to respect enforcers of the law. Crime statistics in town were down, partly because people stopped reporting and partly because the cops stopped recording. Officially it was attributed to more deportations of illegal immigrants.

I asked my father once why people like Pa Gohardy voted for Trump. He replied that our nation, he always called it ours, was founded on business. Individual entrepreneurs and large corporations had built the richest economy in the world. Trump was a businessman, not a politician, so logically he could restore that economy. "Just two problems," said Father. "One, you can't run a country like a business and two, all his businesses failed."

The growth of the town, boosted by cheap housing, the supermarket, and jobs, now that the immigrants had gone, appeared to vindicate its decision to elect then re-elect Trump. None of the new residents went to Ma Gohardy's shop more than once. They found the prices unaffordable because the new jobs paid less. The experience also unnerved them as she kept forgetting to turn on the lights. Delmore checked with the power company; it took a while because of confidentiality, but they confirmed she was up-to-date with her bills. We were there once when one of the people who wanted to build a cafe phoned. Delmore told them to go away. He asked Ma Gohardy first, just in case she had changed her mind. She said that nobody would ruin her business. It reminded me of Trump's most famous tweet: nobody ruins America.

The first man shot was Farmer Stickson. He went in to buy some mints with the money saved from Trump's tax cuts, and Ma Gohardy got him in the arm. He was back at work the next day. As it was just a minor wound, my father treated him without any need to pay. He didn't tell the press either but someone informed the cops. They told Ma Gohardy that she couldn't keep the gun any more. She cited the amendment, proudly telling them that her grandson would become a famous lawyer. He had briefed her well and she knew the details of the pardon given by Trump. Everyone was entitled to bear arms, even an old, black, female shopkeeper. Oh sorry, didn't I say she was black? It's easy to forget. Most of the kids at my school were black, there were a few Hispanic like me and the rest were white. I never once heard any of the white kids talk about race. We all mixed together and plenty got into relationships or less formal situations. Funny thing though, the white kids are all working now, most of them as warders at the new prison.

The prison stands proudly next to the supermarket and came with a second bus through town for staff to get to work. Father signed a petition not to name the prison after President Trump. Instead, Trump's name and poster went on the side of the bus. The gun shop owner tweeted the President, asking if he would attend the naming ceremony. He got a response, a real letter, from Trump's personal secretary wishing every success to the community. It arrived with a signed picture of Trump which owner photocopied and most of the shops that were still open displayed it. One was offered to the surgery. My father refused to celebrate Trump's success, saying he would rather celebrate a patient surviving. The gun shop owner laughed and said that Trump was making it possible for everyone to succeed.

I didn't succeed at anything because of Delmore. Well, not just because of him. It wasn't his fault. Mine for thinking about the past. For not moving forward. Some things just aren't meant to be and some things that go are gone forever. That's what my father said before his heart attack. My father who treated black patients but didn't like me having a black boyfriend. My father who told others how to be healthy but died before them. He didn't survive because the ambulance from the Donald J. Trump hospital refused to respond to an emergency call, without knowing the patient's credit card number. "First rule of business," tweeted President Trump, "is to make sure customer can pay. We're going to end debt, folks."

Anyway, I'm jumping again. Nobody could stop Ma Gohardy having a gun, unless Farmer Stickson wanted to press charges. Delmore persuaded him not to and the cops couldn't be bothered to argue. A few weeks later it happened. Someone went in the shop, intending to rob it. They never identified this man. The police looked in the drug dens later but couldn't find anyone to confess. The neighbor, Reggie Miniter, heard a shot. So did Delmore, who was driving past. Reggie saw Delmore stop the car and run inside the shop. Then Reggie heard a second shot. He found Ma standing over Delmore's body, with the gun.

They let her attend the funeral, chained to two white prison guards. She recognized me and I went over to talk. "When you going to marry my grandson?" she demanded.

"Can't, Ma," I said.

"Why not?

"Because you shot him, Ma. You shot Delmore."

Then we cried together. I've still crying now, even after all those years. Today I caught the bus, without a logo, from the graveyard to the Delmore Cafe and ordered a biscuit. A white kid brought it over, gazing with pride at the Trump memorial poster in the window. I asked him how the cafe got its name. He didn't know.

Paul's published work includes two non-fiction books and over 50 short stories, plus articles on true crime and cryptozoology. Full details are on his website https://paulecwilliams.org/ He can be followed on Twitter.

20 Celebrating the Presidential Election

by Emenual Wolff

Happy day! Happy day,
where everybody gets a say!
Pick your suits of ace, or spades,
and chose the one to lead our way;
to burn in hell or drown in Hades.
And if it's rigged, to our dismay,
we'll play our hands out anyway!

The pot has thinned,
the plot has thickened…
For this to end
our chants have quickened!
And then again come next November,
emptied by elected louse,
We'll all look back to say "remember,
No one ever beats the house."

Cheers.

A Michigan based poet, pianist, and performer who hosts various venues for artists to show off and sell their work, including full bands, acoustic sets, painters, photographers, filmmakers, and other crafts. Emenual has written, illustrated, and published a poetic anthology entitled *MooNlight*

Howling: Poems from An Existential Anxiety Attack, which has been able to sell across continental borders. "I don't consider myself either a democrat or republican, but I'm a skeptic who's passionate enough to express the political and societal dread we all inherently feel."

21 King Donald

by Art Lasky

King Donald the Winner was beloved, brave, and just: it said so on his business card. His only fear was that outsiders were sneaking into his beautiful, rich and green kingdom. For security he sealed the borders North and South of the kingdom with mighty walls, tall, deep and thickly built. But the East and West borders still vexed him, as they were not secure; for Ocean, uninvited and without apology, sent waves to his shores. Waves marching one after the other, an infinite army assailing him.

Forsooth, the King didn't know very much about anything much, but was a self-proclaimed expert on getting things done and on finding 'really smart guys' (RSGs) who could solve any problem. He assembled his team of RSGs and charged them with finding the answer. What kind of a threat were these waves and what could be done to foil Ocean's, undoubtedly nefarious, plans?

The RSGs summoned Ocean for questioning. Ocean brazenly ignored the summons. Finally the RSGs sent lackeys who fetched Ocean in tubs, tanks, bowls and cups. Yesman, the head RSG, asked really important questions.

"Where are you from? Why have you come here?" But, alas, Ocean ignored him.

"King Donald the Winner is not to be denied! If I report your intransigence, he will be sorely vexed. "I ask you one more time: what are your intentions?"

Yet again Ocean returned only silence.

The RSGs listened to seashells and heard the endless mocking susurration of the very Ocean that had stubbornly uttered not a word to them. Yesman summoned every ocean creature from minnow through whale, to no avail. Finally a creature that dwelled near the Ocean and knew it well was brought before the RSGs.

"Why is this creature caged?" said Yesman.

"It is a Seagull and thus a flight risk," answered the head lackey.

"Seagull? Isn't that a Jewish name?" asked Yesman, who was also the smartest of the RSGs.

The lackey shrugged.

The Seagull shat upon the floor of its cage, and brazenly said, "Aah-aah!"

"He mocks us," pronounced Yesman. "He must be punished! Have him thrown from the highest tower in the kingdom."

So it was commanded, and so it was done. Seagull was thrown from the very top of the Tower of Trump. Seagull spread his wings, flew thrice around the tower and with a last mocking "Aah-aah!" gave a final shate upon Yesman's pate before it flew back to Ocean. Ocean ignored all demands for Seagull's return. The fugitive, Seagull, thus escaped all punishment for his final insult to King Donald's minions.

Yesman had no other choice but to report all of this to the king who reacted with his customary speed and intelligence. Thus it was commanded, and thus it was done. Mighty walls that were tall, deep and thick were built to secure the East and the West.

The wise and mighty King rested, triumphant in the knowledge that he had foiled Ocean's scheme, whatever it might have been. Of course, the walls changed the weather pattern and the realm became a dry dusty wasteland. But finally, it was secure.

T

Art is a retired computer programmer. After forty years of writing in COBOL and Assembler he decided to try writing in English; it's much harder than it looks. He lives in New York City with his wife/muse and regularly visiting grandkids.

Art's had stories published in *Drunken Boat, Third Flat Iron, Decasp.com, Forever Night* (the 2017 *ANYDSWPE Anthology*), *101 Words, The Lane of Unusual Traders,* and *Home Planet News Online.* If you'd like to contact him: alasky9679@yahoo.com.

22 Credibility Gap

by Matthew Kresal

The vote was up before the committee. It was not the first time nor would it be the last time, she expected. Once upon a time, the meeting would have taken place in a conference room or a board room. Technology hadn't made it necessary but secrecy still reigned supreme, thus the encrypted video feed. *A pity, given the occasion,* Emily Shaffer thought, as she took a moment to survey her office overlooking the Chicago skyline from behind her desk. She turned her attention back to the laptop screen and the little boxes of human faces arranged upon it.

"Miss Shaffer's motion is that the timetable for EBE disclosure proceedings first adopted by the committee in 1996 should go ahead." The strong, yet soothing Scottish tones of Malcolm Blackwood filtered into her ears through her headphones, his dignified face looking out at her from the screen of her laptop. In person, he was shorter than he looked on screen but his eyes appeared to combined fiercely intelligent with a faint air of menace. "Will someone second the motion?"

"Seconded." Emily felt both of her ginger eyebrows raise at the sound of an unlikely voice. It was Rutledge, the man who had always argued against the very idea of disclosure since before she had even been born. She looked at his little piece of the screen to study his face but the old man with the flop of white hair betrayed nothing to her or their fellow committee members.

"Mr. Rutledge has seconded the motion." Blackwood's voice carried a hint of surprise, enough that he paused for a moment. "The committee will now vote. Please indicate your vote now."

Shaffer leaned forward and pressed the "yes" button on the screen in front of her. Once again, she felt pity for the fact that this wasn't happening with everyone in the same room. She felt the longing to see people's faces, their hands raised in the air, that sense of being there as history unfolded. How ironic it was that it was only because of *them* and the recovered technology that had crashed along with the little gray beings that they were able to have this meeting without being in the same room.

"Thank you." Blackwood paused and she could see on the screen that the Scotsman was tallying the votes. He looked surprised for a moment and she watched his eyes go back and forth as he looked over the results again. Finally he faced the camera.

"As you know, the original Majestic charter from 1947 requires a vote on disclosure to be carried unanimously. Given what we are about to reveal, this is understandable. The vote is twelve for, none against. The motion carries."

Shaffer felt a surge of triumph within her and a slight smile crept across her face. It was what she had been working for ever since she had been brought in to fill a spot on the committee board a decade earlier: the revelation to the world of the secret that this committee, known simply as the Majestic 12, and the agency they controlled had been keeping since July 1947. They could finally learn the truth about Roswell, Aztec, and a number of different events. To know what she knew about the extraterrestrial biological entities (EBEs), the recovered technology from them, and what their presence had helped to bring about.

"We will continue with our business and then discuss the mechanics of EBE disclosure. Onto the next item then…"

T

"Unfortunately, even the draft versions of the Majestic charter did not call for specific disclosure proceedings," Blackwood confessed as he sat across the table from Shaffer. He held a set of ancient looking documents in between hands that were only a little younger than the pages themselves. There was a faint shudder as the private jet carrying them from Nova Scotia to Chicago experienced an episode of slight turbulence. Two weeks had passed since the disclosure vote and the pair were well into working on just how to reveal the truth about Roswell and subsequent extraterrestrial contact to the world.

"Somehow that doesn't surprise me." Shaffer said, reaching up to brush back a bit of her red hair that had come out of place. She picked up the document with her left hand and began to read over the faint yellow page with its dark ink still present. There were only a few copies of what she was holding in existence and she felt humbled by the sense of history in front of her.

"Truman never bargained on this ever coming out. Or it becoming an international project rather than just a US led effort." She sat the page down and sighed. "I wonder what he would think about Majestic being led by a Scotsman?"

"Lord only knows." Blackwood said mischievously. "You think he would ever have imagined the impact of tasking a group of military men and scientists to take apart wreckage from a recovered spaceship and figure out how it all worked?"

"I doubt it." Shaffer looked back down at the documents, shifting them back into their proper order. "How do you explain to someone from World War II that one day that technology will end up building a phone that can also play music and let you read almost anything from anywhere in the world at the same time?"

"Fair point. Maybe that's why they never thought to make serious plans to tell anyone." Blackwood offered thoughtfully as Emily finished putting the papers into their protective sleeves. "That being said, the committee was set up by the United States and I think it's only fitting that it be the sitting President who makes the announcement to the world at large."

"On the Roswell anniversary or Majestic's founding?" Shaffer inquired. Either date would be an appropriate one for the announcement. Especially given that the original fifty year time table had been shelved in the 90s before she had ever been appointed. There had been some efforts made towards disclosure, especially in light of public pressure about the crash of something in the New Mexico desert during the summer of 1947, but the cover-up had continued instead.

"Roswell is the more important and better known one." Blackwood offered as he collected up the documents again. "I assume you'd like to brief whoever the next President is yourself? It is protocol to brief incoming President's on the EBEs after all."

"I'd like you to be there as well." Blackwood looked surprised. "You're MJ-1 after all. It's only appropriate you be there too."

"I've never been to the White House before. I wonder who we'll talking to?"

Shaffer shrugged. "The election's next Tuesday, we'll know soon."

T

The election result had come as a surprise but not enough that Emily would change her mind about disclosure. She had assumed that Rutledge would call for a new vote after their plans had been given to the committee at their December 2016 meeting. Instead, he had barely said a word and it had been others who had objected to the idea of the announcement being made by Donald Trump, of all people. Blackwood argued the case for and the decision was made to go ahead.

She understood the objections. Hell, she had felt a sickening feeling followed by uncertainty in the days after the November 8th election. The idea of Trump telling the world the truth about what had been going on since the summer of 1947 didn't sit well with her. It had given her a few sleepless nights much to the consternation of her business partners at her "day job." In the end, she decided that she had fought too long and hard for this chance.

"Are you alright?" Blackwood's voice brought her out of her own thoughts and back to the lobby of the West Wing. She blinked a couple of times and looked across at the well-dressed man sitting in front of her who was checking his smartphone. "You look a little distracted. Nervous, perhaps?"

"Aren't you?" she answered back before looking down at the folder in her lap. Blackwood shrugged and shook his head.

"Not really. I met him before during the fuss over his golf course in Scotland. He's exactly how you would expect him to be."

"Is that meant to be comforting?" Emily asked sarcastically with a slight shake of her head. Blackwood cocked his head at an angle.

"What do you think?"

"Excuse me?" a female voice suddenly said. Both Blackwood and Shaffer looked up to see an aide, short of stature with blond-hair, standing over them. "The President is ready to see you now."

Blackwood and Shaffer exchanged a look between them.

"Thank you." Emily stood up first, being a good twenty odd years younger than her companion. Together they were led through corridors of closed office doors before stopping in front of the doorway to the Oval Office. Emily allowed herself a last deep breath as the door was opened and she put her life's ambition into play.

T

Emily watched the announcement on TV. Majestic had not been allowed to be present at the White House for the occasion. She wished she had been there though. The press room was silent. Even the clicking shutters of cameras had stopped. President Trump rocked on his feet, leaning from one side of the podium to the other as he had done throughout his presidency in what his opponents had come to term "Donald's shuffle." A heavy silence hung over the room as the President continued.

"The first alien spaceship crashed to Earth near Roswell, New Mexico in 1947."

The press conference deteriorated a little further with every word he spoke. The assembled members of the press stared in disbelief and a low chorus of whispers filled the room. Trump just kept on talking for a minute or so before he began jeering at them. The whispers became shouts and questions about proof became a roar. By the time it had finally ended and cable news returned to its studio, Emily felt the need for a drink.

T

Emily was on her third glass of wine when Blackwood came into her office. Why a government minister from Scotland was in Chicago visiting an American business executive would have made a creative news story, usually something about a trade deal. After the events of earlier today, no one was taking notice.

Blackwood wore a look of concern on his face as he walked in. He had never seen her drink outside of a meal before, the sight of her in her office, staring out onto the Chicago skyline holding a glass of wine, came as a surprise. He sat down across from her.

"I'd offer you a drink," she finally said, "but I kind of finished the bottle already."

"That's quite alright. Looks like it was a good year so at least it didn't go to waste" He offered gently.

She started laughing, softly at first and then progressing to a loud belly laugh, raising a hand to her face as she did so. She finally stopped and turned her chair so she could face him, tears running down her cheeks.

"That is the best thing I've heard all damn day."

"Emily—" Blackwood tried to offer condolences but she merely waved a dismissive hand at him and shook her head angrily. She finished off the glass and sat it on the desk, her empty hands now cradling her head.

"I spent a decade of my life fighting for this and I let him blow it. Someone should have stopped me!"

"Emily—"

"Someone should have physically restrained me and told me just how damn bad of an idea it was, that letting Donald—"

"Emily!" Blackwood's deep voice filled the large office like a bomb going off.

Emily felt her train of thought immediately derail and she took a deep breath the moment her ears stopped ringing. She closed her eyes and dropped her head, causing a crick in her neck which she began to rub.

"I messed up," she muttered. She repeated this twice more before Blackwood finally got up from his chair. He walked behind the desk and put a hand on her left shoulder.

"It's not your fault." He reminded Emily of a father trying to comfort his child. She let out a bitter laugh and shook her head, turning her gaze away from him.

"There's a reason why it was decided in '96 not to go ahead, wasn't there?" Her voice was low, defeated. "Is this why?"

"Back then we couldn't decide what it was we needed to be doing. Those of us not from the US thought the time was right; those in the US didn't want to compromise the efforts the American military was making about keeping the Roswell affair quiet. A couple of them thought the truth would come out without our help. They were wrong though as it turned out. A shame, as it might have saved Clinton from all that nonsense about that intern."

"We threw away our shot, didn't we?" Shaffer asked as she turned her head to look at Blackwood. "We had one chance to get this right and instead we let *him* waste it."

"I think that's why Rutledge let it through." Blackwood offered, removing his hand. "He thought that by the time we reached the anniversary, whoever got voted into office wouldn't be considered credible. Lord knows, Trump's got enough on his plate without this being piled on. Whatever credibility he had is probably lost."

"We offered evidence, things he could show to back up the claim..." Shaffer's voice trailed off as she saw Blackwood shaking his head sadly. She leaned back in her chair and listened to him speak as he crossed over to the window and the sun began to set.

"He was too much of an egotist to let someone else steal the spotlight from him. He'll be begging for our help shortly, of that you can be sure."

"Are you going to give it to him?"

Blackwood turned away from the window with an enigmatic expression on his face. She looked into his eyes and found them unreadable. *What was he was trying to say? Something or maybe nothing at all?*

"What if we do?" He put his hands into his pockets. "It's true that we tried this particular announcement with Trump but that doesn't mean we have to keep propping him up. We don't have to give him anything we've offered before today."

Shaffer was confused. "What about the craft fragments? The tissues slides?"

"Nothing. We bide our time."

"You think there will be another chance to tell the world about all this one day?" Emily shook her head in disbelief. Blackwood's face didn't change but the tone of his voice did when next he spoke.

"Oh, there have been attempts before. Nixon tried to have a documentary made in the 70s and Reagan kept dropping broad hints in the 80s in his speeches after he was briefed. They thought the time was right but they weren't right then either."

"And was I wrong this time?"

Blackwood said nothing. He merely turned to the window and looked out at the city beneath them. Shaffer set down her empty glass and walked over, stopping next to him as they gazed out at the same vista.

"I thought it would change everything." She said quietly. "That's naïve, I know, but we're supposed to believe in humanity, that we can do great things with all the technology they left for us one day."

"Emily, my dear," Blackwood turned to face her despite the fact she was several inches taller than he was. "People are capable of great things. Love, passion, creativity. They're also capable of terrible things. There's nothing worse than those who grab power for themselves. I took on this job because, like you, I thought that the day would come when we could reveal all this. The fact that we aren't alone in the universe, that we can reach out and actually visit the stars would change the world. Today was not that day."

"The real question then, is will it ever come?"

Blackwood looked sideways for a moment before turning back to her, taking a hand out of his pocket as he did so. He handed a plaid handkerchief to the younger lady who took it to dab her tear streaked face. She offered it back but he shook his head.

"The only way to build a better world is to make it ourselves. Majestic, all of what we've done, will survive Trump just as it has everything else. But to answer your question…" His voice trailed off.

"Yes?" Emily Shaffer said with slight concern. Blackwood shrugged.

"Time will tell; it always does."

Matthew Kresal was born and raised in North Alabama though never developed a Southern accent weirdly enough. He contributed the Sci-Fi Review column in the North Alabama arts & entertainment magazine *The Valley Planet* (his review of the novelization of Douglas Adams's largely unfilmed Doctor Who adventure "Shada" is quoted in its US paperback edition). He had also contributed to numerous online publications including *The Terrible Zodin* and *Warped Factor*. His first piece of fiction, "Shadows Of The Past", was published in Nosetouch Press's *Blood, Sweat, And Fears: Horror Inspired By The 1970s* in 2016.

23 #Trumptopia

by Koom Kankesan

4:55 p.m. The time will forever be etched in my memory. My beloved Seahawks were losing to the Rams on their home turf. Frost lay on the grass back home. I was on the phone, texting my friend Jordan who was at CenturyLink Field. Jordan's a doctor too but he's just a GP, not a pathologist like I am. He decided to keep it cosy and move back to Seattle. It was after Coach Carroll made the decision to pull Eddie Lacy out. They didn't put anybody else in and then the game just sort of stopped.

I was at Walter Reed and it wasn't even my shift. I was just nursing that coffee that smells like burned wicker. They have it in the cafeteria. I was watching the players move around, not knowing which way to walk, on the small TV in the corner. We'd been texting but Jordan called me.

"Hey," he said, "do you hear what they're saying?"

A bald guy in a tuxedo had walked onto the astroturf and was reading something. The sound was muted on the TV.

"I can't hear anything," I replied. "What's going on?"

"They just announced that Trump's been shot," Jordan whispered.

I told everyone in the cafeteria to shut up, then stood up on the pleather banquette and turned up the volume on the TV.

T

As you know, president Trump had been shot while going out for a McDonald's run. Why did he go alone instead of sending the secret service? One of the many deranged shooters living in the DC area (of which I am convinced there are hundreds) exited the ammo depot in the strip mall as Trump drove through the drive thru in his gold Cadillac Allante. The Allante's top was down. The shooter, out-of-work welder Malik Malawi, fired four .38 rounds before a driver in the parking lot, Richard Dudman, ran his blue Volvo into him.

President Trump had his head turned towards the drive thru window when the first shot was fired. This is the bullet that the FBI concluded went wide and passed through the Allante windshield, shattering the glass. According to the McDonald's employee serving Mr. Trump, the president then turned to look back, the startled words "I'll tell you what—I'll tell you this—it's a disgrace—" escaped his pudgy jowls before the next shot was fired, entering Trump's trachea and collapsing his windpipe. The third shot was a head wound which entered the right temple and blew out the back of his skull, forcing the president to jerk back and almost stand up. The fourth round caught Trump squarely in the groin, rendering his reproductive organs a mess of spaghetti-o's.

At least, this is what we were told.

T

Walter Reed, or Bethesda Naval Hospital as it is colloquially called, has serviced countless presidents. I was just brought in as a witness to assist in the operating room. Trump's body lay pallid and lifeless on the operating tables as the chief surgeons, Dr. Lennox and Dr. Doyle, operated upon him. Among the EEG monitors, defibrillators, and other equipment, Trump looked tiny. He's supposed to be 6' 2" and grossly overweight. Under the glare of sodium lights, a hive of masked doctors and technicians surrounding him, Trump looked insignificant. His skin, always a flushed overblown Technicolor salmon on TV, was mottled grey. An acne rash below his left collarbone had turned red where he'd picked at it. Lennox and Doyle on the other hand, towering over him with scalpels, light glinting off their glasses, looked formidable.

Trump's head was slung back where the bullet had entered the trachea. A tracheostomy tube had been inserted. A fair amount of blood was on the surgeons' gloves and smocks as they made incisions and tried to repair the severed nerve endings around C6 and C7. Usually a severing of the spine at that juncture is fatal. It effectively severs off all nerves going to and from the brain. The body looked dead. It's true that except for very light breathing, a body in trauma and heavy sedation looks indistinguishable from one that is dead, but I've seen a lot of dead bodies in my time.

This one looked dead.

I was there to observe and corroborate. Nothing more. There are many doctors and senior pathologists who rank higher than me at Walter Reed. The atmosphere verges on militaristic. I kept my mouth shut and nodded whenever one of them spoke and another wrote down what was said. I initialed where they pointed on the forms.

A half hour in, I felt lightheaded and my esophageal sphincter pinched so tight I could feel my belly spasm. I had to sit down. My eyes closed from the pain and when I opened them, for a moment, one second, two seconds, maybe three, the surgeons standing in front of Trump's head parted. I could see where the duckback combover fell down in wispy straw strands. Blood still oozed out of the wound, slowly. In the cold of the operating theatre, the blood had congealed and ran in a slow motion stream, a rusty mould making its way across his head. Bits of brain were carried with it. Through the hole, I could see his brain but it wasn't pinkish like cerebellum is supposed to be. In fact, the exposure, maybe five and a half, six inches at its widest point, revealed grey matter —undoubtedly the occipital lobe.

This was no gunshot through the back of the head. Or if it was, that had long been dealt with.

They began cutting his skull open.

T

After I signed the forms, no one mentioned Trump's body for about two weeks. There was a state funeral; closed casket of course. Nowhere near the number of attendees came out as you might expect. The rain slicked pavements looked as bald as a senator's scalp as the procession inched forward. Melania and Barron trailed behind the flag draped coffin, a Lincoln hearse slowly rolling its way down Pennsylvania Avenue, en route to Arlington cemetery.

What was in the casket? Was it Donald Trump's body minus his head and central nervous system? Was it everything except the brain and the face? Was it a pile of rocks? Was there anything at all under the flag-draped lid?

I didn't talk to Lennox or Doyle for two weeks. One day, I was summoned to Lennox's office.

A meeting was in progress as I got off the elevator and entered his suite. His stuffed armchairs and stuffed birds were hazy in the darkness as a group of people, mostly men, sat in a circle around a shrouded object. On the pull down screen behind Lennox's desk, a projector projected slides containing schematics of something I couldn't quite make out. It looked like a shop vac or one of those new vacuum cleaners with the tubes that stand upright.The top of the schematic looked familiar though —a roundedness and swoop to the contour.

I was introduced to the others briefly, although no introduction was needed. In the midst of the group, projector light glinting off Lennox and Doyle's glasses, someone removed the shroud. As the brown vinyl tarp slid off, Lennox stood up and turned on the light. We adjusted our eyes to the brightness.

The brightness caused my esophageal sphincter to tighten yet again. Not a fear so much this time as a frisson. A shock at how small we were. How inconsequential and ultimately, worthless. The tables had turned. On the chair underneath the tarp was something made out of titanium alloyed parts, fluid mechanisms, and exposed ribbed tubing.

Something huge and invulnerable. Something sophisticated and elegant. Atop the fiberglass and metal and wires was a head. A humanoid head with a wispy combover and duckback swoop that could only belong to one being.

The hair was recognizable but the face was not. Gone were the pudgy jowls. But if one stared, you could see the tight mouth, that puckering rictus of pride.

No one spoke until Lennox pointed to a lanky man, youngish, bearded, standing against the wall. In designer jeans, white t shirt, and a motorcycle jacket, this young man pushed himself forward, approaching us, a digital tablet in his hand.

"Gentlemen," announced Lennox, "I present you Jack Dorsey, CEO of Twitter."

A muted applause and many puzzled frowns sprouted in the room. "No need," said Dorsey quietly, "no need." I realized I'd seen photos of his face before. He was stiff yet louche at the same time. For someone who commanded our interest, he didn't speak much or look anyone directly in the eye. Instead, he stared in awe at the creation which sat dormant on its gold electronic throne. The chair was some sort of resting station, something that Trump 2.0 (that is what I called him in my head) was plugged into. A small series of monitors at the back of the chair indicated vital signs. A button pulsed blue in the shape of the Twitter logo. I thought of the flatlines on the monitors that day in Walter Reed when I'd been sure he was dead.

Dorsey talked in short epigrammatic bursts, not unlike tweets. "As you gentlemen undoubtedly know, our former president was a big fan of our platform.

"What you might not have known was that he left a proviso—in case of this very scenario. We at Twitter have been working on exciting things.

"The next stage in integration between human and computer. The president was excited, very excited."

Dorsey looked around the room.

"You mean he's an android?" someone ventured.

"We prefer the term *fully linked in*." Dorsey was terse. "Imagine—the next step in human/software integration."

"But you and the president..." someone else proclaimed doubtfully, "you're known for being a strong liberal, you've publicly supported the Democratic party."

"Well, we've made a few tweaks," replied Dorsey, looking at Trump 2.0, "besides the cosmetic enhancements your colleagues Dr. Lennox and Dr. Doyle have so skillfully enacted, we at Twitter have made operating system upgrades.

"Our president desired nothing more than to live on, electronically if necessary. He wanted to find a way to tweet directly from his brain to his millions of followers.

"That is how the conversation started. For what is Twitter if not an ongoing conversation? He signed papers allowing us significant advantages. Google's working on a self-driving car but we've been working on this!

"A personality is nothing more than a network of neurological connections, a matrix or an operating system. We can now code on a complexity that rivals DNA. We simply enhanced him. Greater logic, compassion, and altruistic tendencies."

So there was the trade-off. "And you just paid for all this? How much did Trump 2.0 cost?" I found myself saying. Everybody turned and looked at me. I might have blushed. Lennox and Doyle both frowned and tightened their eyes.

"Ah, that is where we had to make a concession," smiled Dorsey ruefully, scratching his beard, "the third party in our partnership."

He retreated and a burly man in a military uniform stood up. The man had the salt and pepper buzzcut favored by so many in the military. The folds in the back of his neck were pressed against the tightness of his collar.

"General Armbruster Fung," puffed the red faced general. "The boys in Defense put together the portfolio to create... well, Trump 2.0, as you whizzes put it. We're primarily interested in hardware. Our nation's at the greatest risk it's ever been since WWII: ISIS, foreigners, Putin and North Korea, a vulnerable economy..."

"I don't think that's true."

"...cost of living in big cities, rising tuition rates, cellphone plans that are outta control, phishing emails, drunken behavior and low GPA scores in an ever competitive job market..."

Somewhere the general was losing his train of thought. It sounded like he had a kid in college.

"Anyway, we've outfitted Trump 2.0 with jet propulsion boots, short range ballistic missile capabilities, scanning and tracking software that's virtually foolproof, hydraulically enhanced strength, and automatic . 50 caliber cannons in his shoulders."

"Not to mention the processing power of twenty computers," chimed in Dorsey.

"So—he's invulnerable?" someone asked.

"Better than anything the Chinese have," replied General Fung, looking sharply at Dorsey. Dorsey looked away.

"Is he going to resume the presidency?" I wondered. Again, everybody stared at me.

"Well, the country's in chaos, as you all know" admitted Fung, "let's fly this up the flagpole and see what happens?"

Dorsey took his cue and pressed the blue button on the back of Trump 2.0's gold sprayed throne. An image of what looked like a cellphone battery reserve indicator flashed on the screen and intense buzzing filled the room. Trump's powerful atomic generator kicked in. A fusion engine warmed the plexiglass and ribbed tubing and the creature's blue irises began to open. His midriff which consisted of little more than a spine screwed into a titanium pelvis (all of his bulk was top heavy) radiated an eerie luminescence.

"State your prime directives," whispered General Fung dramatically.

Trump 2.0 pursed his tight lips:

"Uphold the office of President.

Help the Economy.

Serve the Public Trust."

It was impossible to read the expression in Trump 2.0's eyes.

T

We all know what happened next. Trump not only helped the economy and served the public trust: he revitalized the country. He healed the divide between North and South. He united the Democrats and Republicans. With the neo-liberal programming installed by Dorsey and the hardware provided by the military, Trump plugged in electronically to the defense grids, the complex networks of banks and finance that clogged up the country's economy; he even controlled the traffic patterns of the U.S.A.'s major cities so that everybody got to their destinations faster. And safer.

Dorsey had a team of technicians working on the president twenty-four seven. The full capacity of the neural networks of twenty linked computers was put to maximum effect. He only needed to recharge once every hundred hours. A new heightened processing power allowed him to see that the only way forward was to increase social spending. To repair the great schisms and cracks in American society, he put money into neighborhoods that needed it most. He created job programs that were labeled by the media as the '*new* New Deal.' Over-congested prisons were shut down and an increase in rehabilitation programs, like those in Norway and other Scandinavian countries, helped smooth the transition of felons back into society. Public health clinics, community centers, and immigrant services were created. Affordable housing and sound mortgage options returned. The disenfranchised were supported on a level never seen before. Corporations and politicians were made liable for their crimes. For the first time, bosses were responsible to their employees and voters. Tax havens and graft became a thing of the past.

For those on the right, Trump gave them the work programs and blue collar opportunities that had become scarce in the heartland. He was tough on crime and built an army of police droids that he controlled. Singlehandedly, he put the fear of law into criminals' hearts, both on the street and in office towers. The force's resources and power were insurmountable.

All the while, he tweeted about it. Our phones constantly buzzed and flashed at Walter Reed and around the world as Trump 2.0 updated the entire nation as to what he was doing, on the hour every hour. And he always used the hashtag #Trumptopia.

He plugged in directly to all the cellular networks and acquired even more followers. His popularity rose. A team was put together to run his campaign for re-election. Their motto:

"Taxes, Transparency, Tweets. Trump 2.0 for 2020. #Trumptopia."

T

I had signed off on the forms so I was present, albeit on the fringes, of the group at Walter Reed that monitored him and checked the big man's vital signs. I wasn't invited to the sessions where he rested in the recharging chair in Lennox's office.

But I was around. And I kept my eyes open. The scientists at the hospital were excited. It was a new age: Trump 2.0's changes heralded a new era in technical advancement, scientific discovery, and space exploration. Learning and curiosity became popular for their own sake. The only people who really objected were the plutocrats. They numbered less than five percent of the population. Their objections were easily quashed. Wealth was redistributed to pay for all the new benefits, and once Americans saw the increase in their quality of life, the increase in happiness and neighborliness and contentment and basic felicity that existed, they didn't wish to go back. It was the end of that illusory and hollow *American Dream*. It was instead replaced by a new *American Health & Happiness*.

There were still rich people and Trump and his family numbered among that class. I did too, to be honest. But now that the very very rich had been seen to, that virus of greed that made people aspire to the unnecessary and lavish excesses of *that* toxic class dissipated and lost its hold. Trump and his family even donated half of their fortunes to cancer research and inner city schools. Instead of espousing golden edifices, the Trump brand became synonymous with a gold standard. Trump Tower itself became a temporary shelter, a mission if you will, for the dwindling homeless population in New York.

#Trumptopia had been achieved. And it was huuuge with everybody.

T

Three years into his presidency, Trump's hardware had been built over and redesigned by the military and Dorsey's team so often that it was hard for any of us to say which version we were dealing with at any given time. He no longer needed to recharge every hundred hours—a cooling/generating system filtered nutrients and minerals from the air while he flew—like *Iron Man*, he had hundreds of duplicates taking care of whatever needed attending to. One body took care of earthquake victims in California while another spoke to prisoners in Idaho about reforming their lives while yet another aided Kurdish militants in Syria. We could not call him Trump 10.0 or 20.0 or even 100.0 because numbers meant nothing. We might as well call him Trump Infinity.

I saw him rarely, just when one of his bodies visited Lennox and Doyle's hangar. The clanking of his jet propulsion boots rang through the halls. The armored boots left impressions in the concrete as he walked. And always, that smell of jet fuel and oiled machinery, the ionic heat of fibre optic cables pushed beyond burning point, cloyed to the walls. It was ironic in a way—so much of our energy came from solar panels and turbines now—renewable sources of energy had been worked into the electric grids—America had become a world leader in reducing carbon emissions—and yet, Trump Infinity was still made of gears and wires and oil and machinery and silicon and fibre optic, all crowned with that iconic face with the tight blue eyes and puckered lips and swoop of hair that become his trademark. Only, the hair on the versions I saw now was not original hair—it had been replaced by an aestheticized alloyed skull plate, painted gold, that swooped over the back of his head.

Sometimes he erupted from Lennox and Doyle's lab in a cloud of what seemed like urgency, flying away on jet fumes into clouds, the plexiglass flashing an electric shade of neon, reverberating some emotion beyond the ken of ordinary folk. Sometimes there were four or five of him descending from the sky at the same time. A visual reminder of how exactly things had changed. If we felt trepidation or fear during those times, we didn't talk of it.

T

With everything running smoothly, Trump Infinity had all but become an anachronism. Though he was no longer the bloated representation of a cancerous America, as he had been before his death, with his long range missiles and nuclear capability, he inhabited bodies that were out of step with the world he had created. The Trumptopia he engineered was at dissonance with the microwaves emitting from his eyes and the strategic protocols that linked his hard drives.

I was no longer in the loop but had been given a promotion and significant bump in pay. I used it to fly back to Seattle often. To remain in touch with reality. Or I bought tickets for myself and Jordan to stay at hotels and see away games, so we could witness the Seahawks get trashed firsthand.

We were at the newly-opened Las Vegas Stadium where the Seahawks played an exhibition game against the Raiders. Trump, or one of his manifestations, sang the national anthem. At first, he stood erect and sang in perfect pitch, albeit modulated by autotune. But when he got to 'the land of the free and the home of the brave,' his voice cracked and something rusty came out, a wailed croak or a sob, as Trump's plexiglass and metal frame crumpled. He then ripped the gold alloyed skull plate from atop his scalp and flung it into the Nevada sky. It traced a perfect screaming parabola and crashed back down, almost maiming one of the players. Coach Carroll tried to approach the great hulking droid but Trump suddenly straightened and shot off in a cloud of jet exhaust, singeing Coach Carroll's face.

The exhibition game that night began after a delay.

I felt a troubling sense of deja vu.

T

It wasn't too long after I returned to Walter Reed that the anonymous texts began.

"I know you were there," read the first one.

"I'm in pain. You're a doctor. A stand-up guy. Help me…" read another.

A later one still flashed: "I know you're a patriot. One of this nation's heroes. Not a loser. I can sense it… this isn't right and you know it—in your heart."

I didn't answer and quickly deleted the texts. After all, there was no number attached to them and I didn't know where or whom they were from. They simply appeared on my phone. I was enjoying the fruits of my promotion. America was enjoying renewed prosperity for the first time since the sixties. The world was a better place. Where was the loss?

So I switched cellphone plans. And bought a new phone. But I transferred my contacts from my old phone and in that split second, he grabbed hold of the signal and whatever essence was left, whatever smidge of human consciousness still remained, rode the electrons from one device to the other. I say 'he' because it could be no other. The compulsive four a.m. tweeter. The unreluctant reality star. The ghost in the machine. Trump 1.0. The original.

"I'm in pain," he texted, "I miss having a penis... I miss the thrill of taking Viagra... I'm in anguish... you're my doctor. Help me!" The time was 4:55 p.m.

I reminded him of his directives:

Uphold the office of President.
Help the economy.
Serve the public trust.

The ensuing silence was worse than a heart-wrenching sob.

No matter how I reasoned with myself, I could not deny that he was right: I was his doctor and since I had signed those forms on that fateful day, he was my patient. He was right. The man was in anguish and I must help him. What did he want? Nothing short of death, it turned out. The sweet release of oblivion. A respite from consciousness, from the weariness of serving an immortal term. He had died on that fateful day he placed the McDonald's order from within his gold Cadillac Allante and he now wished to ride the great Cadillac in the sky. There was no real relationship between him and Melania or Barron or Ivanka or any of the others, only photo ops.

He was a copy of a copy of a copy.

Don't you understand? He did not really exist anymore and yet, he could not die. His was a soul caught in purgatory.

The more he worked at me, the more he wore me down. In the end, the texts not only infiltrated my phone, they infiltrated my mind. I became loyal to him. Let's be honest. I worshipped him like everyone else.

T

You know by now what happened. How the nuclear fallout came about. It's not easy to kill a program, a copy of a copy of a copy. Simply breaking into Lennox's hangar and burning it to the ground would do no good. Neither would attacking Jack Dorsey and demanding he erase the code. The code itself was as sophisticated as DNA and possessed both sentience and resilience. Would I then approach Armbruster and demand back the bits of Trump's brain they'd copied? No, Armbruster only served others.

He served the public trust.

There was only one way to defeat Trump Infinity's existence and that was to carry out a plan Trump himself designed. His software had protocols that stopped him short of harming himself, erasing or deleting any of the work Dorsey had done. But there was nothing to stop him downloading the information, the code created by Dorsey, the schematics I had seen that day in Lennox's office, the automatic video and memory logs that were kept, everything that could be compressed into a series of files. It all existed in the cloud. Using an anonymous routing process, he set up a meeting between me and his adversary. No, not Putin. Kim Jong Un. The president of North Korea.

"Why not Putin?" I asked, "you two were rumored to be friends at one time. Why not have him and the SVR carry out the job?"

"Putin's an android himself," came the cryptic reply. "You think those muscles are real?"

I didn't want to know more.

Kim Jong Un, according to the deal, was to use the schematics and updated files I provided to find Trump's weaknesses and destroy him. But Kim, being the jealous madman that he was, set out to build an army of flying 'droids that would serve himself, counter Trump, and commissioned a very special exoskeleton for himself. While Trump felt less than a man, Kim Jong Un armed himself with penis projectiles and ballistic balls.

The battle over the Pacific has been recorded and commented upon by smarter people than me. It rivaled the war between the Greek Gods and Titans. It left a nuclear fallout that we are told will last decades. Perhaps a century and more.

T

So now you know the story. How a simple doctor like me could do a thing like that. I turned myself into Armbruster and that's how I ended up in here. It's a good thing that the death penalty was abolished nationwide while Trump still assumed his presidency.

I know there are a lot of conspiracy theories out there, like I was a sleeper agent working for the Russians. That I was born Korean and had my face surgically altered. That I was hired by the consortium of plutocrats taxed heavily by Trump 2.0. That I was in collusion with Malik Malawi, the person who killed Trump the first time. That I worked with a team of people who belonged to a cult that considers *The Apprentice* their religious text. That I've hidden a memory key with Trump's consciousness on the grounds around Twitter's campus, to be dug up and implemented later. That they froze his brain and keep it in a safe in the Arctic. That Lennox and Doyle were alien ambassadors sent to Earth with alien technology. That the mafia bankrolled the whole thing.

No! For goodness sake!

It was just me and this is what happened. Not a lone shooter exactly, but a lone something. I'm not even sure that I was in control when it all went down. I was as much swept away as everyone else. By him. It seemed like the right thing to do. His voice was so urgent—like a child's. Then it was gone.

Now, I know I wasn't the only one being reached out to. There were others. At the time, I didn't know that. I felt special. He asked them all to do the same thing. But I was the only one who went along.

Was I special or stupid?

You tell me.

Me! A lonely doctor from Seattle who likes the Seahawks. The only reason I haven't been shanked in prison is because of the prison reform *he* created. This place is almost humane. It's certainly better than the world out there, with the fallout. And the riots and the looting. And the burning buildings.

Like the medieval ages now.

T

Jordan's gone too. I miss him. Ah well. I wish the radiation hadn't destroyed the whole western seaboard including Seattle. And my beloved Seahawks.

And the NFL.

Why did I sign off on those forms? It wasn't even my shift.

People told me to sign those forms, that's why.

Nobody told me to be a hero.

Koom Kankesan is the author of The Panic Button, The Rajapaksa Stories, and The Tamil Dream. He contributes comics journalism to Deconstructing Comics Podcast and Comicon.com. Feel free to listen or read at: deconstructingcomics.com and comicon.com.

24 Avoiding Eye Contact on Main Street, USA

by Jacob Guyon

Like every weekday for the past seven years, I slip on my surgical mask and set out down Main Street on the mile-long walk to work. I used to take the bus, but a heavy tax cut pretty much gutted public transportation services. Small price to pay, I'm told. The Dow is certainly soaring, not that I can afford to invest.

I cast a quick glance at the mangled front of the Hernandez family's house next door. They were internally rendered a few days ago. They'll probably be deported; they're only three generations removed from being Mexican immigrants and the regional prefect is unlikely to place much value on their birth certificates and decades of taxpaying citizenship. The local branch of Immigration and Customs Enforcement jumped at the chance to call out their SWAT team and rolled in heavy, backing their armored vehicle into the front of the house. I had to duck away from the window so I didn't get shot when the rifle-toting cops spilled out. They dragged the parents and their siblings out and threw them in the back of the van. They took the children a bit more gently. After all, they can't be cruel. The kids will be adopted by a celebrity couple in all likelihood.

The last reporter who called attention to the deportation of American citizens was sent to debtor's prison after a series of libel lawsuits bankrupted her. Her claims were completely true and reinforced by a lot of evidence. She was an excellent journalist, but that was less relevant than her inability to afford an excellent lawyer.

My route takes me through the downtown business district, the two opulent blocks between Trump Avenue and Trump Boulevard, with its shiny buildings and heavily armed guards. I avoid eye contact. No sense in risking a spark to their notoriously short fuses.

The first time a young activist was shot for vandalism it was a big federal case. It was in the newspapers for a whole week, but all the major outlets dropped it when a White House representative hinted that they were in danger of making the dreaded Fake News List. Even CNN and Fox News couldn't survive that unofficial designation. The Not-So-Supreme Court—so named a few months into the President's third term when they pursued their investigation into the election with a little too much enthusiasm—made a show of deliberating but ultimately reached the unsurprising conclusion that destruction of property could be considered an attempt on the lives of the people in the building. There have been a lot of legal precedents in the past few years for the sanctity of property. After all that, the thick layers of graffiti faded and were covered with shiny new paint and posters of President Trump, his chin nobly inclined. His fourth term started a few weeks ago.

The chic cafes are practically empty, but thirty dollars for a small black coffee means they keep more than enough of a profit to stay in business. I avoid eye contact. No sense in risking the ire of Those More Fortunate. One sideways look could result in a call to my employer and my own one-way ticket to a bug-infested bunk in debtor's prison.

I pass a gas station. A couple of wannabe hillbilly types are trying to look rustic, tilting their spotless Stetsons and hooking their thumbs behind their polished belt buckles while shelling out eight dollars a gallon to gas up their trucks. All the real hicks drive energy efficient little sedans now out of simple necessity. One of them cast me a hairy eyeball for some reason. Maybe it's because there's an anti-mask fad going around that crowd after a couple pundits made fun of people who wear them in public with a few almost-racist jokes about Americans wanting to turn Japanese. Their ratings dropped until they made the jokes obviously racist. They would probably call me an environmentalist, which is almost as bad as being called a terrorist, communist, or illegal immigrant. I avoid eye contact. No sense in risking the informal investigation that would likely result from their jibes. I've been a hard-working law-abiding citizen my whole life but that wouldn't count for much if the Neighborhood Watch decided to take issue with me. I've had too many demerits lately, especially considering how nice I was to the Hernandez family.

The next few blocks are spotted with prostitutes and panhandlers outside the barred windows of dead or struggling shops. I look away quickly when I see my brother among them. After his third tour in North Korea, he was more than a little off and had trouble getting a steady job. His grace period ran out and it was illegal to let him stay with us so we had to throw him off our couch. I hope in vain that he won't recognize me, that the mask will hide my shame if I avoid eye contact. It doesn't work, and he obviously recognizes me. He looks sallow and ragged, like he hasn't seen sunlight or a good night's sleep in years. His eyes seem to be half a mile away. Without a word, he watches me pass, a stained coffee cup half full of coins jingling slightly in his shaky grip. I expect, maybe even hope that he'll launch into a foul-mouthed tirade accusing me of abandoning him when he was most in need, but his silence is worse.

As I round the last corner before reaching my office, I get coal-rolled by one of the guys from the gas station. It's a very popular insult nowadays, considering no one has to worry about passing emissions tests. They only left a tiny number of the environmental regulations, and that didn't make the cut.

I clock in for a fourteen-hour day, the first of six this week. Hard work is all the rage, they say, and the slightest complaint would have worse results than failing to retweet one of the president's Twitter posts. I'm lucky they didn't fire me for my union membership. Right to Work state and all. I avoid eye contact with my boss and get to work.

I thank God every day for my fortunate situation, and not just because it's mandatory.

Jacob is a Colorado native who grew up in and around Ogden, Utah. He is a student at Weber State University, where he also works as a stagehand and sound designer at the Val A. Browning Center for the Performing Arts. He's had poetry and short fiction published in the campus undergraduate literary journal, *Metaphor*. He's been writing his entire life, inspired in part by a counter cultural social consciousness to which he was first introduced by the punk subculture. His efforts are usually in the form of poetry and short fiction, though he has a novel nearing completion.

25 The Cure

by Aaron C. Smith

"Open your eyes, Agent St. Claire. Playin' possum insults me. It's gotta be borin' you."

The honey-on-steel voice carried the faint tones of the Texas oil fields, decades after the speaker had stopped wildcatting.

J. Anson Galt. Mad scientist. Or, more accurately, mad engineer whose billions funded an army of scientists.

I opened my eyes.

There was no other choice. My infiltration of his Rocky Mountain fortress had failed. His security robots had captured me in the facility's power plant, as I attempted to cause a catastrophic failure. The explosion was the only possible way to stop Galt from releasing his weaponized smallpox virus.

I expected to find myself in a cell and instead faced my captor in a padded leather chair. The lack of restraints spoke to his confidence. An LED screen filled the wall behind Galt. Books lined the walls, their cracked spines illustrating many readings. Cases throughout the room held swords, shields, armor and firearms, testimony to Galt's love of military history.

The billionaire wore an unbuttoned Oxford shirt, sans tie. The vast redwood desk separating us was bare, save photographs of two blond children. Galt's wide, bluff face was evidence of his years working outdoors.

Galt polished a pair of glasses before placing them on his head. "These belonged to Benjamin Franklin," he said. "Some reporter writes a butt kissing piece about me and how smart I am, I just think about what Franklin did. Now there's genius, Agent St. Claire. *Agent St. Claire.* That sounds so formal. Can I call you Peter? You can call me Anson."

"You may call me whatever you wish. I am rather hard pressed to object," I said.

Americans think we Brits lack emotions. They are wrong. Some of us are simply raised not to let those emotions control us. At this moment, Galt's emotions mattered far more than mine.

"You're right. I could kill you if I want. But I wanna talk. It's just you, me and 482 here," he said, nodding to the robot valet at his side.

The humanoid machine lacked the false flesh Galt's killing machines normally wore. Wires looked like veins, titanium rods resembled bone. "I told my staff to let us be. This study's soundproofed."

Soundproofing sounded rather ominous, as was the marble floor. In all aspects, except for one, this office mirrored Galt's study in his Homewood estate. The polished floor in this room made for far easier cleanup than the carpet at Homewood.

There would be no rescue.

Circumstances required my violation of American sovereignty. President Trump's accusation that our GCHQ helped President Obama spy on his campaign cooled relationships between our nations. Even absent that insult, his intelligence agencies leaked like sieves. If the Home Office informed him of this operation, the odds did not favor his authorization of a mission to liberate me.

"It's an honor to be speaking with you, Peter. I've read your files. That business with Wilson DeVries and his moon laser was amazing. And meeting the man who put the Butcher of Beijing in the ground is… It's just an honor."

Galt's casual discussion of files that only three people in the world had read sent shivers down my spine.

"Guests can leave whenever they please. Am I free to leave?"

"Peter, y'all were breaking into my property. I coulda just shot you and called it a day. It's pretty gutsy to complain about your treatment," Galt replied. His features softened. "Ah, that's not the foot I wanted to get off on with you. This is just supposed to be a friendly chat."

"I presume we are talking about *the Cure*?"

Dropping the name did not impress Galt. My presence meant I knew his game. He waved a hand, inviting me to continue.

"You are planning to murder the human race, Anson," I said, loathing such informality. "I fought your robots from England and the Continent to Sri Lanka and now here. But I cannot answer a simple question."

"What's that, Peter?"

"Why?"

The billionaire smiled. He picked up a remote control from the desk. "Thought you'd never ask. Take a look here, Peter."

A video began playing, beginning with a black screen. A low, rumbling bass rolled through the room as images appeared.

A former Vice President of the United States warned that the earth had a fever. Images of forest fires followed.

Scientists stood before legislatures, TED Talks and cable television shows, delivering dire predictions of mankind ravaging the planet. The screen shifted to piles of dead animals.

The presentation ended with a burnt-out Earth spinning in the darkness.

"Thoughts?" Galt asked.

"You are a bloody lunatic."

"Lunatic? No. Dying? Yes. Cancer. Started in the lungs but decided to spread. I've got grandchildren." He slammed his hand down and the pictures on his desk jumped. "I will leave them a better world than this one. Anyone who stands in the way of that can burn!"

Galt shook his head.

"Hell. I'm lecturin' you and haven't you offered you a drink. What'ya want?" He pointed to a full bar in the corner of the room.

A drink? I knew this game. After a sip, my innards would turn to liquid or some such thing.

Or would they?

If Galt wanted me dead, he did not need poison.

"Scotch," I requested.

"Single malt?"

"Is there any other?"

"Good man," the billionaire said and chuckled. "482, a Pappy Van Winkle for me." The robot nodded.

"Neat or on the rocks, Agent St. Claire?" 482 asked.

"Do you have stones?"

"Yes, sir."

"Two please."

482 made us our drinks.

The malty scotch was exquisite.

"There now," Galt said. "We can be civil. Now tell me, Peter, do you honestly think our world's not in danger?"

"Your proposal is to kill nine in ten humans."

"The planet's full up, Peter. Population management's necessary. I save the best of humanity, spread 'em all over the world so they can take care of 'emselves and not bump up against each other, startin' wars and such. They learn a new way of living, with the proper guiding hands. Heck, with the robots, most folks'll be free to follow their dreams."

"And you would lead these guiding hands?"

"You know someone better?"

"Have you listened to yourself? You hate humanity but want to save it?"

Galt strode over to a display case, withdrawing a revolver from its mount. "This, my friend, is a Colt Peacemaker. Custer carried this weapon, though he left it in his tent at Little Big Horn. Amazing piece of engineering. We go from banging rocks to make fire to building this.

"Beauty. It's why I love humanity and why I will save it."

482 replenished my Scotch as I finished it. "You show your love of humanity by its slaughter."

"I've built an ark. I'm saving what can be saved! Of course, our new world'll need others of vision and strength. You and your colleagues've thinned my ranks of Tin Men. That's left me in the need of able humans in my employ." He smiled at me, hands opened wide to offer me Heaven and earth.

I shook my head. "Never."

Galt returned to his desk with long, purposeful strides. Each step bounced his bushy mustache. "Never's an extremely long time, Peter."

I sipped my Scotch, saying nothing.

"Your efforts were magnificent, Peter. But the Cure is happening, whether you want it or not."

"You can still be stopped."

"What y'all're looking at there is why the Cure can't be stopped." Galt pressed another button. The screen split to show half-a-dozen different views.

Galt's prison.

I recognized many of the prisoners in what could only be called gilded cages. Some I had met. Others I knew simply by reputation as fellow players in the great game, such as Nadya Romanov, an FSB agent currently practicing her yoga. Some were the politicians. A Tory MP engrossed in painting a watercolor still life. The daughter of a reality star reading an actual book. These were the sort of people whose disappearances triggered my investigation in the first place.

The screen changed, showing feeds from a first-person point of view, similar to a shooting simulator. The most chilling image came from England, the Cabinet Room in 10 Downing Street. The camera angle made it clear that the footage was being broadcasted from the Prime Minister's own chair.

Only the Prime Minister sat in that chair.

"Who is sending this video feed?" I asked, forcing power I did not feel into my voice.

"You're looking through the eyes of the Cure. Politicians. Generals. Heads of companies. Media types. Scientists who see the coming apocalypse. They were the first. But not the most important. Peter, you ever hear the term 'deep state?'"

I had. It referred to the lower level, entrenched government bureaucrats who stayed in their positions no matter which party controlled the government. They possessed the bulk of government authority, enforcing or failing to enforce policy as they saw fit. No matter the election results, they remained and answered to no one.

"Leaders were just a first step. They gave me the money we needed to set this up and recruited the bureaucrats that'll manage things when the plague hits. They'll send resources where we need 'em, away from unproductive populations the world won't need."

"How?" The scope of this treason nearly left me speechless. I blinked and saw dying cities that could be saved, if they hadn't offended Galt's agents.

"All kinda reasons. Some believe. Others want pull in the New World.

"Mostly they want this."

The screen showed an injection gun, loaded with a clear ampule.

"A vaccine," Galt said. "Given to my supporters and folks they want to survive with. Real interesting, seeing who some of them picked. That gal there, Minority Leader in the House over here, she didn't give it to her husband. Said losing someone she loved would help rally the country around her.

"So think on this. A gal like her is gonna reshape humanity. You want to leave it in her hands? Mine? Suit up with us, you get a say in things. Balance her type out. Don't you get why you're here, son?"

"I am here because your robots used a Taser on me."

Galt smiled.

"Was talking about why you were in my house in the first place. I mean, here I am in a fortress designed and built by the best engineers and architects money could buy. Why do you think they built air ducts large enough for a person to fit in?"

"Maintenance?" The excuse sounded weak, even to my own ears.

"Son, I have android assassins. I have robots deliverin' meals. You're honestly tellin' me you don't think we could build a machine to run repairs small enough that our ducts don't have to give every operative from the CIA, FSB or MI-6 a way in? We built three hatches for y'all. You know how much they cost to fix when one of you guys bust in?"

My mouth opened but nothing came out.

Bloody hell.

Why had none of us seen the trap?

"Do you get it now, Pete? We've planned for every way the dice're gonna bounce. You can't win."

I shook my head. I had beaten a man seeking to use a laser on the moon to extort humanity. I had convinced the head of the People's Liberation Army to kill himself instead of launching a nuclear weapon from North Korean territory at Japan.

Galt sighed and shook his own head. "Okay then. One last pitch."

He rose from behind the desk. The Colt Peacemaker hung at his side.

The madman slid a round into the revolver.

Then another.

And a third, until he loaded each chamber. Then Galt looked up at me, a weariness in his eyes.

"Y'all want to reconsider signing on?" he asked and stepped behind me.

Galt snapped the cylinder into the revolver.

Cold steel pressed against the base of my skull.

I could not make a play for the gun before he fired. Better to end this with dignity.

Eyes closed, I contemplated my regrets.

I am a soldier. I have fought around the world for Crown and country.

But I cannot say I am proud of all my choices.

The abused trusts.

The shattered hearts.

The bodies left behind.

Given a chance to relive my life, I would make the same decisions. They saved more lives than they destroyed. My honor may lay in tatters but the Crown's stayed intact.

I was a soldier. I did my duty.

My epitaph.

The hammer cocked.

If an afterlife existed, I would not meet it under my birth name. I would not see my mother and father. They would be in Heaven.

I possessed no illusions about my fate.

The hammer fell.

Click.

"Very good," Galt said. "Very good."

He stepped back into my sight line, clapping as if admiring a skillful putt.

"You're one of the good ones," the billionaire said, laying his pistol on the desk. He produced the round that should have killed me. "Bit of stage magic I learned a few years back, like pulling quarters out of my son's ear."

"What?" My heart pounded. I tried to understand why it still beat.

"You didn't take the offer, to kill all those people just to save your skin. You passed."

"What are you talking about?"

Galt sat back down. "482, freshen our drinks please. I believe Peter here's earned himself a double."

I must admit I took a far more liberal belt of the Scotch than I would have under normal circumstances.

"What was the purpose of that little game?" I asked. Anger burnt through confusion. "A bit of fun before you kill me and release your plague? Our files did not indicate that you were a sadist."

"I'm blushing that your people think so highly of me, Peter. What'ya think they'd say if I told you that there ain't a plague at all?" Galt tossed back his whole drink, motioning for another.

I tried to process the statement. "But all of the resources invested in this facility, the others you mentioned, the robots. Your 'backers.' You said they invested fortunes with you..."

Galt tapped his nose.

It became clear. "It was a confidence game, separating your followers from their millions, wasn't it?"

"Getting close, Peter. Those funds sure helped us develop some pretty fun toys. But that's just a side benefit."

"What was the point of this. The destruction you have caused. The lives you have taken."

"I'm dying."

"You have said that."

"And I'm going to leave a better world for my grandchildren."

"Now you are simply talking in circles."

"Nah, you're looking at it in circles. If I'm not really killing the world, what have I done?"

I considered the question. "You have identified those in power willing to kill the world."

"Exactly!" Galt said. "And you've seen I can get a view through their Mark 1 eyeballs."

"How?"

"Well, we didn't need to waste money ginning up a plague or a cure. We worked on another project. Nanotechnology. Tiny robots. We put them in the 'vaccines.' When we gave out the injections, the nano settled into optic and aural nerves. I can see, hear and record everything they've been doing."

"My God," I said.

A record of this treason would tear down governments. The scope of what Galt had done was breathtaking.

So was the cost.

"Was it worth it? The lives you have taken to move this deception forward?"

"How many lives've I taken? Son, I could've hired mercenaries from anywhere and everywhere. Ex-Delta Force, Shin Bet, Spetsnaz, whatever the Chinese call their commandos. I can afford 'em all, for bucket loads cheaper than one of my Tin Men. But I didn't. You know why?"

"They are fun toys?"

"They are!" Galt said, slapping his thigh. "But you know what else they do? They keep down the collateral damage. My robots could've killed you easy. I told 'em not to. I wanted to see you in action."

"So you have evidence of the world's most powerful individuals planning its greatest crime. I assume you plan to release it."

Galt nodded. "In time."

"Then why take so many prisoners? If someone spurned your offer, why take them hostage?"

"Couldn't let them let the cat out of the bag before we found all the scoundrels. Besides, the folks who turned me down needed protecting."

"Protecting from what?" I asked.

"The Cure and its aftermath."

"You said there was no Cure," I said, my stomach tightening.

"No. I said that there was no plague. There's a Cure. It's just not what these folks expected. See, the robots in their heads don't just broadcast signals. They receive 'em too."

"And what do these signals do?"

"They instruct the nano in those traitors' heads to blow their brains out."

When I stood up this time, 482 did not stop me. "What gives you the right to kill all of those people?"

"The fact that they were willing to slaughter the human race."

"It is still murder!"

"You're a soldier, Peter. You've killed. How many people were you going to kill blowing this place up? When they said yes to my offer, these monsters declared war on humanity. They chose the wrong side and get to pay the price."

"But why not simply let the authorities deal with it? Your video footage is incontrovertible"

"What authorities? Is the Prime Minister going to meekly let himself be cuffed? Will Washington allow a purge that hits both parties? No sir, just releasing this information is guaranteed to start more than a few civil wars. If I lop the heads off this beast, the rest will be easier to deal with."

"What gives you the right?"

"Peter, before anyone got the shot, they saw video of folks 'dying' from the plague. CGI but horrifying. They still signed on for it. Some were downright giddy, put little kids on Christmas morning to shame. An actress who called me a murderer for eating a steak was willing to slaughter cities."

Galt removed his glasses and shook his head.

"If I don't put them down, then I am a monster."

"What about the children? You said that families were inoculated."

"Kids got saline solution. My computers make sure no heads blow up if someone's driving or anything like that. I'm not evil or stupid. I am willing to do what's necessary. Look at the casualties after World War II. Millions dead in the fighting and it makes us sick. But that was also the last war we won decisively against barbarians looking to kill us.

"You see that surgeon's saw, from the Civil War?" Galt asked, pointing to one of the glass cubes. "Battlefield medicine back then was ugly. Docs cut the whole limb off to save someone's life. War is the same thing. This ends here and now, in one shot. Then I release my guests from protective custody. Since folks who were in it for the money or from pressure didn't get the shot, there's still be work to do."

The words hung in the air.

I considered them. For a few seconds, I considered that he might be correct. His solution possessed the elegance of simplicity.

But at what cost? The Crown had not executed anyone since Peter Allen and Gwynne Evans in the Sixties. Aside from Belarus, Europe had abolished the death penalty. Even if the conspirators were taken to The Hague for trial, they could not face execution.

"I cannot let you do this," I said.

"You can't stop me," Galt replied.

I lunged forward and grabbed Galt's revolver from the desk.

He had kept one round out for his test. When I pulled the trigger, the hammer landed on a live one as did my next shot. I pivoted and fired the rest of the rounds into 482's head, destroying the robot.

I walked over to Galt, who lay against his giant screen. Blood bubbled from his lips.

"How do I stop it?"

"Too late," he said. "My grandson showed me the Evil Overlord List once. I mean, all the mistakes evil geniuses make in one list? I'd've paid a billion for that and it's free on the Internet? I triggered the devices before I brought you up here. Showed you recordings."

"Then why all this talk?"

"Wanted to take your measure. Like I said... meeting you's an honor. Besides, kept you occupied while the signal went out."

His chest jumped with a weak laugh.

"I am sorry," I whispered.

"Don't be, hoss. This way, I beat the cancer."

He died with a smile on his lips.

My hands tightened into fist. Galt represented another useless death.

I stood, staring at the monitor.

It was time to free the prisoners and enter the future Galt had given us.

Aaron Smith is a family law attorney practicing in San Diego, CA where he lives with his wife, son and two pit bulls. He has previously been published in *Microhorror.com, Liberty Island* and *PJ Lifestyles*. His short story, "Agency Cost," is included in the anthology *California Screamin'*. Follow him on Twitter @AaronCSmith1 and on Facebook at https://www.facebook.com/aaronsmithauthor/.

26 Alt.Death

by Joanna Koch

"Hi, everyone. This is Donny. Say hello, Donny."

"Hell-lo."

The audience of obsolete bots chuckles at the canned voice.

"Cute, isn't he? Donny here is our newest TransitionBot from Crematorium Productions, a subcontractor of Trumpczar Holdings United Group. Donny's here to relieve some of your anxiety about your next step forward on the corporate ladder and help you move on up to that great golden tower in the sky. We appreciate all of your hard work over the years, and we can't wait for you to grab your reward. Go on folks —give yourself a round of applause."

The retirees applaud. As reliable old worker models, the TransitionBot on stage strikes them as a bit twitchy. They're impressed by the human speaker. He's well-fed, dressed like a slick professional, and he sports a broad smile even though Donny's bleeps and tweets interrupt his speech.

"You're all here because of your hard work, but mostly because of your loyalty. Commitment and loyalty like yours set you apart from the rest when you supported the first incarnation of Trump in the pre-truth era. You made the choice to keep that legacy alive into the 22nd century, and here you all are, alive and kicking. More or less." The speaker nods.

Donny punctuates the silence with motorized cooing. "Pretty impressive, yes, indeed."

Donny spins and blasts waste heat from the flue in his head. White steam billows up to the rafters. The speaker takes a swig of bottled water. The retirees imagine a parched mouth blissfully hydrated. They don't need to eat, drink or sleep in their mechanical bodies. Although their uptime is unlimited since the switch, human memories often intrude on their productivity. When the power's out and battery supplies run low, they're tempted to question if they made the right choice.

"Choose life!" The speaker raises his voice and his fist. "That's what you did when you voted for the second incarnation of Trump, and for the third and final revelation of his Really Big Greatness that we all know and love today. You weren't like those fake protestors, those zero nothings whining about whatever lives matter. Boo-hoo. You supported the Open Ballot Act of 2019 and ended election fraud with one-hundred percent transparency. You knew your vote really mattered. Your vote meant so much that it was archived in a military database in Colorado Springs for your own protection. All those nothings disappeared pretty fast after the 2020 election, didn't they? A vote for Trump is a vote for life —your own! Give yourself a big cheer!"

A stray voice belts out "Amen!"

Donny seems to stop and nod, but it's hard for the retiring bots to tell. He's modeled on a memory from the template brain's formative years, rendering him less expressive in appearance than the obsolete models. His Really Big Greatness rejected the advice of his designers, engineers and publicists. He didn't trust the experts. Despite modern advances in ergo-robotics and the potential of organic-digital tissue processing, Donny looks like a big shop vac.

"Now folks, as much as we wish we could abolish term limits—so to speak—for everyone one of you, I'm sorry to say it's just not practical. Sure we have the science, but who's going to pay for it? Your contracts already renewed once, and the upkeep on old models is unbelievable! You don't want a hand-out, do you? No, you want what you've earned. You want what's fair. And I think it's fair to say, it's time for you to clock out."

Audience members exchange worried glances and nervous laughter. Restless, they rub phantom aches in their joints or tongue the idea of missing teeth. Freedom from health care exacted small sacrifices from their bodies before their memories and identities were uploaded into robotic frames. Most of them are women who outlived their reproductive and erotic utility. Their aluminum hands stray across abdomens filled with wire cables and circuitry as though the ghost of a uterus still dwelled within.

The speaker's smile shines bright. He's a charmer. "I don't need to show you this little four-foot tin-can bugger Donny here to convince you that moving up's nothing to be touchy about, but he certainly doesn't hurt, does he? You don't hurt, do you Donny?"

"Ouch. I hurt." Donny's metallic voice whines.

"Oh no! Big guy, what do you mean you hurt? What's wrong?"

Donny waves his vacuum hose arms and whirs in a circle. "I'm sad."

"Aw, Donny here is sad. I wonder what will make him feel better. Does anybody have any ideas? You there, ma'am, in the fourth row. You look like a sympathetic type. What's your classification? Amrel2015, eh? Now that's some serious vintage liberal juice right there, some real old-school sympathy. Give yourself a round of applause!"

Necks crane to spot the Amrel2015, the oldest classification still running.

This one was born before the country became a corporation: before the elderly president refused to die, diverted massive funds into bioengineering, and became CEO in perpetuity. Her early human memories, long repressed and obscure, gain new life as her short-term memory degrades due to age. She's not listening to the speaker or looking at his smile. She's lost in a memory. She's listening to her mother's voice and falling asleep in her father's lap. Amrel2015 doesn't understand why grown-ups make such a big deal about everything, as though talking about an election is more important than dinner, more important than dessert. All Amrel2015 wants is some of the baklava she helped her mother make earlier that day. She can still taste the sting of the sugar at the edge of her lips.

"Yes, indeed. Old-school tolerance and sympathy. Just what our little Donny needs. Why don't you hop up on stage, Amrel2015?"

The younger model retiree beside Amrel2015 rouses her from reverie and points her to the stage. Amrel2015 powers up her actuator and wobbles forward, favoring her right axle. The auditorium is quiet except for her grating gears and the hums and clicks of other aging bots. Though some recognize her effectors and worry about her outcome, they can't risk getting involved.

The retirees remember what happened to people with loud mouths, dark skin or questionable gender in the early days. Churches were granted tax funds for purity control, and gangs of Right Boys delivered transgressive bodies to the pyre. Competition and paranoia staunched revolt. Today, the group remains fractured like the land they drill and the wall they re-build as it falls apart under its own weight. Workers got the jobs they were promised: jobs for life, jobs for after-life, jobs building barriers against immigration, travel, trade, art and education. De-funding and deregulation cut all science programs except the military. Outside, everyone is the enemy. Inside, the protective border shrinks. Shortages and extreme weather deplete resources. Coastal states secede, driving the nation deeper into the dust bowl.

The speaker winces and paces around the stage as Amrel2015 creaks forward. Her frame shakes as she rolls up. "Well, that was quite the journey you just made there." The speaker mimics her gait with exaggerated gestures and pneumatic sounds. She feels embarrassed even though no one laughs.

"Ahem, just kidding, seriously, that was great. Thanks for all your hard work. We don't see commitment like that every day. Well, actually we do. It's all we see because there's no other choice. But you know, that was great, honey. Really, really great."

The speaker thumps Amrel2015 on the back. She nearly topples off the stage. He steadies her by reflex, grabbing her manipulator arm and rotary joint to prevent a fall. She hasn't been this close to a human in fifty years. Her optical sensors detect his sudden scowl and the sweat from his pores. She thinks he's a liar, and that he's afraid of his own lies. She's known men like him. A man like this once called himself her friend. She was five years old when the police kicked down the door of her home. He picked her up and said to turn away and watch the pretty lights. She looked out, and her neighborhood exploded with fires and sirens. She's still afraid of flashing lights.

Donny's control panel blinks faster and changes from amber to red.

The speaker seems amused. "Hey folks, I think little Donny here is about to blow a fuse if someone doesn't make him feel better. We don't want that to happen, do we? You don't want that, do you Amrel2015?"

Amrel2015 nods.

The speaker rolls his eyes. "Other way, honey. You don't want that, now do you?"

She shakes her head back and forth, remembering the men. A man such as this taught her the liberal race war would end when all the bad dogs were put down. Such a man praised her for having light skin. He declared the religion of her parents was a poison. The men in unison stamped Amrel2015 on her wrist, and later replaced it with a chip. She graduated from reform camp with honors, and the men in power declared her set free from the bondage of history, set free to build the future.

She had faith her hard work would pay off in the end. Survival required it. She worked to give her children a better life, and accepted the burden of silencing her memories as the price of her children's safety. She accepted the replacement of her body as the price of living long enough to see them succeed. When letters came that her children died fighting against terrorism in the wars in Afghanistan and California, Amrel2015 stared at the barbed-wire fence of the president's signature sealing her sons in a mass grave. She wondered about the bodies, both hers and theirs. She secretly prayed they might rest together someday.

Amrel2015 shakes her head as she meets the speaker's eyes. He's not handsome like the soldiers and executives she knew when she was young. He's flabbier, more desperate. Not her type. If she'd learned to live with a man like this, learned to live with his fears and lies, she might have escaped a life of labor fortifying the wall. She might have been privileged to embrace a natural death rather than living fifty extra years in a standardized, sexless body hauling load after load of grey-green modular bricks.

The speaker says, "That's more like it, honey. Now go over to Donny and make him feel good."

Donny's metal cavity is split into two stacked sections. The top displays the corporate American logo, a gold star and letter "T." The lower section has a latched door with a thin oblong window.

Through the window Amrel2015 sees flames.

The speaker takes her arm like a concerned father guiding a nervous bride. "Keep on going, honey. You're almost there. We're all about repurposing at Crematorium Productions, as you'll see in a minute. Or maybe a week or two at your speed. No one cares more about the people than we do. When you work for CremaPro, you don't just build the wall, you become a part of it. That's it honey, keep moving, you're doing fine. How are you doing, Donny?"

"Sad! I need hugs." Donny's vacuum hose arms slump from his rubber gasket shoulders. His control panel lights flash faster and brighter.

"Aw, poor little fella. All he wants is a hug. Go on, honey, give Donny a fucking hug already."

Inside Donny, the flames burn blue.

Amrel2015 can't move. The glare on her sheet metal is like the heat of the sun. The resistance in her wheels is like running in sand. Once upon a time, she fought to run in the sand, and played on the beach in the sun or under the stars. She lived in a home instead of a tent camp covered in coal ash. She ran until she collapsed in giggles, until her small celestial body was exhausted by its own joy and her mother scooped her up to safety and tucked her into bed. Her father, his face is lost to her now, but she heard his voice, his shouts when the men tortured him for a wrong vote. She heard the animal sounds from her mother. She looked away at the pretty lights and understood the same might happen to her.

"Hello, is there anybody in there? You still with us, honey? Donny needs you. Don't you, big guy?"

Donny whines and burns and holds his arms out with insistent greed. "Hug me! Hug me!"

The speaker leans low, dampening Amrel2015's aural sensor with his breath. "Look honey, this is harder for me than it is for you. I have to do this every day. Face it: you're junk, you're scrap. I've got a real live wife and kids. What happens to them if I don't keep Donny happy? Show some fucking sympathy, alright? Give the little metal fucker a hug and get this over with right now."

Amrel2015 notes the internal heat warning from her failsafe and disables it. Her name isn't honey. Her name isn't Amrel2015. Her name is a gift her parents gave her, a name rich with tradition, meaning and hope. She leans into the heat, leans into the memory. She's on vacation in her mother's homeland, at the beach. Her parents call her name. They're overreacting, as they always do. She swims too far from shore and, stunned at her absence, her parents shout out her name, wailing and beckoning over the sound of waves. Amrel2015 hears her forgotten name and signals success across the breakers, across the millennium that divides her family. They needn't worry. She's an excellent swimmer.

Amrel2015 meets the speaker's grasp with metal fingers. "My name is Najat."

Najat hurls the speaker into Donny.

The effort causes her to stumble offstage. She moves unnoticed to the abandoned control terminal as its guard rushes the stage with the other security detail.

Donny clamps the speaker in place. His cremation cavity swings open. Blue flames incinerate the speaker in seconds. Vacuum arms sweep up the ashes, and Donny metabolizes the speaker's mineral compounds through a sensory production chute grown from stem cells and pig DNA. Donny squats, grunts and extrudes a new grey-green modular brick.

At the control terminal, Najat fumbles for a USB-Q port compatible with her identity stick. She finds a receptacle in the machine that fits, flips open her thumb, and plugs it in. Nausea overwhelms her.

The Trumprocessor inside Donny uploads his pleasure to the home server, linking with hundreds of copies that share his delight in relieving himself. The original body of His Really Big Greatness, preserved and integrated within the system, participates through a neuro-digital connection that stimulates his pelvic splanchnic nerve. Simultaneous barks of fecal orgasm boost the signal to amplify its power, bouncing from one TransitionBot to the next, perpetuating the febrile brain's fantasy: as the wall grows bigger and thicker, the borders of the nation shrink around him like a small puckered mouth. The wall holds him, a womb of offal, a circle of flesh. He dreams of a country in the shape of an O, the middle letter of God, the Arabic zero that affronts Number One, the great oval toilet seat atop the wall that he shall cast out of solid gold. A toilet seat such as the world has never seen. A toilet seat only the ass of God is fit to shit upon.

Donny waves his shiny new brick with pride. Steam rises from the surface.

Najat installs her identity code, corrupting the template brain with her memories and emotions. The system formulates a query based on Najat's experiences: Who is the terrorist? Where is the threat? An error-detection process responds, calculates a correction and loads it into the network.

Donny flashes red, white and blue in patriotic eulogy to himself and all Trumps as he executes his final command. Before he explodes, he proclaims, "Thanks for your lifetime of service. I love you! You're fired."

Joanna Koch's short fiction has been published in journals such as *Dark Fuse* and *Hello Horror*, and in the anthology *Game Fiction, Volume One*. In addition to writing, Joanna is a visual artist and organic gardener, providing habitat for native insect fauna in her backyard near Detroit. She is an MA Contemplative Psychotherapy graduate of Naropa University and works as an advocate for women's rights.

27 The American

by G. Gray

Al eased himself onto the rough wooden bench, elbowing others aside to give him space to eat. They were being served a burnt slab of what he thought was meat drowned in the piss-colored gravy. The potatoes were lucky—they floated. He ate hunched over his bowl, dirty elbows protecting his food. He forced the food down in silence, knowing it would be some time before he ate again. He had already lost so much weight that his threadbare trousers were held up with string.

"Right, all of you. Dinner's over... get moving!"

The guard's brisk demeanor brooked no argument, yet no one at the table moved. The tension was palpable. Al stole a quick glance at his fellow prisoners—his bunkmates: all branded undesirable in the new regime, rounded up like sheep ready to be herded away. No one moved.

"I said move, you bastards!" The guard unslung his rifle and cracked it into the skull of the nearest man to him, knocking him to the ground.

Al recoiled as the sound of splintering bone reached his ears. He started to rise but the rough hands of the men on either side pushed him down. He eased himself back onto the bench, head down, with sweat running down his back.

The guard raised the rifle and aimed at one of the other men. "I have no problem pulling this trigger on any of you."

The silence in the food tent was louder than any explosion. As one, the group of twenty stood and edged away from the table.

"And take this piece of shit with you." The guard nodded toward the prone man.

Two of the group hauled their bunkmate up and carried him from the tent. The group walked over the frozen mud back to their flimsy, wooden hut in silence, under the disgusted stare of the perimeter sentries. Al glanced at the barbed wire fences, and the manned guard towers.

How in the hell did this happen?

T

"Get up! It's time."

Calloused hands shook Al awake and one hand clamped over his mouth in case he cried out. Opening his eyes did little to improve his sight.

The night was dark with no moon.

Everyone huddled together in their room, twenty men in the space for four. He hopped down from his bunk and shouldered his way toward the door.

"What about Miguel?" Al indicated their unconscious friend with the bandaged head. The Mexican had been the first person Al met when he arrived in the camp. Despite their differences, if hadn't been for Miguel, he might not have survived. Al had been badly beaten, but Miguel took care of him.

"He's staying here. He can hardly walk after that shit Carson hit him," Hiro responded.

"What'll they do to him when we're gone?"

No one answered, nor met Al's gaze. The likelihood of treatment was slim and without it—

Al took a long, slow breath. "Go. I'll stay with him. Get as far away as you can. Head north just like we said."

"What about you?"

"I'm an American. I'll be fine."

Cracking open the door, Al checked to make sure that the way was clear and ushered his friends out into the cold night. He led them to the perimeter fence, near the sewage waste ditch, where over the last few weeks he'd been sneaking out to loosen the fence posts. He dug the last bits of stabilizing dirt out with his hands and lifted the pole out far enough for them to crawl under. Once they were safely on the other side, Al wedged the post back in and stomped dirt around the base before smoothing it flat with his hands.

T

Al awoke the next morning to the breakfast bell. He rolled off the cot and helped Miguel get ready. The two of them shuffled toward the food hall as fast as Miguel could manage. Al settled him at their allotted table before queuing up for food. On his way back to the table, he noticed the group of guards making their way through the hall in his direction.

Carson stepped in front of him, demanding, "Where are your friends?"

"I don't know."

Carson slapped the two bowls of watery porridge from his hands and grabbed him around the throat. "Answer me!"

A hand clamped down on Carson's shoulder, pulling him away from Al, who stood in silence as the guards huddled and whispered amongst themselves. Carson stepped away from the group and circled behind Al, shoving him in the back. "Move!"

Al followed the guards to the sewage ditch. Carson pushed him into the ditch and made him walk through the waste in the direction of the damaged fence post. As they neared the scene of the escape, Carson yelled, "Stop."

Carson unslung his rifle, sighting Al down the barrel. "Now, anything you'd like to say, Muslim-boy?"

"You can't do this! I'm an American."

"You're a shifty, deceitful, brown-skinned bag of shit!"

"But, this is America!" Al Hussein yelled.

"Yeah, President Trump's America, and this is war," Carson sneered as he pulled the trigger.

G. Gray is a Northern Irish writer who likes to blur the boundaries between genres. In 2015, he achieved an honorable mention in the L.Ron Hubbard's "Writers of the Future" competition. He has also published through Robocup press—*Revenge; Hindered Souls* anthology; and the upcoming *Kids: Second Grade* from Dark Chapter Press. A published author in both the horror and thriller arenas, he is working on his first full length science fiction novel. https://www.amazon.co.uk/Gareth-Gray

28 Swan Song to a Gold-Plated Mausoleum

by Priya Sridhar

Her heart rattled with a rhythm that made her stomach ache. It thrummed at a rapid pace, making her chest jostle.

Swan brushed a strand of hair off her forehead. Her makeup sweated. Her lips were a dull red color with an added hint of gold eyeshadow. Swan thought she looked like last year's enamel evening bag. She stood in front of the studio audience, focusing her gaze on the camera.

"Welcome to another wonderful show!" Swan announced. "We have a great line of guest stars lined up, including Rue Morgue and Goldie Channing!"

The audience applauded. Swan fought the instinct to cover her breasts; she was wearing a teal ball gown that was better fit for a dance floor. Everyone was eyeing the low cut; they remembered the green bikini from that show. Swan wished she could forget the green bikini.

"There are hints that a certain flock of birds may also join us..." Swan said suggestively.

The audience cheered.

"It's amazing to be up here," She said. "Back when I was a kid growing up in the Florida backwater, I thought I would just be flipping burgers at McDonalds. And you know I don't have the wrist for that. You have to have the coordination. It's like being the MVP of Big Macs!"

She mimed flipping a burger. That got a few weak laughs.

"And also, we're all still here!" she said. "You may have heard that a certain president passed away today."

Boos greeted her in response. Swan grinned widely at them.

"Yeah; that was me—ding dong, the witch is dead! They say you shouldn't speak ill of the dead, but frankly, who is going to defend the Hairy Orange anyway? Are you going to honor him today?"

"Nooooo!" There was more laughter.

"Good! Neither are we. You know he's getting the full ceremonies? A full marble mausoleum and gold toilets on this tomb." This earned her first real laugh. "Also you have to bribe guards to even get a glimpse of the gold. I know I'm going to New Jersey with a chisel! Who else is?"

Some people cheered.

"But think of it this way!" she told the crowd. "We made it. We survived: black people, immigrants, people with disabilities, and LGBTQ! And guess who didn't? Ex-president Donald Trump. His hands tried to squeeze the life out of us, but they were too small!"

Swan staggered and walked. She pressed a manicured hand to her chest.

Her heart gave a lurch; the pacemaker thrummed uneasily. There was a pause. Swan's smile became a grimace. Then she stood tall.

"I know I'll be celebrating." She pulled a tiny champagne flute from her padded bra and a tiny hot pink bottle of champagne pops. "To outliving the Hairy Orange!"

T

Construction of the mausoleum didn't finish until late winter. It stood at nineteen feet and had creamy marble walls. Multiple obelisks cluttered the space.

The people that worked on the mausoleum had bad tempers. They were men with missing teeth, beard stubble, and hacking coughs. They wore blue uniforms embroidered with the Trump emblem.

"Outta my sight!" they yelled at people who strolled onto the site without helmets. "You're trespassing!"

Jared Kushner took questions from Fox News and Breitbart. Ivanka went to Iceland to promote her clothes and shoes. Tiffany vanished, along with the sons.

They said Melania had confined herself to one of the many Trump hotels. Hotel clerks hung up on hearing the name. ICE denied the allegation that it had receiving orders to deport her.

Someone left a tiny guillotine outside a Trump hotel. It had a beheaded doll under its minuscule blades, with a smashed china face.

"The queen is dead," a tag attached to the guillotine read. "Long live the queen."

T

She sat at the prop desk. This set had been used before, in skits about the harried bureaucrats that had held onto their jobs the way some houses during hurricanes held onto the ground.

Beau Gray was guest-starring in this episode. He wore a bald wig with a camel hair comb-over.

Kendall, the director, made the motion to start. Swan crossed her legs under the desk, as they had discussed during commercial. She took a deep breath and assumed a rigid pose. Beau swaggered over to her and chewed gum loudly.

"I'm here to vote in the upcoming election," he said in a nasally Brooklyn accent. Then he swallowed his gum loudly, before hacking.

"Good morning to you too," Swan recited, while she made a show of shuffling around papers. "May I have your ID?"

"Sure thing." Beau took out a prop ID made for this purpose. He dropped it, grabbed it, and dropped it again. Then he mixed it up with other props pulled out from his pockets: a string of paperclips, a paper doll with a white hood, a purple dildo, and a wad of dollar bills. These went up into the air, and down. After a vast amount of juggling, he finally set the ID on the prop desk, next to the dildo.

The audience had already started to laugh. Swan remained stony-faced. Mirth bubbled against her heart, and against the throbbing pacemaker. She picked up the dildo and scrutinized it.

"This isn't a valid ID," she said, biting her lip.

"Aw nuts," Beau moaned.

"Nuts are also forbidden. We operate on a cock-blocking policy," Swan said with a straight face. She bent down and revealed a large saw from the desk's bottom left drawer. "So I would suggest not taking any of those out."

"What about my license?" Beau gestured at the plastic card.

"Let me see…" Swan pretended to type. "Johnny Smith, aged 35. No criminal record, birth certificate on file, citizenship undisputed…"

She stopped dead cold. The silence made the audience laugh. Swan turned.

"What?" Beau asked.

"I'm sorry, I can't allow you to vote." Swan gave an exaggerated, sarcastic shrug. "New rules."

"What rules?"

"You voted for Donald Trump in the 2016 and 2020 elections." Swan gave a fake smile that showed off her whitened teeth. "Anyone who voted for Pussygate is determined unfit to vote in future elections."

"But that's not fair!" he protested. "I have the right to vote for whomever I want!"

"Not when it decimates our country's financial and social institutions, as well as destroying Net Neutrality." Swan kept smiling. "You allowed Verizon and Comcast to charge online lanes, Johnny! How did you think the surviving lawmakers would respond?"

Beau opened his mouth. He was supposed to protest here, but nothing came out of his mouth. He wasn't reading the cue card. Swan decided to go to the next line before the audience realized his fumble.

"Oh don't look so dour. Now you're among the ranks of Americans abroad, convicted felons, and black people." She spread her fingernails and grinned. "Welcome to their world!"

"I'm going to challenge this in court!" Beau said, regaining his thunder.

"And what do you think you'll get, Johnny Smith?" Swan clicked a computer. "Settlement money? Oh that's right; it got eaten up when Trump spent taxpayer dollars on golfing weekends and sending Barron to private school."

The laughs became more uncomfortable.

"Oh. I almost forgot. There is one way you can vote again," Swan said.

"And what's that?"

"You have to run the Gauntlet. It's a test of durability to see if you have the stamina for another election."

"Oh. Okay." Beau put on an air of confidence. "I've always been athletic."

Swan pressed a fake intercom button.

"Officer M, we have another contender."

There was a loud thumping. That came from the machine off-camera.

Beau looked around. He ran a hand across his lips to stop the smile that was blooming.

A large female officer dressed in a bulky uniform came on, wielding an ice pick and a prop Taser.

"Where is the fresh meat?" she shouted.

"You have to outlast Officer M for at twenty four hours." Swan made sure not to smirk.

Beau managed to cover his laughter with a high-pitched scream. He managed to run off stage, before doubling back to grab his dildo. The screaming continued.

"This is for motherhood being a preexisting condition, bitch!" The cop shouted and gave chase to him. They eventually ran off the set and into the audience. The cameraman adjusted the lens and videotaped Beau jumping over entire rows.

"And may the odds be ever in your favor," Swan said in a pronounced British accent.

T

The mausoleum was finished in the fall. Most of the project overseers went away, replaced by guards who also had missing teeth. Millions attended the funerary service, which was held before the first snowfall. News casters compared the millions to the paltry numbers that attended both inaugurations. It was a pathetic sight that a man's death was better attended than his life was.

The newest guard for the mausoleum was heavyset, with a twitching cobalt blue eye and brown scruff. He had been hired from a temp agency, from outside of the region. Before he had worked in the mines, and before that he had worked in his family's restaurant. The restaurant had closed after his father's hospital bills had bankrupted the family. His mother called him Ben, but his work ID read Benito.

No one was allowed into the mausoleum anymore; the coffin had developed nicks that the most skilled smiths couldn't smooth. Twitter was filled with pictures of faceless users that had scraped handfuls of gold for themselves from the coffin. One user even claimed to have Trump's middle finger from his right hand.

One day, in early spring, a skinny, freckled man in a blue business suit showed up. He walked up to Benito with other men wearing sunglasses and black business suits behind him. They appeared to be an escort entourage.

"Who are you?" Benito asked.

"I'm Eric Trump," the man said. "I'm here to pay respects to my father."

"You don't seem to be grieving," Benito said.

"I grieved a long time ago." Eric looked down. His blond hair was combed into spitball curls. "You saw me at the funeral."

Everyone had. The funeral had been televised, with a crowd of only Trump's family and a few advocates. People on Twitter livestreamed a violent confrontation between protesters, some of whom dressed as blue Munchkins from the Wizard of Oz singing, "Ding dong the witch is dead!"

"I spent a lot of time in Africa," Eric continued. "I just want to pay my respects."

Benito scrutinized him. Something was off, and the air seemed to crackle with that sense of wrongness. But the man did look like Eric, and he didn't rattle with chisels to steal a piece of gold.

"Very well, Mr. Trump," he said. "I do have to advise you that there are security cameras. We monitor the mausoleum 24/7."

"I know that." Eric looked irritated.

"I'm sure you do," Benito said. "It's part of our training to inform everyone who visits, even family."

Benito stepped aside. Eric's business shoes clicked against the marble floors.

Eric knelt alone in front of the large golden coffin which was now surrounded by a glass cabinet. The glass was several inches thick, with fingerprints coating most of it. Benito kept his hand on his walkie talkie.

Eric positioned himself into an odd squat. He spread his legs and bent his knees. It looked like he was sitting on a chair. A few pieces of paper came out from his breast pocket.

A flurry of brown hair flew into the air. It was a wig, which had belonged to the escort. The escort who tossed it passed by Benito, moving quickly toward Eric. He met Benito's eyes briefly.

"This is nothing personal," the escort mouthed.

He went to Eric, and whispered a few words. A knife appeared between the escort's fingers. The blade gleamed under the mausoleum's old-fashioned bulbs before it plunged into Eric's chest.

Eric screamed. It was a loud wail, followed by moans. His knees buckled inside his trousers.

Benito's fingers on his walkie talkie wouldn't press the button that called for backup. Instead, his legs decided to bolt. He found himself running away and screaming.

If he had turned back, he would have seen the silver lenses poking out from the other guards' lapels. He would have heard the rumbles of laughter coming from the bodyguards, as they covered their smiles.

Eric got up. He wiped off the fake blood and examined the knife. He pressed the dull tip with sweaty fingers to make the blade retract before popping it out again.

"Let's do that again," he said in a thick German accent. "The lighting's shit in here."

T

Swan watched from backstage, hugging her chest. She had changed into her outfit for the next skit, corset and all. Rue Morgue was on the center stage, singing an Elton John cover. They all wore shimmering golden and black suits.

> *So goodbye yellow brick road*
> *Where the dogs of society howl*
> *You can't plant me in your penthouse*
> *I'm going back to my plough*

Swan wiped her eyes. Her heart seemed to beat in time with the a capella group's rhythm, however, the pacemaker gave a few alarming jolts. She remembered the news of Elton John passing away peacefully in his sleep, by his partner's side.

When they finished, and the cameras stopped rolling, she came out and hugged the lead singer. He was surprised and hugged her back. He smelled of deodorant, sweat and dry cleaning fluid.

"Hey, where's my hug?" a tenor with curly brown hair demanded. He stood a head shorter than her.

Swan hugged him as well. The choir group started to line up, and she managed to wrap her warm arms around all of them.

"I was a big fan of *Alexandria*," one of the boys told her. "Your character was really brave."

Swan smiled at him. The corset wasn't visible under her jacket.

"You're going to like the next skit, then," she replied. "We'll be revisiting her."

T

The video of the mausoleum incident went up online, on one of the art websites that corporations hadn't been able to gouge out of existence. The video included morbid background music, and an old French song. The captions added context: the Death of Marat turned Marat into a martyr during the French reign of terror, and his murderess into a femme fatale. Charlotte Corday had marched to the guillotine with grace, justifying her act. Her knife, plunged into a sick man's chest as he pondered in a bathtub, would liberate the people.

Benito stopped working and turned to collecting food stamps. Meanwhile, the local libraries with Internet-linked computers were closed to the public. No one in government appreciated that an artist had gotten access to Trump's mausoleum, by posing as Trump's son.

Benito moved back in with his parents. His father needed caring for anyway, with his injured spine, and his mother had gotten a job as a cashier. He sometimes worked shifts next to his mother at the same store. They needed the money.

A check came in the mail every few weeks. A note next to the signature read, "My apologies, always."

The handwriting matched that of the signature on the artist's website. Even so, Benito never put the pieces together. He just thought someone cared about him, finally.

T

"Beverly Lovelace!" Beau was dressed in green from head to toe. "Fancy seeing you again, in the Land of Oz!"

"Oh stop that, Wizard." Swan kept her stern demeanor, in character as the librarian from *Alexandria*. "You knew you'd see me again. You sent me this invitation."

"*I* sent you an invitation?" Beau raised an eyebrow. He was trying not to laugh.

Swan wanted to smack him then and there, but held back. She didn't understand how men like Beau could break character and keep their parts, while she sometimes didn't make the cut before she could spoke a word.

"I got your card." She showed him a small red balloon with an elegant card tied to it with an emerald green ribbon. "I noticed you included an old costume of mine."

She shook the card and a green bikini top fell out of it. There were holes in it, and looked ratty, but it was obviously a bikini. Beau blinked. He then tried to look seductive.

"I was wondering who took it. I was using it as a pillow case."

Swan remained stern; they had dug up the old square glasses from that show, and had done her hair in the messy top knot. Her outfit was a knee-length green ballet dress with a sheer pea-green tulle skirt, and sequins on the bosom of the corset. The wardrobe artists had gone wild recreating an outfit for the grand finale skit that would bring the house down. Swan supposed it was more graceful and flattering than the infamous green bikini had been. She wished that the writers hadn't put it in the script. It reminded her of Carrie Fisher hating her slave girl bikini from *Star Wars*.

"Oh, so no hard feelings then?" Beau spoke. "You came back, so you must feel something."

"You tried to make me an Oz slave girl and dance in front of your Wizard court." Swan made her voice rise. "I came because this card promised an apology."

"Why should I apologize? Victoria with her secrets never apologized for her lingerie." Beau gave a knowing sniff. "I still love that black lace."

Swan's pacemaker lurched. She opened her mouth. The audience kept laughing. They hadn't registered her look of alarm. But the cameraman did.

She stood firmly. The show had to go on, and it had to end. In all honesty, she ought to have known that her pacemaker battery would act up on the day that Trump died.

"I'm more of a boxers woman myself," she said in a loud whisper. "Where is that apology? For the slavery issue."

"Oh come on, Beverly." Beau exaggerated his eye roll. "You enjoyed showing your ass as much as we did. You wanted something only Oz can give."

"I came for literature!" Swan barked, making dismissive hand gestures. The trick was to keep it in character, so that those off-camera realized she was signaling for help. "I came to find the great books of Oz. But you turned all the libraries into strip clubs?"

"And you fit in so nicely!" Beau leered. "That song about rainbows and bluebirds, utterly pleasing on the ears."

Swan hiccuped. It came out involuntarily. Beau stopped. He had another line.

The audience laughed.

Then Swan hiccupped again.

"Believe me, I'm not as desirable as I was," she ad-libbed between hiccups. "You see, I also went to visit the Tin Man."

"The Tin Man?" Beau looked genuinely confused. They were going off-script. "Why?"

"He said he wanted to give me his heart," Swan said, her head feeling faint.

She didn't hear her body collapsing to the floor, or her head thudding against the set's carpeted floor. The audience gasped and screamed. The scenery blurred and sounds became muffled.

"I gave the Tin Man a defective heart!" Beau said from above, his voice dissolving into gurgles. "He didn't have the right to love you!"

T

A few months later, the libraries opened up again. One of the millionaires that banked in Ireland paid the deficit so that the doors could open to the public. They had done it in Swan's name.

Benito watched the video of Swan collapsing mid-sketch on one of the computers while sipping a Coke he had smuggled in, thanks to his overcoat. At the moment this video was overtaking the views of the mausoleum video. Benito felt guilty and relieved that the mausoleum video was slowly losing popularity. He tried to review his Italian, but it was hard to learn it from old books with dog-eared pages. One of his mother's Italian friends wanted help in a hardware store, and that job paid better than being a late-night cashier. It required a fluent speaker, and Benito had never learned.

There were rumors that a white supremacist had hacked into Swan's pacemaker, and caused her to collapse. An arrest was made, of a hacker named Jude Asher who belonged to Rue Morgue. He had hugged her last during the show. Rumors had it that if Swan died in the hospital, he would be charged with murder. Her heart kept beating. The doctors said she would recover within the year.

In the early days of the Trump presidency, people were warned about pacemakers being hacked by terrorists. No one expected that a white boy would hurt Swan. Benito wouldn't have imagined it.

People cited her donating album royalties to foster care, and to heart research. They talked of her doing seven seasons of *Alexandria* despite needing a pacemaker, and how she still gave hugs to fans.

Benito didn't know what to think. He had watched *Alexandria* because he had liked the green bikini. He couldn't think of someone hurting Beverly Lovelace. On the other hand, the libraries were open. Trump was dead. His mausoleum was a laughingstock.

There only seemed to be one thing to do. Benito swigged some Coke and watched Swan's last TV appearance. She looked lovely in that green dress while making fun of a dead president.

T

A 2016 MBA graduate and published author, Priya Sridhar has been writing fantasy and science fiction for fifteen years, and counting, as well as drawing a webcomic for five years. She believes that every story is a journey, and that a good tale allows the reader to escape to a new world. One of Priya's stories made the Top Ten Amazon Kindle Download list, and Alban Lake published her novella *Carousel*. Priya lives in Miami, Florida with her family and posts monthly at her blog.

29 The History Changers

by Ross Baxter

Despite his splitting headache, Karam's mouth was dry with excitement. He panted while he was shown the way into the plush office. Having run for nearly four blocks, his t-shirt clung to his thin chest and sweat glistened in his unruly dark mop of hair. He had failed to realize how big the Pentagon was, and going to the wrong entrance had made him even more late.

"Better late than never," frowned a bullet-headed man from behind a huge mahogany desk, making no attempt to hide his irritation.

"Yeah, sorry," Karam replied sheepishly. "I celebrated a little too hard last night."

"Well, I suppose I can forgive you that," conceded the smartly-dressed man. "Los Angeles 2028 has been the most successful Olympics for the United States for half a century. The closing ceremony last night was truly incredible."

"Absolutely," Karam agreed, though actually unable to remember much of it.

"It makes me even more proud to be an American, which is actually why we are all here this morning," said the seated man with conviction.

"Right on!" cried Karam, rather too enthusiastically.

"Take a seat," the man requested.

There were three chairs facing the desk, two of which were already taken. Karam nodded nervously to the occupants of the other chairs and quickly sat down. The blond woman next to him wrinkled her nose, making Karam think that he should have put on a clean shirt before he ran out of his apartment. He guessed that the man behind the large desk was in his fifties, and had a very senior position given the size of his office and the cut of his expensive suit.

The women he sat next to were much younger, probably in their early twenties like himself, but that was where any similarities ended. To his left sat a woman dressed in an immaculate business suit with perfect makeup, nails and flawless long blond hair, looking like a contestant on The Apprentice. In contrast, her neighbor sported a severe crew-cut through which the black ebony skin of her scalp could be clearly seen, multiple ear piercings, faded black jeans and a t-shirt depicting African art.

"Before we make any introductions, I need you all to sign a Non-Disclosure Agreement," said the man behind the imposing desk, pushing three large sheaves of paper towards them. "Once signed, you cannot disclose anything you do, see or hear to any person outside of this office. Everything regarding your employment will be covered by Federal Law, and any transgression will be prosecuted to the maximum possible extent."

Karam nodded, trying not to show how thrilled he was to be there. He had started working for central government as a junior administrator after flunking college barely six months previously, and now it seemed he had been recognized as someone special. Apart from his brief encounters with sex and drugs, this was the most exciting thing to ever happen to him. Finally, he had an achievement to make his parents proud and give them something to boast about to his extended family back in India. He immediately signed his name on the front page of the thick document, without even reading past the title.

"There are over sixty pages in this agreement," complained the young women sat next to Karam. "I'm not going to sign without reading it!"

"I wouldn't expect you to," nodded the man behind the desk sagely. "The document will determine exactly what you can and cannot do for the next two years of your life. Take as much time as you need."

Karam felt his cheeks flush with embarrassment, although happily he knew the others probably would not notice it given the darkness of his skin. He swiftly scooped up the heavy document up again and began read it. In the silence that followed, the only sounds were those of pages being turned, together with the quiet taps on glass from the man behind the desk as he returned his attention to his tablet screen. Within minutes, Karam's mind started to wander: reading anything other than that on the screen of a smartphone, tablet or laptop was rare for him, and he quickly started to lose interest in the dull and long-winded legal text before him. By the time he reached page five, his eyes only blindly followed the words. As he unconsciously picked at a piece of food stuck in his crooked teeth, his mind wondered who the two women who sat with him were, and what was so special about his secondment that he had to endure reading the longest printed document he had ever seen in his life.

"I'm done," said the black girl curtly, signing the paper with a flourish.

The blonde frowned, clearly not wanting to be rushed, but aware that all eyes were on her. She went back to reading. Silence resumed, and the minutes started to slowly tick by again. After what seemed like an age to Karam, she finally signed the document and placed it carefully on the edge of the large desk.

"Thank you," smiled the man behind the desk, "now we can make a start. Firstly, I'll get the introductions over with. My name is Elijah Court, and I head up the Asymmetrical Information Project. We deliberately told you very little about the project or the team during the interviews, mainly because it is a very secret undertaking. I can tell you now that you were the only successful candidates; we selected you very carefully, and were sure from the start that you are exactly the people we need. We will make huge demands on both your time and your lifestyle over the next couple of years, but I believe the remuneration package will more than make up for that."

Karam smiled to himself, still absolutely staggered with the amount he would be earning.

"I also believe that the contribution you will undoubtedly make to the security and prosperity of our nation is worthy of any sacrifices required," continued Court. "You each come with particular strengths and weaknesses, but together you are perfect for the Asymmetrical Information Project."

"Weaknesses?" questioned the blond woman sitting next to Karam.

Court nodded. "We all have weaknesses, but our strengths are greater. For instance, although it is unlikely that Karam here can even spell 'asymmetrical,' he is unrivaled when it comes to hacking and system coding."

Karam nodded uncertainly. Although a little harsh regarding spelling, Court was correct regarding his strengths.

Court turned to look at the blond woman. "Next to Karam, we have Kate. Kate can spell 'asymmetrical' in at least five different languages. She has a doctorate in history, and what she doesn't know about books and librarianship is not worth knowing. Next to Kate we have Ashanti, expert in communications and a whiz on all things social media. Together, I believe you three will take the Asymmetrical Information Project to the next level."

"But what exactly is the Asymmetrical Information Project?" Ashanti interjected.

"Over the past few weeks at the Los Angeles Olympics the United States has proved itself the world leader in terms of sport. But our long-term identity as a nation is firmly rooted in the past. History affects every context of the way we act, and how we consider ourselves. The events of the past shape each nation, and determine the national character of its citizens. A simple example would be the United States: a nation born from struggle. Colonialism, geographical expansion, civil war and external threats all made a mark on the character of this country, forcing us to be independent, hardy, capable and self-reliant. Our place as the leading economic and cultural power in the world is a direct result of that history. It determines how we see ourselves in the mirror, and how we live our everyday lives," concluded Court, pausing to gauge the reaction of his audience.

Kate nodded, Ashanti looked thoughtful, and Karam stared back blankly.

"America has so much to be proud of, and that makes us stronger," Court continued. "But some countries have more historical negatives in their history than positives. There are many other countries with little or nothing to be proud of, and who struggle to known for anything other from losing wars, governmental corruption, ethnic intolerance, and religious bigotry. Imagine how difficult it is to have pride in such a nation? Failure for such nations and people becomes a self-fulfilling prophecy, stemming directly from their own history."

Kate nodded, Ashanti frowned, and Karam still stared back dumbly.

"But remember there are plenty of negatives for America!" Ashanti challenged, her dark eyes flashing. "What about slavery, the persecution of native Americans, or Vietnam?"

"Exactly!" beamed Court. "However, those historical negatives are more than outweighed by the good things of the past."

"I'm not sure my African ancestors would agree that the evils of slavery can ever be balanced out," Ashanti counted.

"Perhaps not, but the election of a black President to be the most powerful man in the world must have gone some way?" suggested Court. "Even though the next one maybe undid some of that positive."

"I'm still not convinced," replied Ashanti.

"And that is why we have the Asymmetrical Information Project," explained Court. "Imagine if we had the ability to go back in time and change parts of our history, to rewrite some of the negatives, and thereby increase our national pride?"

"Dude!" stuttered Karam, suddenly waking up. "Are we going to be time travelers?"

"Only figuratively," said Court with a stoical smile. "How we view ourselves has changed massively in the last few decades. We no longer learn about history through word-of-mouth, lessons or books. Now we learn through via internet streaming, virtual reality headsets and sound bites. Traditional media such as newsprint is long gone; the previous few sources of information are now replaced by thousands or millions of alternate views. History has become far less rigid, and far easier to manipulate. By changing a few selected details, we can actually alter the way a nation thinks about itself, and how that nation is regarded by others."

Court paused, scanning the faces of Kate, Ashanti and Karam to gauge their reaction.

"So, it's a propaganda project then," scoffed Ashanti.

Court smiled. "I describe it more as a way to change perceptions in order to improve national self-confidence, leading to economic growth and social prosperity."

"I think I understand what you're saying," said Kate thoughtfully, "but changing perceptions would take years, maybe even generations."

"Technology advances so quickly now that I think the term 'generation' is not as rigid as it once was. People learn differently, and apply themselves in different ways now. There is no one in this country today who doesn't use the internet, including those born decades before it was even conceptualized. It's the same picture all over the world. Everyone is part the internet generation, which makes things much easier for us. Changing history is still difficult, but it is now be possible."

"Sounds more like science fiction to me," Karam offered, brushing a strand of his long dark hair from his eyes. "But still pretty cool."

"Well, I can tell you that it's science fact, not fiction," Court cut in. "This project began seven years ago, with a small team of gifted individuals just like yourselves. Our aim then was to see if we could change a few small details relating to the Spanish-American war of 1898, specifically the spelling of the name of the Commanding Officer of the USS Texas, Captain Phillip, spelt with two 'l's. I can tell you that we succeeded; as far as the whole world knows, the Commanding Officer of the USS Texas was, and has always been, Captain Philip, spelt with one 'l'."

Court paused once more to scan the faces of the three. Kate looked fascinated, Ashanti unimpressed, and Karam confused.

"So," he continued, "we proved that we could actually change history."

"But how did you do it?" challenged Ashanti.

"With experts like you. We virally changed internet databases, deleting and amending where necessary. The biggest challenge was changing physical evidence such as books, newspapers and art, but everything is possible if you have the right team and the right resources," said Court.

"That is impressive!" gasped Kate, her blue eyes now wide and sparkling.

"Oh, come on," Ashanti groaned, giving Kate a hard look. "I don't think that a minor name change, in a war no one has even heard of, is that impressive."

"It was proof of concept," Court countered. "We then got bolder and took out an American President. Deleted him completely from history."

"Oh yeah," said Ashanti flatly. "Sure you did."

"It took us over four years, but we managed to delete Millard Fillmore," said Court matter-of-factly.

"Who?" asked Karam.

Court smiled at the unintentional irony. "Millard Fillmore was the thirteenth President of the United States. He held office from 1850 to 1853. But we changed that."

"Impossible!" said Ashanti scornfully, reaching for her mini-tablet.

"The challenge was not to delete the person completely from history, but just to delete him from the presidency. History still knows him; he was still born in 1800, married in 1826, and died from a stroke in 1874. We changed nothing before July 1850 or after March 1853. We simply squeezed out his presidency by increasing the terms of his predecessor Zachary Taylor, and his successor Franklin Pierce."

"Wow!" exclaimed Kate, obviously shocked by the magnitude of what Court was telling them.

"It was a challenge, both intellectually and financially," Court conceded, "but we succeeded. As far as history is concerned, there was no President Fillmore."

"Wait a minute," Ashanti cut in. "I want to check this for myself."

"Go ahead," Court nodded.

Ashanti started to search, her fingers a blur as she flew through a myriad of databases and searches, her African wrist bangles jingling loudly. The others watched her as she worked, Karam noting she preferred the old-fashioned way of screen input rather than thought-generated searching using an ear implant. After less than a minute she looked up, her face betraying her surprise and wonder.

"Well, if Millard Fillmore was ever a President, it doesn't seem to be recorded anywhere," she acknowledged grudgingly.

"So, if you've already managed to do the impossible, what do you us to do then?" asked Kate.

"We managed to change history in Fillmore's case because the actual events took place almost two hundred years ago, and nothing we changed has any bearing on how our country is viewed by its citizens or by the outside world. Our next task is to change recent history, to modify and tweak events which took place between 2016 and 2020, taking the challenge to a whole new level."

"You want us to delete President Trump!" Ashanti laughed. "Now, that's something I could get behind."

"That would be impossible," replied Court. "Although if we managed to melt down half of the statues he commissioned of himself during his presidency, the scrap value alone would probably pay for the project. No, we'll have to be much subtler than that; instead we'll concentrate on slightly changing some of the things he said, some of the things he threatened to do, and the reasoning behind some of the things he managed to do. We need to make him a more sympathetic character that he actually was, and thereby reduce the embarrassment and ill-feeling he caused during his term of office."

"I'm not sure I understand," said Karam.

"Let's take the example of the Great Wall of America," explained Court. "Seen by many as a monument to Trump's racist views about all Mexicans being drug dealers or rapists. In fact, that was not the real reason it was built, but that is what the perception of many other nations is. That perception is damaging to the image of our country, so we could work to change it by replacing the rhetoric with more reasonable reasons for building it. We therefore make subtle changes to show the idea behind it was wholly to inhibit the flow of drugs, thereby helping the populaces on both sides of the wall. We make the reasons for the wall positive rather than negative. Other nations will then view the US more favorably, Americans will feel better regarding their own history, and national pride increases. Everybody wins."

Karam finally nodded his understanding.

"That's just bullshit," challenged Ashanti. "He built the wall to get and keep the votes of a certain minority. And you're forgetting that Trump is still around; he's ancient but his history has not yet finished."

"True," countered Court, "but that is to our advantage. The years took their toll on him; his reclusiveness and obvious mental fragility are things we can use to our advantage. I believe he'll go with our version of history rather than the one he probably only now vaguely remembers. What could be better?"

"So, you want us to work with your existing team who changed Captain Phillip's name and deleted President Fillmore?" asked Kate.

"No. Those people have moved on now. To make this work each project has a new team; that ensures freshness and safeguards against people getting burnt out by the enormity of the challenge. Expecting people to work in secrecy and isolation for long periods of time is not really feasible."

"And you think that just we three can overwrite things that happened for real only a decade ago?" asked Ashanti with incredulity.

"I absolutely do," affirmed Court. "You've been chosen as being the three current government employees most likely to succeed. Your skill-sets and personal dispositions were identified as being ideal for this extremely well-paid, ground-breaking and secret role. You will be given all the resources and finance you could possibly need. I have great faith in you pulling this off."

"Awesome," smiled Karam, once again thinking of the size of his future paychecks.

"So, are you all up for the challenge?" asked Court. "Up for dedicating the next two years of your lives solely to the Asymmetrical Information Project?"

Karam nodded enthusiastically, whilst Kate gave a single nod. Ashanti considered it for a few moments, then finally assented with a smile.

"Then let's get to work."

T

The first month on the project proved difficult. All three shared a large out-of-town house where they were expected to both work and live, with minimal contact with the world outside of the project. It took them a while to adjust to the personal limitations and constraints imposed by the secret nature of their work, and even longer to get used to each other. Both women were constantly frustrated by Karam's untidiness and seemingly juvenile delight at his constant flatulence. Karam and Kate struggled with the vagaries of Ashanti's vegan cuisine and lifestyle, whilst Kate's compulsive desire for absolute order and hyper-cleanliness did nothing to endear her to her housemates.

But all three were completely taken by the challenge of their work, which was enough to keep them together until the Asymmetrical Information Project became a common obsession. After that, the trials of communal living and the insular nature of their existence became increasingly insignificant.

For most of the time they worked alone in their separate offices. Karam hardly ever left the building, the huge array of powerful and cutting-edge technology being all he needed to code and hack multiple systems, networks and databases across the world. It was all Karam had ever wanted to do, and he quickly started feeling uncomfortable if he became separated from his beloved computers for too long.

Kate spent her first month learning how to create expert forgeries of book pages, pages she would then use to covertly replace original sheets in any protected historic documents. She split her time between researching and creating forgeries in the house, and visits to various governmental departments, libraries and academic institutions. In many respects, her work carried the most risk, often requiring her to steal or substitute documents from under watchful eyes. But the buzz of her covert work quickly drew her in and soon she was addicted to it.

Ashanti also learnt new skills, becoming a proficient and astute participant in political debates, both online and in person. With the powerful backing of the Asymmetrical Information Project she became an authority on the Trump period, and a popular speaker often called upon by the media for opinion. When not engaged in debates Ashanti immersed herself in social media, skilfully managing hundreds of accounts across dozens of sites and platforms. Any mention of Trump's presidency on any social media was immediately flagged for Ashanti, who quickly swung into action and covertly countered if the message was contrary to the one desired.

Court gave his protégés as much space as they needed, ensuring they had any resource they requested and any comfort they craved. He was pleased with his selections, and delighted that the Asymmetrical Information Project completely satisfied the various obsessive or compulsive tendencies each individual displayed. Progress was quicker than he expected, and as the months went by, the presidency of Donald Trump became less and less contentious, his historical aspect becoming increasingly statesmanlike, and his achievements more liberal and philanthropic. Fewer comedians made jokes at Trump's expense, and even the most hard-bitten political satirists moved on to some extent.

T

Eighteen months after their first meeting, Court took Kate, Karam and Ashanti out for dinner at an expensive Michelin-starred restaurant in Washington. He wanted them to eat whilst watching the now ancient Hillary Clinton being interviewed on Justin Bieber's Tonight Show. It was a crucial test of what they had achieved, and a potential tipping point. Since the show had first been announced the three had worked tirelessly to try and limit any possible damage, but all knew the risk.

The four of them sat alone at the single large table in the private dining room of the restaurant. Although it was a place where a main course could cost an average weeks' salary, Court seemed to be well known to the staff. Kate, Ashanti and Karam wasted no time in sampling the best wines and ordering the most lavish dishes. Court seemed not to notice, his attention focused instead on the large television screen and the build-up to Clinton's appearance.

As they reached the end of their sumptuous main course main course, the elderly ex-Secretary of State and failed presidential candidate took a seat next to the popular host of the Tonight Show. Talking ceased at the table and everyone quietly put down their cutlery; all listening intently as the initial pleasantries were exchanged. Bieber quickly covered the early parts of Clinton's life, her husband's presidency, and swiftly moved onto the crunch year of 2016. They waited for the sting, for the rhetoric about the most divisive campaign in history to start, but instead Trump's old rival seemed to gloss over the scars. Rather than talk about the years of ruin, she concentrated more on her later role with the United Nations, and her new book, a romantic novel. It was perfect, the Trump years being side-lined and down-played, the bogeyman kept at bay.

"A toast!" announced Court, standing and raising his glass. "To a dull and uneventful Trump presidency!"

T

Ashanti glanced at her exquisite Cartier watch and frowned. Kate smiled to herself, still admiring her Manolo Blahnik shoes in the full-length hall mirror.

"Karam would be late to his own funeral," Ashanti muttered darkly.

"He would," said Kate, still smiling. "But I'm sure Court won't mind this time; it is the final meeting of the project."

"Yeah," mused Ashanti. "I can't believe how quickly the two years passed. I've been so tied up in all this that I've had no time to think about anything else. But I'm really going to miss it if Court tells us our contract is finished."

"I can't see that he will. It's been too much of a success, plus there are hundreds of other historical boo-boos which need tidying up. I think we have a job for life," said Kate happily, her thoughts filled with the joy of expensive footwear.

"I'm not so sure," murmured Ashanti. "I don't trust that man. History only remains changed if the people who changed it remain silent, and there are four people who could instantly reverse all the work that has been done. What if Court doesn't trust us to keep quiet?"

Kate glanced up from her shoes. "What do you mean?"

"What if Court thinks that one of us three could let out the secret of our work at some time in the future, and effectively reverse everything that has been achieved? It would be catastrophic."

"But we're all covered by perpetually binding non-disclosure agreements; we'd land in front of a federal court for prosecution," replied Kate.

"We would," continued Ashanti, "but the secret would still be out, and the damage would be done. It would be like having President Trump all over again."

Kate stared at Ashanti, her mind working on the implications of what she was saying. "But we're federal employees. We're on the inside."

"The inside of a secret cell," said Ashanti darkly. "Remember, we've never actually met the team who worked before us, the three who stripped Millard Fillmore of his presidency. Court only told us that they'd moved on to bigger things. With national pride at stake, how important do you think we really are? And Court doesn't strike me as someone who like to take risks; wouldn't it be simpler and safer for him to have us disappear?"

"You're just being paranoid," said Kate. "I'll ask him first thing when we see him at ten."

"Not if Karam doesn't get a move on," grumbled Ashanti.

"Karam!" Kate yelled from the entrance hall. "We're going to be late!"

Karam appeared a few moments later. He stood at the top of the stairs and yawned, looking as if he had just got out of bed.

"Sorry," he shouted down. "I was doing a final web check on our dear Donald."

"And?" shouted up Kate.

"Well, it turns out that he wasn't such a bad guy after all," Karam replied with a broad smile as he shambled down the stairs, showing off the results of his expensive dental work.

"Are you really going to this meeting dressed like that?" Kate sighed, looking in disgust at Karam's faded t-shirt and ripped baggy pants.

"Why?" Karam asked in genuine puzzlement.

"You're incorrigible," chided Kate. "With the money you now have in the bank you could at least buy a decent pair of trousers."

"Or get a haircut," added Ashanti, frowning at Karam's unruly mop of black curls.

"These pants are Calvin Klein!" Karam protested.

"Whatever," said Ashanti picked up the keys to the Porsche SUV She then paused, sniffing the air. "What is that smell?"

"Come on, guys," Karam pleaded. "You're always on my case; I did have a shower this morning!"

"No," said Ashanti. "Not you. I think I smell gas?"

"I smell it too," said Kate. "We'd better check the kitchen."

As the three turned, there was a blinding flash. The explosion that ripped through the building was huge, taking out every window in the luxury cars parked two hundred yards away in their multi-car garage and even felling a couple of nearby trees. The ensuing fire quickly engulfed the shattered remains of the buildings, consuming everything intensely enough to vitrify the sandy soil in the nearby lawn.

Court watched the flames for a few seconds from his car at the bottom of the long drive. He returned the tiny remote control to his shirt pocket and pulled away, finally satisfied that another chapter of history would now remain forever changed, and hoping that the three would be the last chapter of Trump's forgotten history.

After thirty years at sea, Ross Baxter now concentrates on writing sci-fi and horror fiction. His varied work has been published in print by several publishing houses in the US and the UK. He won the Horror Novel Reviews Creation Short Story Award in December 2014. Married to a Norwegian and with two Anglo-Viking kids, he now lives in Derby, England. Ross's author page can be found at on Amazon. His twitter address is @rossbaxter1.

30 A Town Called Unity

by Ira Nayman

"Say, fella," the tiny blond woman in the pink striped uniform of the professional waitress said, "I know it's not quite closing time, but it's been a long day, so, if y'all wouldn't mind…"

The fire hydrant with limbs and sandy hair's smile was electric. "No problem," he said, taking one last slurp from a long empty milkshake (vanilla—don't judge). "It's just been a lazy kind of day… <u>Mona</u>," the man read the name tag on the woman's uniform. "The kind of day when contemplating the world's problems is much more inviting than making any kind of effort to solve them—know what I mean?"

"You're tryna talk your way to closing time?" <u>Mona</u> smiled.

"You got me," the fire hydrant with limbs raised his hands in mock defeat. <u>Mona</u> watched admiringly as the muscular man shimmied across the booth, stood and walked out the door of The Wayward Diner.

The WD (it'd be a real hoot if the eatery made it to its thirtieth birthday) was situated on the outskirts of Unity, North Dakota (town motto: "The howl you hear in the middle of the night is the cry of unity!"). The WD (not to be confused with the WC… in any of its various meanings) boasted that it offered: "The best chicken fried potato salad in the tri-state area!" (the sign had to be changed when the Disambiguating Diner, with its disgraced four star chef from the big city—Dayton—who specialized in chicken fried potato salad, opened up down the street, but the WD's owner—Philboyd Studge—never quite had the time to get around to it). The exterior could use a new coat of paint (couldn't we all!) and deep fryer three wouldn't melt a snowball in a heat wave, but the fact the Diner had seen better days was attractive to some people. Tourists, mostly, out-of-towners who confused seediness with authenticity.

Mona locked the door behind the last customer of the day (who, for the sake of narrative completeness, I should point out had paid his bill about an hour earlier). Ordinarily, Moe, who was even shorter than she was, but, to be fair, was a lot hairier, a man who sported the face of a seventy year-old even though he claimed to be forty-three, would turn the neon OPEN sign in the front window to CLOSED at the same time; after six years of working together, they had developed a kind of lunch counter synchronicity. Mona waited three seconds... seven seconds... nineteen seconds—nineteen seconds! Their timing hadn't been this off since before Mona had started working at the diner. She turned to see Moe talking on the phone behind the counter—the one in these settings that was always on the wall next to the window that allowed customers to see into the kitchen, (although only the bravest of souls would avail themselves of the opportunity) opposite the cash register. He looked old and confused and desperately in need of a hug.

Mona walked up to the counter just as Moe hung up. "Everything okay?" she chirped.

"I am a traveler of both time and space," Moe darkly responded. At least, it seemed dark to Mona, although she couldn't be sure because his deep voice lent darkness to everything he said, including, "I just won the lottery!" and "Good morning."

Mona was stunned. "I—you—what?" she sputtered.

"I am a traveler of both time and space," Moe, composing himself, repeated.

"But that—"

"If you know the counterpassword, say it now," Moe commanded. <u>Mona</u> had never noticed it before, but the way he played the spatula from one hand to the other looked vaguely threatening. Perhaps, now that she came to think of it, not so vaguely. "I am a traveler of both time and space."

"I'm moving to Kashmir," <u>Mona</u> glumly responded.

Moe shook his head in disbelief. "I often wondered if headquarters was going to send backup," he commented. "And if they did, who it might be. But in all the years we've worked together in this heartless universe, I never expected my contact would be you."

Taking off her apron as she walked to the counter, <u>Mona</u> answered, "Likewise." She dropped the apron, along with her pad and pencil, on the counter with finality.

"So," Moe said. "I think it's time to submit our final report and get the invasion of this Earth started. Agreed?"

"Agreed," <u>Mona</u> agreed.

Nodding, Moe opened the till and took out a single dollar bill. After he closed the till, <u>Mona</u> asked him what he was doing. "Souvenir," he explained.

"You can't do that," <u>Mona</u> admonished him.

"Why not?"

"It's stealing. The owner could have you blackballed from every diner in the tri-state area!"

A moment later, the pair broke out laughing.

A moment after that, Moe said, "I feel like celebrating. How about I make us a couple of steaks? It will be a long time before I eat anything that good after I rejoin my unit of the Extradimensional Military Pacification Force."

"Yeah. A steak sounds great," <u>Mona</u> agreed. Only, she was frowning as she said it.

Moe got a couple of steaks out of the meat locker and threw them on the grill. As the smell of burning flesh ("How can people in this universe trust meat if it doesn't taste of charcoal?" Moe reasoned) filled the kitchen, <u>Mona</u> considered possibilities.

"Moe?" she finally asked as the fry cook threw some fries into the fryer (number two, for those of you keeping score at home—one of the still functioning ones).

"Mmm?" He had been humming Elvis Costello's "Oliver's Army."

"What is the Extradimensional Pacification Force?"

Moe looked up from the fryer. A stray bit of grease splatted against the top of his hand, but his people had developed the ability to ignore pain when astonished, and he was utterly flabbergasted now. Over the years, he had seen <u>Mona</u> standing in the doorway to the kitchen uncountable times (it was actually eight hundred thirty-seven, so obviously it was only uncountable for some), stray wisps of yellow hair falling across her tiny face; but it was like he was looking at her for the first time.

"The Extradimensional *Military* Pacification Force," he emphasized, flicking the grease off his hand, "is the branch of the Armed Forces that invades American territories in other universes. You must know that. The EMPF will be sending a full fleet of battle ships here as soon as we report. That is the plan."

"That is not the plan," <u>Mona</u> argued.

"What?"

"The plan is to replace key people in the government, business and entertainment realms of this universe's America so that when, in a few years, warships appear over this country, it will capitulate to our control without a shot ever being fired. The Infowar Directorate has studied the options for decades and has thoroughly vetted this operation."

"We don't have an Infowar Directorate," Moe coldly stated.

"We don't have an Extradimensional Pacification Force."

"Military. Extradimensional Military Pacification Force."

"Whatever!" Mona shouted. "We don't have one of those things, whatever the hell you call it!"

Moe's eyes narrowed and his left cheek began to twitch. "Who are you?" he quietly demanded.

Mona self-importantly pulled herself up to her full five foot two inch height. "I am Per Monashem Avartheusus, of the House of Altoidreides. Who the hell are you?"

Moe was about to pull himself up to his full height, but realizing he was one and a half inches shorter than the woman he was confronting, decided that the effect wasn't worth the effort. "I am Lieutenant Colonel Moricious von Stuffenstein of the Fourth Fighting Bokol Birds Brigade."

"Never heard of you," Mona, nee Per Monashem Avartheusus, sniffed.

"Nor I, you," Lieutenant Colonel Moricious "Moe" von Stuffenstein replied.

The steaks were emitting a semi-urgent charcoal scent which both parties chose to ignore.

They quickly came to realize that they had come from different universes; the fact that they were researching an invasion of the same

Earth was what people who were unfamiliar with multiverse theory would call "a coincidence," and what people who did understand multiverse theory would call "an amusing nuisance." Using the child's decision-making hand jive game infiltration-invasion-negotiations, they agreed that, under normal circumstances, Lieutenant Colonel von Stuffenstein's invasion force would quickly overtake Per Avartheusus's infiltration force. But these were not ordinary circumstances.

"Our people have been monitoring the communications of this country since before I arrived," Per Avartheusus haughtily informed the Lieutenant Colonel. "We believe, with a ninety-three percent degree of certainty, that they have the strongest military in the world—quite possibly the history of the world—in order to repel outside invaders—no, to annihilate anybody who would even consider attacking them. Your frontal assault is a suicide mission!"

"With all due respect," Lieutenant Colonel von Stuffenstein stiffly replied, yet still managed to insinuate that the due respect was very little, indeed, "our people have also been monitoring the communications of this country for a very long time. *Our* research indicates that it is rife with internal enemies, a society in moral decay on the verge of collapse. Our intelligence unit assures us with a ninety-eight per cent degree of certainty that if attacked, it will crumble with little or no resistance."

Per Avartheusus frowned. "They... both can't be right. One of us must be wrong..."

The pair contemplated this for a few seconds. Then, Lieutenant Colonel von Stuffenstein slapped his forehead so loud it drowned out the sound of liquid sizzling out of meat. "We've been compromised!"

"No." Per Avartheusus shook her head.

"That's the only explanation," Lieutenant Colonel von Stuffenstein insisted. "They have been feeding us both misinformation in order for us to underestimate the strength of their civilization."

"That simply isn't possible," Per Avartheusus argued. "This country does not have the technical capability to determine when somebody from another universe has arrived here. Furthermore, this country has a primitive communications system that cannot monitor communications between dimensions, so my communications with headquarters—*my* headquarters—could not have been intercepted. There is no way they could know that I was here!"

"I would have agreed," Lieutenant Colonel von Stuffenstein disagreed. "But, if they haven't been running a disinformation campaign against us, how do you explain how we came to such vastly different conclusions?"

Per Avartheusus had no reply. Making a decision, Lieutenant Colonel von Stuffenstein went out of the kitchen area to the bar, picked up the telephone and dialed (because if rotary phones were good enough for the 1950s, they were good enough for The Wayward Diner!) a twenty-seven digit number. "Yes. It's me," he said after a couple of rings. "I'm ready to go home and make my final report. No—don't say anything. This line might be monitored. I know—I know—it will all be in my report. Yes. Give me thirty seconds. Right."

After he hung up, Lieutenant Colonel von Stuffenstein went back into the kitchen and said to Per Avartheusus: "I'm going to recommend that we abort our plans to invade this planet. If you value the lives of your fellow soldiers, I would suggest that you—" Then, he shimmered out of existence. We'll never know if he had time to appreciate the metaphoric value of the charred remains of the steaks on the grill.

Thinking furiously, Per Avartheusus twisted an opal ring on the second finger of her right hand and took a small red pill out of the resulting hole. She swallowed it; then her body spasmed ninety degrees to the left, then one hundred thirty degrees to the right, then collapsed in on itself.

Seven minutes passed. Then, the sandy haired fire hydrant with limbs looked into the diner through the glass front door. By his side was a dark-skinned woman whose hair stuck out in so many directions that physicists were hoping she would donate it to science after she died so that they may prove string theory once and for all. (Spend billions of dollars building particle accelerators? Pfft! Waste of time and money!)

The man tried the handle, but found the door locked. He bent on one knee, ready to pick the lock with a toothpick that had appeared in his hand out of nowhere. Smiling, the woman said something to him that we can't hear. Standing up, the man shrugged pleasantly (not an easy feat— try it some time) and handed the woman the toothpick.

The woman went down on one knee and picked the lock of the front door to the diner.

As they entered the building, the man* commented, "Twenty-seven seconds. Not bad. Did you learn that at the Alternaut Academy?"

"Catholic girl's school," the woman*** replied.

Crash went to the booth where he had been sitting and retrieved a black lacquered ball with brown streaks that fell in size between cricket and croquet from the floor where he had surreptitiously dropped it.

"Something's burning," Noomi sniffed.

The ball***** was laughing uproariously. "Did you—hoo, man!— did you see that? I haven't had this much fun since Doctor Alhambra******'s experiment on transdimensional flux resistance stopped up all the toilets in headquarters for a week!"

"We didn't see it," Noomi pointed out. "We weren't here."

"Not to worry," TOM, its mirth undiminished, assured her. "I've got the most amazing thermal video footage—when we get back to Earth Prime, look for it on my Farcebook page!"

"Seriously, something's burning," Noomi insisted. As Crash and TOM giggled at each other, she made her way to the kitchen.

"Did they make the gotcha face?" Crash was like a kid at an all you can eat gummi bar for the first time (kids who make subsequent trips tend to be a bit warier).

"Naah," TOM replied. As Crash's face began to fall, it continued, "They made a maximegabiggiegotcha face!"

Noomi grabbed a fire extinguisher off the kitchen wall and used it to blow out the fire that was about to start on burner two.

Crash grinned as if it was Christmas, Chanukkah and Kwanzaa all rolled into one. Which, technically, did happen once a year on Earth Prime. But ChristmaKwaanzUkah was in December, and it was only June! "TOM," Crash enthused, "I would high five you if you had hands!"

"Aww, Crash," TOM gushingly responded, "you're one of the least annoying semi-evolved ape creatures I've had the displeasure of working with!"

Noomi dropped the fire extinguisher and rejoined the boys. She was uncertain what was being celebrated, so she didn't know how much bonding she would be interrupting if she interrupted. She interrupted: "So, what, exactly, have we accomplished, here?"

"We just stopped an invasion of Earth Prime 4-3-4-6-2-8 dash Chi without firing a shot!" Crash enthused.

"Technically, two invasions," TOM pointed out.

"Only one of them would have succeeded," Crash countered.

"Right," TOM countercountered, "but it's a case of Schrodinger's alien invasion, isn't it? Until the box is blown to bits by a laser-guided cluster bomb, both invasion conditions are true."

"That's one way of looking at it," Crash recountercountered. "Another way of looking at it is that both invasion condition make up a single invasion system."

"But—" TOM started to disrecountercounter, but Noomi cut him off.

"So, you stopped the invasion or invasions," she demanded, "by feeding both sides fake news?"

Crash bristled at the term. "In the multiverse, there is no such thing as fake news. There's just news that didn't happen in your dimension. But, no, what happened here today was much simpler than—"

"I hate to interrupt a good exposition," TOM interrupted the interruption, "but you know you tripped a silent alarm when you broke into this diner, right?"

Fortunately, the Dimensional Delorean™ ("The classier way to travel between universes!") was parked several blocks away, so, after locking up the diner (out of reflex—now that all of the staff had left without notice, it wouldn't be opened for a while), Crash had plenty of time to explain that the aliens had monitored communications on Earth Prime 4-3-4-6-2-8 dash Chi for a long time. Funny thing about that, though: decades earlier, the right on this Earth felt that its point of view wasn't properly represented in the media, so it decided to establish its own news and information outlets. Over time, the reality portrayed in the two sets of media diverged, to the point where the realities they portrayed may as well have been two completely different universes.

This reached its nadir during the Presidency of Donald Trump, when the right-wing media's war on... well, everybody else, found a sympathetic ear in the White House. That was three Presidents ago, all Democrats. Despite their best efforts to breach the divide, it remained as wide as ever.

When the aliens first came to this world, they probably monitored a wide array of communications. However, over time, each alien drifted towards the media that conformed to their own understanding of the way the multiverse worked. As a result, they each chose an attack plan to conquer this Earth's United States that played to the strengths of their militaries. And you saw how well that worked for them.

"We discovered their plots soon after they arrived on Earth Prime 4-3-4-6-2-8 dash Chi," Crash explained. "We could have closed them down at any time, but we wanted to interfere as little as possible. As it happened, all it took to derail the invasion plots was a single email."

"Which was...?" Noomi prompted.

Since the Dimensional Delorean™ was still conveniently a few blocks away, Crash had enough time to explain that the Transdimensional Authority sent a message to the cook's boss changing the contact password to that of the waitress and advising him to break cover with her at once. He immediately passed that information on to the cook. In fact, neither of them needed a second person in the field, but—

"Won't they realize that they have been tricked as soon as they get back to their home universes?" Noomi questioned.

Yes, Crash answered, but it won't matter. If they had employed a black market Dimensional Portal™ to travel to this universe, or if they had built their own, they were in contravention of the Treaty of Gehenna-Wentworth. If they had legitimately purchased their Dimensional Portal™ for the purpose of invading another dimension, they were in contravention of their End User License Agreement. Either way, they would find that their devices no longer functioned. The Transdimensional Authority just had to wait until all of their terrestrials had returned to their proper place to shut them down.

"This seems over-elaborate," Noomi caviled. "Once you had enough evidence, couldn't you just have deported the foreign agents to their home universes?"

Crash frowned. "Where would the elegance be in that?"

TOM, comfortably ensconced in Crash's pocket, grunted and scoffed, "Yeah, yeah—you investigators and your stupid ideas of elegance! I can't wait to get back to headquarters on Earth Prime and forget I was ever a part of this ferkakte mission!"

Ignoring the fact that TOM believed that every mission he went on was ferkakte, Crash investigatorsplained: "TOM, you know we can't just allow invading armies to cross dimensional boundaries willy nilly! The Transdimensional Authority, which licenses interdimensional travel, requires everybody to have a plan to deal with the displaced matter and information complexity that they bring with them when they cross dimensional boundaries."

"Crash, we know all of this," Noomi tried to stop the flow. She may as well have tried telling Niagara Falls that it was informationally redundant.

Crash continueinvestigatorsplained: "Without these offsets, the universe, and a small number of universes surrounding it, will become unstable. Linear causality will break down. Life in those realities will become a constant flood of non-sequiturs. We refer to these clusters of dimension as * UNHINGED ZONE *s. I shudder just thinking about it. Does anybody want that?"

Before Noomi could formulate a response, the trio even more conveniently arrived on the tree-lined lane in the small city where nothing much ever happened where the Dimensional Delorean™ had been parked. "Would you like to drive?" Crash asked Noomi.

All negative thoughts about the case vanished.

T

NOTES

* His name, for those who are obsessed about such details, is Crash Chumley. He is an investigator for the Transdimensional Authority.**

** The Transdimensional Authority is the organization that monitors and polices travel between universes. If you're somewhere you shouldn't be, doing something that is illegal, immoral or fattening, it is the TA's job to find you, stop you and take you back to where you belong.

*** Noomi Rapier. A newly minted Transdimensional Authority investigator. This is only her second case after graduating top of her class at the Alternaut Academy****, because in these kind of stories there's always somebody fresh out of the Alternaut Academy, isn't there?

**** The Alternaut Academy trains investigators for the Transdimensional Authority and Time Agency agents. To date, its alumni have featured in twelve novels, twenty-seven short stories and a line of poseable, eco-friendly disposable drinking cups.

***** TOM is a Transdimensional Oddity Monitor. It is an artificial intelligence that can trace traveling energies across dimensions. Its personality module has a love of humanity rivaled only by Don Rickles.

****** The Transdimensional Authority's Chief Scientist. His personality module has a love of humanity rivaled only by TOM's.

IraNaymanisaTorontohumouristwho... forgets to use spaces when he gets excited about a project. He has had five humorous SF novels published by Elsewhen Press, the most recent of which is *The Multiverse is a Nice Place to Visit, But I Wouldn't Want to Live There*. His seventh collection of satirical news from alternate realities, *Futures in Mirror Are Closer Than They Appear*, has appeared on Amazon. New humor is published weekly on Ira's website, Les Pages aux Folles.

31 The Brief Reign of King Donnie the Awesome

by Will Morton

'Tis much when sceptres are in children's hands
— King Henry VI, Part 1: Act IV, Scene I

Chapter 1
Donnie is the new King of Merrycow

"But I want ice cream *now!*" Donnie Clump whined.

"We're late, Donnie. You'll have to wait until after the funeral," his mother, Queen Melanoma, sighed, her attention waning. "There will be ice cream at the wake."

"I'm awake *now*," Donnie argued, beginning to pout.

"Oh, let him have some ice cream," said Michael McPrince, Regent of Merrycow, as he strode through the doorway without waiting to be announced. "He's the new king—and you're not!"

McPrince motioned to a nearby robot guard, which immediately pressed buttons on its torso. A microsecond later, its tummy door slid open and it pulled out a dish of quibble-berry ice cream.

Queen Melanoma opened her mouth to speak, but Donnie cried "Uncle Mikey!" and ran to him, accidentally bumping the robot's hand and knocking the dish to the floor.

"Tell your mother: you're not only a king, you're a star, and stars can grab ice cream anytime they want."

Donnie turned to glare at his mother. "Yeah, Mom!"

"Donnie, you know your father didn't…"

"Daddy always put me in time out!" Donnie interrupted. "And kings don't have be in time out!"

He turned an anxious glance to Uncle Mikey. "Do they?"

"Absolutely not! Kings are above the law."

Donnie pumped a tiny fist in the air.

Queen Melanoma stared at the two of them, attention gradually fading from her eyes. "Ice cream," she said, looking away, "it's just boy talk."

Donnie resumed playing a virtual Tweety game on his handheld, thumbs jabbing furiously.

"I know what King Donnie wants to do…"

Donnie jerked his head up. "What, Uncle Mikey?"

"I'll bet you want to talk on holovids like your daddy used to!"

"Oh, can I? Really?"

"Certainly! Kings can talk whenever they want. And you know what?" He leaned down and whispered conspiratorially. "Everybody else has to listen!"

"Listen to me me me?"

Uncle Mikey nodded, grinning. "You *could* speak after your father's funeral..."

"More boy talk," said Queen Melanoma.

T

Chapter 2
King Donnie's first holo speech

"Hello, Merrycow. Everybody has to listen because I'm the king and you're not..."

Donnie looks at something off to the side. His voice can be heard saying: "Cool! I can see myself standing right there!"

Donnie tilts his head as someone speaks to him off-camera. After a moment he nods and turns to the holo imager again.

"Uncle Mikey said to call him Regent. He's the one that put the crown on my head, remember? After my daddy fell off the top of the castle.

"Anyway, I'm King Donnie now and I get to eat ice cream whenever I want, which is so cool. I'm gonna eat two gazillion dishes of ice cream!

"Uncle Mikey—I mean, Regent Mikey—says everybody has to call a king Your Majesty, but I don't like that. I like 'awesome' better 'cause I'm sooo awesome!

"That's what I want everybody to call me: King Donnie the Awesome!"

T

Chapter 3
King Donnie is briefed on current affairs

"What's the matter, Uncle Mikey?" King Donnie asked, stopping his virtual Tweety game for the first time that morning.

The regent turned his eyes away and sighed. "I hate to trouble you with trifles."

"Rifles? Can I have a rifle?"

"Wait until you're grown up," Queen Melanoma said.

"Aw, Mom," King Donnie whined. "That's won't be until...uh... forever!"

Uncle Mikey glanced at King Donnie out of the corner of his eye and sighed again, more melodramatically this time.

"What, Uncle Mikey?"

"Well," the regent said, slowly turning to face the infantile monarch. "It's about the aliens."

"Green men from Mars?"

"Actually, they're from the moon."

"I want green men from Mars!"

"We-ell...they *are* green! Sort of."

Queen Melanoma rolled her vacant eyes. "Your father wanted Merrycow to be the first country with a moon colony."

"Yes, he did," agreed the regent, "But the colonists keep coming back to Earth—illegally! They're illegal aliens!"

"Green aliens from the moon? Here in Merrycow?"

Queen Melanoma yawned. "Our moon colonists are human, Michael."

"Oh, they're green, alright!" Regent Mikey met King Donnie's eyes. "You see, the moon is made of green cheese."

"Like Green Eggs and Spam?" the king asked.

"Sort of…" The regent drew his brows together. "And they eat the green cheese because it has chlorophyll."

"Glory-fill…?"

"Plants use it to get nourishment from sunlight—" Queen Melanoma began.

"You mean, these aliens drink the sun?"

"Exactly. And then they come back to Earth and eat up all our food when they don't even need to eat!"

"We should keep them out!"

"Yes, but how?" Mikey asked, looking away and patting one hand against the wall.

"I want to build a wall. A great, big wall—between Earth and the moon—in space!"

"That'll be expensive," Queen Melanoma murmured in a bored tone.

"I'll get the *moon* to pay for it!"

"Brilliant!" cried Uncle Mikey and the little boy beamed.

"What about illegal aliens already here in Merrycow?" asked Queen Melanoma.

"They won't be hard to find, since they're a different color," retorted Donnie. "I want them, you know… reported!"

"Do you mean: deported?" asked Uncle Mikey.

"That too!" agreed King Donnie the Awesome.

T

Chapter 4
King Donnie meets with his royal advisors

King Donnie's gaze swept the assembly seated around the huge mahogany table. More than half were holo projections—as was the table itself, which Donnie discovered when he tried to climb up on it and fell through.

The Duke of Security stood to speak, his face deeply lined from continual scowling. "Your Majesty…"

King Donnie stamped his foot. "I told you not to call me that!"

The duke cleared his throat, his scowl unchanged. "King Donnie the Awesome, we have no evidence that there are three million illegal moon colonists in Merrycow."

King Donnie stamped his foot again. "I told you there were. Do what I say and *disport* them!"

The duke cleared his throat again, his scowl still unchanged. "May I ask how, Your, um, Awesomeness?"

King Donnie rolled his eyes. "They're green," he said as if speaking to a dim-witted infant. "Duh."

The Duke of Security opened his mouth, then closed it again. His scowl did not change.

The regent spoke up. "I believe a blood test would reveal the presence of chlorophyll, wouldn't it, King Donnie the Awesome?"

"*Glory-fill*, yes," the king agreed. "I'm told it's in their pee-pee too."

"Am I to understand that we should conduct random urine testing throughout Merrycow?" the Duke of Security inquired.

"Didn't I just say that?" King Donnie whined.

Regent Mikey called up a virtual document above the center of the mahogany table. "I've prepared a list of suspects," he said to the Duke of Security, indicating the list. "Interrogate them first and put them on the next ship to the moon."

The regent glanced sidelong at the child. "With King Donnie the Awesome's permission, of course."

The Duke of Security turned his scowling face to the infantile king.

"*Terror-gate* them on the way to the moon," King Donnie decreed. "To save time."

"Hmm," the Duke of Security murmured to himself, turning to the hovering list. "The Earl of Federal Investigation, the Lord of General Attorneys, the entire province of Social Services..."

As he sat back down, several others stood, raising their arms.

Regent Mikey, chewing a piece of Shawn's Spiced Gum, pointed. "Yes, you, the Marquis of Science."

"King Donnie the Awesome, I have an idea for a teleporter. I need royal funds to build a prototype."

"Teleportation is impossible," Queen Melanoma, looking bored, whispered to Donnie. "Your father put him in jail for embezzling research money."

The marquis heard this. "King Donnie the Awesome, it's not impossible, merely expensive." He exchanged a glance with the regent. "Your father put me in time out!"

King Donnie exploded. "I hate time out! I command you to build me a teleporter, no matter how much it costs!"

"Thank you, O King. You are indeed Awesome!"

Removing the spiced gum from his mouth, Regent Mikey pointed again. "Yes, Baroness Bleeding Heart."

"King Donnie the Awful—I mean, Awesome…"

Regent Mikey caught the attention of the Duke of Security, then moved his eyes to the virtual list still floating above the mahogany table.

Baroness Bleeding Heart continued, unaware of this exchange. "Throughout Merrycow, thousands of your faithful subjects are unemployed."

"What does that mean: *un-deployed?*"

The regent whispered in the king's ear. "They don't work. Because they're lazy."

King Donnie bristled when he heard this. "If they won't work, they shouldn't have new cellphones."

"A lot of them are illegal aliens," the regent mentioned.

The Baroness bristled. "That's simply not true! Most of them are Merrycow natives."

"I order them all *deployed*—I mean, *disported*. The moon only sends us their problems." Donnie whirled to the Duke of Security. "Build that wall! Build that wall!"

For the first time, the Duke's scowl relaxed ever so slightly.

The Baroness was turning red in the face. "But, King Donnie the Awf—uh, Awesome, there aren't enough jobs to go around and many of their families go hungry!"

"So? They can drink the sun!"

"Drink the—? Are you insane? These people are desperate. Poverty and homelessness lead to crime and worse. It's our duty to help them!"

"Send 'em to the moon. After we've built that wall. Who's next?"

Regent Mikey said, "I believe Baron Alternative Energy is next."

Again he caught the attention of the Duke of Security and glanced to the virtual list. The Duke's scowl relaxed a tiny bit more.

"King Donnie the Awf— I'm so sorry, I heard the Baroness say it and now it's stuck in my brain. King D. the A. Anywho, we have lots of pollution in Merrycow, which could be greatly reduced by replacing carbon-based fuels with solar power. I propose creating an infrastructure —"

"There's no such thing as pollution," King Donnie proclaimed.

The assembly gasped. The Queen woke up.

For several moments there was total silence—not counting the din of jet-car traffic outside the castle, each blasting out great gusts of choking exhaust.

Finally the baron said, "But, the air, the rivers."

"Planets need food."

"What are you talking about?"

"The Earth eats garbage and drinks chemicals. How else would it stay alive? Duh."

"Nonsense! We might as well try to build a teleporter!"

Regent Mikey cut in. "You have one more person, King Donnie the Awesome."

"Thank you, I'm Lady Pedantic de Floss. I'm here to talk about the *deplorable* state of Merrycow schools," she said, snickering. "Kids today can't read, can't spell, can't add or *detract*."

"So?" King Donnie argued. "I can't do any of those things either."

"You're the king, you don't need to be smart," Regent Mikey said.

"It's the teachers' fault," Lady Pedantic went on.

"A child shouldn't get bad grades, no matter how stupid they are," King Donnie agreed. "Kids just need the right encouragement."

"Do you mean vouchers?" Lady Pedantic asked expectantly.

"Ice cream," King Donnie proclaimed.

"Ice cream is a good motivator," said Regent Mikey.

"Indeed it is," agreed Lady Pedantic de Floss.

"Yeah, and if they still don't learn anything, teleport their teachers to the moon!"

Satisfied, King Donnie resumed eating his dish of quibble-berry ice cream.

T

Chapter 5
King Donnie meets with the royal treasurers

"Your Majesty," began the holo image of the Duke of Exchequer.

"I'm King Donnie the Awesome!" shrieked Donnie, enraged at this distraction from his Tweety game, which was not going well, the buttons being sticky with ice cream.

"Pardon me, Your Maj— I mean, King Donnie."

"King Donnie...?" Donnie said, tapping his toe.

"King Donnie... the Awesome."

Young Awesomeness beamed. The holo sighed.

"Well?" King Donnie asked.

The Exchequer's assistant, physically present, answered. "The biggest problem facing Merrycow right now is inflation."

"Invasion?"

"Inflation, Your Maj— uh, money isn't worth as much."

"Let me explain," Regent Mikey suggested. "You know when you blow up a balloon?"

"I like balloons!"

"Of course you do! And what happens when a balloon gets too full?"

King Donnie looked like he wanted to cry. "My favorite balloon popped on my birthday!"

"I know," Regent Mikey soothed. That's why inflation is so bad."

"But, if you let some of the air out, the balloon won't pop," King Donnie reasoned. "Why haven't you done that, Duke?"

"Er, uh," babbled the Duke's holo.

"What we mean to say is," his assistant explained, "The national economy is a bit more complicated."

"The *e-colony*?" King Donnie asked. "Like the moon colony?"

"All the money," the regent whispered.

"Merrycow's money?" the king asked.

The Duke of Exchequer looked smug. "Much of it is yours, Your Maj—uh…"

"You mean, I'm rich?"

"More than we realized."

"I'm *sooo* awesome!" The infantile king tried to pat himself on the back, but couldn't, his hand being too small.

"About inflation…?" asked the Duke of Exchequer.

"Oh, that!" King Donnie's face lit up. "I command you to let some money out of the *e-colony* before it pops!"

"Let money out…?" croaked the holo.

"…of the economy?" croaked his assistant.

King Donnie rolled his eyes. "Money is made out of paper, right? Gather big piles of it in the center of every village in Merrycow."

He looked around, smirking.

"And set it on fire!"

The duke's holo emitted a noise like a strangled rhinoceros.

The duke's assistant's face turned a putrid shade of green.

"No more popped balloons!"

He beamed awesomely.

"Of course, we won't burn any of *my* money. I'm really, really rich!"

"Sheer genius!" Regent Mikey exclaimed, applauding. "Three cheers for King Donnie the Awesome!"

"Let's all have ice cream now!" the king commanded.

T

Chapter 6
King Donnie deals with a hostile enemy

General Bellicose snapped to attention, clicked his heels together, and saluted. He spoke in a shrill nasal voice. "*Bed* news to re-*pot*, King *Dennie* the *Ass*-some."

"Tell us," Regent Mikey said, ignoring King Donnie's reaction to being called 'ass-some'.

"Madeessa."

"The country where quibble-berries come from?" King Donnie asked.

"The very *wan*," replied General Bellicose. "They're the *sauce* of all the terrorism in Merrycow."

"There's no more terrorism here," sighed Queen Melanoma, almost asleep. "Your father got O-Sammy."

Regent Mikey spoke. "Our king knows of 78 incidents the holovid networks refused to report."

"I do? Well, ban 'em!" roared King Donnie.

"Ban whom?" asked General Bellicose, "The *hallow*-vid network re-*pot*ters?"

"Banning holovid folks isn't a bad idea," murmured Queen Melanoma.

"Ban all Madeessa-ners," King Donnie snapped. "There's a new sheriff in town."

King Donnie questioned General Bellicose. "Why are Madeessa-ners sending *Tarot*-ists here anyway?"

"You rule a better kingdom than they do," the general explained. "They're jealous."

King Donnie stamped his foot. "They need to be put in time out!"

"They certainly do," Regent Mikey agreed. "Do you remember the sanction agreement we talked about?"

"*Spank-em* agreement?" King Donnie looked blank, but rubbed his small hands together anyway.

"We stop buying quibble-berries."

"Ah!" said General Bellicose. "Madeessa goes bankrupt and we win at Monopoly!"

His face fell. "Without a single shot fired."

"Quibble-berries encourage domestic *Tarot*-ists," Regent Mikey said smoothly. "We solve two problems at once."

"Really?" King Donnie asked hesitantly.

"You told me, remember?"

"I did? Oh, right, yeah. I'm *sooo* smart!"

"You're King Donnie the Awesome!"

T

Chapter 7
King Donnie talks to his loyal subjects

When King Donnie stepped onto the balcony overlooking the courtyard thronged with peasants, a loud cheer went up.

Actually, it was a loud *boo*.

Well, not loud, either, since hardly anybody was in attendance. Most peasants were demonstrating in the streets, chanting *pee-pee on that wall*.

King Donnie raised his tiny hand for silence, but the booing continued, along with hissing, and the occasional thrown toupee.

"King Donnie the Awful!" someone shouted. The other two or three took it up as a chant.

King Donnie stamped his foot, which caused him to teeter, almost losing his balance.

Regent Mikey held out a megaphone. King Donnie took it and spoke into the wrong end.

Queen Melanoma turned it around and showed him which button to press.

After an ear-splitting shriek of feedback, Donnie said, "You're supposed to call me *Awesome!*"

"You promised us health care!" another peasant shouted.

The puny crowd chanted: "Health care! Health care!"

"King Bamma-bamma promised that, not me!" King Donnie whined.

He started to stamp his foot—then thought better of it, and said, "I have something even better!"

Silence reigned—except for the chants of demonstrators all over Merrycow: *pee-pee on that wall.*

"Yes, you will all have the *Wonder Cure!*"

The micro-crowd looked bewildered.

Regent Mikey took the megaphone. "It's a genetically modified virus."

King Donnie snatched back the megaphone. "It'll cure anything! Everything! I've commanded all diseases and injuries to be cured, because I'm the king!"

A huge cheer erupted—well, huge for them.

"When will we get the Wonder Cure?" someone shouted.

"As soon as it's invented," King Donnie explained. "We're working on it right now."

"We like King Bamma-bamma's health care!" someone shouted.

King Donnie ignored this. "I admit it's taking longer than even *I* expected—especially after Paul Cryin got teleported to the moon. He was a filthy greenblood, you know."

They booed and hissed, still unable to drown out the demonstrators' *pee-pee on that wall.*

"We invented that teleporter in record time," Regent Mikey told them.

Queen Melanoma sniggered in her sleep.

Forgetting his balance, King Donnie stamped his foot, shouting, "If you don't stop chanting pee-pee on that wall, you won't get any ice cream!"

The king lost his balance, skinned his knee, and cried pitifully. Queen Melanoma refused to hold his little hand.

The chanting continued.

T

Chapter 8
King Donnie learns the truth about ice cream

"But I want ice cream *now!*" Donnie Clump whined.

"I'm sorry," his mother droned. "There is no more ice cream anywhere in Merrycow."

"But there has to be—because I want some!"

He glared at the robot guard until it pressed buttons on its torso. Immediately its tummy door slid open and it pulled out a dish, holding it out to Donnie.

The dish was empty.

King Donnie stamped his foot.

"Ice cream is made from quibble-berries," Queen Melanoma explained in her now-famous bored tone. "You ordered a sanction on Madeessa."

"I did?"

"Because you're concerned about terrorism."

"You said there's no *Tarot*-ists, right, Mom?"

Queen Melanoma gave a vacant glance at the robot with the open tummy door who lifted both hands palms up.

"Cancel the *spank-em* agreement," Donnie cried.

"Right away," the robot spoke in a monotone. "Should we stop banning Madeessa-ners too?"

"Yes!" cried the king. "Anything to get back my ice cream!"

"Boy talk," Queen Melanoma said.

T

Chapter 9
King Donnie learns the truth about teleporters

Regent Michael McPrince stormed through the doorway without waiting to be announced.

"Uncle Mikey!" King Donnie exclaimed and ran to him.

"Seize him!" the Regent bellowed to several robot guards.

King Donnie stopped in his tracks, mouth agape.

The robots approached the child.

"Uncle Mikey!" King Donnie whined before collapsing onto the floor in a royal tantrum.

"His bored mother, too," the regent said, ignoring the young king. "They're both greenbloods!"

"You have been the real ruler of Merrycow ever since Donnie was crowned," Queen Melanoma yawned. "Why do this now?"

Regent Mikey glared at King Donnie. "Order the quibble-berry sanction reinstated."

For answer, the king renewed his royal tantrum.

The regent shrugged. "Take them to the teleporters."

The royal tantrum ceased. "We're going to the moon?"

"It's a scam," Queen Melanoma said, still inattentive. "People he puts in a teleporter are killed, or thrown into a dungeon, or something."

King Donnie looked at Uncle Mikey, sniffling. "But, you promised! You said kings who are stars could grab as much ice cream as they want!"

"You pathetic baby," the regent said, his voice rough and quavering. "You spoiled brat. *I'm* the king of Merrycow. Or, rather, I *should* be."

King Donnie sobbed. "You… you said I was an awesome king!"

"You!" The regent snorted. "You're an imbecile. A complete failure as king, and a total loser as a person."

"Not to mention, Lady Hilarious won the popular vote," the robot with the open tummy door said in a monotone voice.

McPrince took a deep breath and bellowed: "You're by far the worst king in Merrycow's history!"

"I know you are, but what am I?" the king stuck out his tongue. "You're the one who should be teleported to the moon!"

The robot with the open tummy door spoke again. "Some demonstrators sneaked in and re-programmed me to teleport all of you."

"Have the Merrycow people *finally* come to their senses?" the other obviously reprogrammed robot guards asked, seizing Regent Mikey.

"But, but," the regent sputtered, "those teleporters'll *kill* me!"

The first robot closed his tummy. "We're actually sending you to the moon on *real* spaceships."

The robot then turned to King Donnie. "You're fired!"

Born in the US, Will Morton lives in the Los Angeles area with his wife Yvonne. He has received Honorable Mention three times from the Writers of the Future contest. His story "The Molly Armband" was selected for the Australian anthology *All the King's Men*. His stories have also appeared in the ezine *Third Flatiron* and in small press anthologies. Visit him at his website www.willmorton.com.

32 In Trump We Trust

by Livia Finucci

I voted for Trump and I'd do it again.
The press says awful things about him,
But I know they lie through their teeth.
Alternative facts must be true, and I
Snap my fingers at the Russian connection.
As for climate change, I am with Trump;
It only exists in the minds of conspiracy theorists.

I voted for Trump because he is sincere,
He speaks his mind; he is not afraid.
He doesn't mince words; he doesn't have
The foul vice of political correctness.
He doesn't put on airs and try to be cleverer than he is.
Much to the contrary, he is like us,
The unprivileged, law-abiding,
Hard-working average Joe.

The press harps on corruption, but our president is filthy rich.
Can people not understand that he is above
Petty corruption? He doesn't need more money!
If he hired his children for key positions, he did it because
It is much more efficient to work with family. If I were the
      president,
I would do the same, and so would you.

Trump is practical. He doesn't sugar-coat

The bitter pill, and I like him for that.
At the start of the Third World War
He told us to wait for destruction and mayhem.
He was sincere. Destruction and mayhem is exactly
What we are getting now. Nobody was unaware.
From my shelter I saw the tall buildings of New York City
       collapse
One by one like giant houses of cards. I was there. I saw
       everything.
I saw when that wicked missile smashed the Statue of Liberty
       into smithereens.
I saw all the carnage, the smoke and the despair.

Every day I wait in this underground shelter. I wait for the end.
I know sooner or later it will come. No, I'm not angry about it.
We were all prepared. Our president didn't lie to us.
He said it would be the end, and the end it will be.
But this will always be the land of the free.
Our president was brave. He never yielded.
Some say he escaped in a rocket ship when war broke out. I don't
       believe it.
I voted for Trump and I'll do it again
If we're still around for a second election.

Livia Finucci has had prose and poetry published in anthologies and magazines such as *Scifaikuest, Tales of the Talisman, Kepler's Cowboys, Gears and Levers* and *Here There Be Dragons*. She was nominated for the Dwarf Stars Award in 2014. She writes at the blog http://liviasmicrocosmos.blogspot.co.uk/ and in her free time enjoys botanical painting.

About the Editors

JF Garrard

JF Garrard is the author of *The Undead Sorceress,* an Asian-themed horror novel where the vampires suck *chi* instead of blood, and the ultimate self-help guide for self-publishing, *The Literary Elephant.* She is a contributor to *Ricepaper Magazine* where, maybe by the time you read this, she will be hosting a podcast called "Tea and Bun Talk." She lives in Toronto with her very tall husband and her much shorter baby.

Jen Frankel

Jen Frankel started writing early in life and never figured out how to stop, no matter how much havoc it plays with her social life. She is the author of the *Blood & Magic* series and the Vegan zombie satire *Undead Redhead,* among other literary and semi-literary works. She has a podcast called "Jen Frankel Reads Random S#it," the title of which was enough to get her a coveted *Explicit* rating on iTunes.

www.ingramcontent.com/pod-product-compliance
Lightning Source LLC
Chambersburg PA
CBHW020405260626
47156CB00007B/2247